FROM ASHER, WITH LOVE

BRITTANY TAYLOR

Cover Design by Amanda Shepard of Shepard Originals
Editing by Vicki James
Formatting by Brittany Taylor

Want to be notified of Brittany's upcoming releases?
Sign up for her newsletter here
https://www.brittanytaylorbooks.com/contact

DEDICATION

To the one who told me
emotions were a sign of weakness.
Fuck you.

INTRODUCTION

Hello dear reader!
I hope you enjoy this spicy billionaire second chance romance.
Charleigh and Asher's story is the first in the NYC Billionaire
Series.

Xoxo,
Brittany

P.S. This story was originally published as *Paper Hearts* but has
undergone massive revisions.
If you read *Paper Hearts*, I hope you enjoy its glow-up!

ONE

CHARLEIGH

August 17, 2014

Four words can change everything.

Unless you're my mother, screaming, "*I want a divorce*" to my father for the millionth time.

The echoes of her cries can be heard from my favorite spot behind the large oak tree in our expansive backyard. The soft, damp soil is pressing into the knees of my overpriced, torn, faded jeans. Absentmindedly, I half twist my body to face the tree and push my finger under a piece of loosening bark. The sharp edges dig under my nail as I lift it free from its home. The deep, earthy scent fills my nostrils, warming the places in my soul wishing I were far from the mingling shouts and bellows of my fighting parents.

Four words can change everything. Unless you're my mother.

My finger is laced with shredded bark while I beg for it to ground me to this place. I close my eyes, feeling my connection to the earth. The peace it brings. As I do every time, I close my eyes and imagine myself somewhere far from here. For as long as I can remember, I've dreamed of escaping my small town in Connecticut and making it to New York City. While the city isn't far from my home, it's always been the one place I've felt is within reach. A place I've always known that, if my lavish upbringing as the only daughter of Michael and Florence Keeler was suddenly ripped out of my hands, was still possible. If I didn't have a penny to my name and couldn't afford to go to my dream school, I could still make it in New York City and build a place for myself—one surrounded by flowers and plants and earth.

So, for the past several years, I've convinced myself that even in a jungle of concrete and metal, I can bring nature to its gray expanse. Senior year is the only thing left standing between my dreams and me.

I'm imagining the dozens of arrangements I'll create in my future flower shop, when my eyes snap open, immediately darting to the sound of the enormous, glass, French door sliding open. My mother's shoulders rack with sobs as she darts down the stone patio and into the backyard. She runs, her long legs stretching with every step. Her long, brown hair whips behind her, and her bare feet meet the damp grass with fevered measure. She's wearing a long, flowing skirt and a silk blouse—a staple for her everyday look. Tears streak down the front of the blouse, staining the shiny, pale blue material.

My mother is beautiful. She always has been.

To the entire world, she's poised and perfect, but behind closed doors, or even in our backyard, she's anything but.

With a broken heart, she eventually slows, collapsing once she's made it fifty feet away from the house. She falls to her knees and covers her face with her hands, muffling her cries.

I stay where I am, tucking myself farther behind the safety of my favorite tree, even though I peeled a piece of its bark. I cling to that piece, hoping it can feel how much I appreciate it in this moment. Every time I hear the first words of my parents arguing, I sneak out to the backyard, using this tree as a shield from my reality until the coast is clear. Within those minutes or hours of they're fighting, I simply don't exist. A fact I've grown to appreciate.

The sky is blanketed in heavy, gray clouds, not quite yet giving way to more rain. My skin prickles with a chill as the late summer breeze blows in the air. I grip onto the bark and peek around the trunk, watching my mother, who is hunching over. Her perfectly long, manicured nails dig into the dirt as she screams and cries, not caring if our neighbors on the other side of our wrought iron fence can hear her.

A knot builds in my chest, and a magnetic force tugs at my heart. Instinct pulls at me to crawl out from behind the tree and go to her. In another life, I could wrap my arms around her and tell her it will all be okay, but after years of the same old argument and problems between her and my father, I don't. I stay in the safety of where I am and watch in silence, as usual.

My mother's long, dark hair curtains her face, shielding her from me, but I can still make out how wide her mouth opens with another sob.

After a few seconds of crying, she keeps her head low as her breathing evens out. Once she's calmed down enough, she finally lifts her head and looks up at the sky, gasping for air. She inhales, counting to ten with every breath she takes, then looks down at her hands. Holding them in front of her, she stares at her dirt-covered skin. With shaking fingers and a trembling chin, she slips her four-carat diamond engagement ring off her fourth finger, and she gently drops and traps it in her palm. Silently, and with more calm measure, she uses her free hand to dig a hole into the soft ground. Satisfied with its depth, she sets her ring in the hole and slowly sweeps the dirt back over it.

I'm watching my mother stare at the mound of dirt she's used to bury her wedding ring when I spot a familiar bit of black from the corner of my eye. Air sucks deep in my lungs when I snap my head toward the front of the yard.

I rest my face against the jagged bark and watch as the boy I've come to know over the past few months makes his way down the street.

This is my favorite part of my day.

He's walking slowly, his worn-down boots scraping against the asphalt. His faded black shirt hangs loose around his torso, and his jeans have far too many holes to be considered fashionable. It's the same outfit I've seen him wear every single day, and each time I see him wander down our street, it's as though he doesn't stick out like a bright, neon flashing light, screaming he doesn't belong here. *I* know he doesn't belong here, but my heart races every time at the sight of him. Like my favorite tree, he's my escape from the ugliness that hides inside the four walls of my parents' idyllic mansion. Even if his presence lasts only a matter of minutes. He's still a glimmer of light in my dark world.

Thunder rolls in the distance, and my fingers claw into the bark a little deeper, anticipating the boy's next move. We've never spoken to one another. I don't know what his voice sounds like. I don't think he even knows I exist.

The boy stops in the middle of the street and, sticking with his usual routine, he reaches into his back pocket and pulls out a small, spiral notebook and pen. He slowly spins in a circle until he stops and faces the neighbor's house next to ours. Although his hood is up covering the top of his head, his gorgeous face is still visible, but covered in shadows. I study him as if I'm trying to ingrain him into my memory. The sharp plane of his nose to the shape of his bottom lip to the smooth curves of his jaw. He looks the same age as me. I don't know a single thing about him. Until a few weeks ago, I'd never seen him before. Not even at school.

Biting on my bottom lip, I watch him as he studies the

neighbor's house before looking down and scribbling across the furled pages of his worn notebook.

When he's done, he looks up to study the house again, but stops when he catches me staring at him. His eyes dart in my direction, finding mine. Heat immediately consumes my cheeks, and I slink back, tucking in to myself with embarrassment.

He's never noticed me before. He's never once looked at me. I feel the heat of his stare from this distance, and although he's far away, it's as if he's peering inside my soul. Like he's able to see and touch every feeling and thought I've ever had. It's both terrifying and exhilarating.

My nails dig into the bark as I hold my breath. Same as my mother, I count my breaths, whispering them into the cool breeze. The boy just stands there with his pen poised over his notebook, his eyes narrowed as he studies me.

Then without looking down at his paper, his pen resumes gliding across the paper. Once he's finished, the corner of his mouth turns up in a small smile. With the pen still pinched between his fingers, he lifts his hand and gives me a gentle wave.

A sharp burst of air slams into my lungs before I find myself returning his gesture. I lift my shaking hand, knowing I can hear my heart beating loud and clear, reminding me to keep breathing.

This is the first time. The first time he's acknowledged me. The first time we're looking at each other.

I give him a smile before my attention is stolen, once again, by the sound of the back door sliding open.

Quietly, I move to the other side of the tree and peek over the side to find my mother still in the same position, kneeling against the soft ground. Her knees and hands are covered in wet dirt, but she doesn't care.

"Florence," my father says, slowly walking up behind her.

He stops just short of meeting her, stuffing his hands into the pockets of his tweed slacks. "What are you doing out here?"

"I want a divorce, Michael," she mutters in response. The same words she screamed to him only moments ago.

"We both know you don't mean that. You should come inside. You're only embarrassing yourself here." Three lines crease my father's forehead as he frowns, knowing my mother won't follow through on the same threat she's told him for years.

"I do mean it." Her voice trembles. She's staring off in the distance with a resigned expression. A tear slips from her eye, sliding slowly down her cheek.

"No, you don't." He doesn't once move to comfort her as he towers over her, looking over her shoulder with annoyance, as if he's tired of convincing my mother to stay with him when she has every reason not to. "We both know you won't divorce me. You won't leave Charleigh here, and I won't let you take her from me. I'll fight you to keep her."

My stomach roils at the thought of either scenario playing out. A life with only my mother. A life with only my father. Neither bring me happiness. Neither bring me closer to my dream of living in New York City surrounded by flowers.

"You... you don't want her," she sputters out on an exhausted breath. "You've never wanted her."

Her confession is a gut punch, making me wish I wasn't a fly on the wall.

"How dare you?" he seethes.

My mother's head finally swivels, looking up and over her shoulder to pierce my father with her daggered eyes.

"No, Michael," she bites back. "How dare *you*? How dare you do this to us time and time again?"

This time, my father bends at his knees, resting his arms over them, bringing his eyes in line with my mother's. He traces her cheek with the back of his hand before tucking her tangled hair behind her ear. She recoils at his touch, but he pulls her back before she can look too far.

"It was one time, and she meant nothing," he says quietly. "I told you that none of them have ever mattered to me. Not as much as you."

"Then, *why* do you keep doing this to me?"

"Florence." Her name is all that falls from his mouth, sending her a silent message.

My mother squeezes her eyes shut, blowing out a resolving breath.

He cocks his head to the side in satisfaction. "That's right, my love."

Four words can change everything.

My mother's eyes open, and my father stands. He narrows his eyes and sniffs before shoving his hands back into his pockets.

"Now, dig your wedding ring out from the ground, and clean yourself up," he orders before spinning around on his heel and making his way back into the house. "We're hosting the board members tonight, and you need to look absolutely perfect."

He slams the door shut behind him, and my mother slowly turns her head back around, looking down at the mound of dirt covering her ring. Her tears fall there as she quickly digs through the dirt again, finding the large diamond resting on a thin, gold band. She slips it back onto her finger and pulls herself to a stand. Streaks of dirt coat her cheeks as she swipes her tears away. Then, as if she hasn't threatened my father with divorce for finding out about his hundredth affair, she walks back into the house with a fake saccharine smile.

I feel her absence as soon as the door slides shut, and it isn't until I look down at the cold ground that I realize I'm shedding my own tears.

Four words can change everything. But for my parents, they never do.

Their love isn't love at all.

And I'm convinced I'll never find true love of my own. At least not here. Not when I'm forced to be an audience to the theater show they put on over and over again while trapped in a dysfunctional, loveless marriage for reasons I don't understand.

I wipe my tears and try to quickly mend my fractured heart when I remember the boy standing in the middle of the street. I look up, hoping to find his golden eyes still staring at me.

My shoulders deflate in disappointment. He's gone, though hope remains tethered to my heart at the thought of seeing him again, especially after today.

For now, my life remains the same. I pluck a wild daisy growing near the roots of my favorite tree, and rub the soft petals between my fingers. At least I have nature to keep me grounded, reminding me four words never change anything.

Ever.

TWO

CHARLEIGH

Present Day

Nothing makes me question my life choices more than standing on the street in the bitter cold, bared legged in only a mini skirt and high heels. I wrap my arms around my middle and tighten my peacoat around my body, hoping it will ward off the permanent chill that has embed itself beneath my skin. I can practically feel my hardened nipples cutting through my silk blouse, too. I sigh, breathing in the intensely cold New York air, feeling it prick its way down the back of my throat. The street is busy tonight. People of all types pass me in a hurry as I stand outside the bar Julianna picked for us to meet at. Nerves bundle inside my stomach, weaving themselves into a tighter knot. My uncertainty still lingers when I think about why she wanted us to get together tonight.

"What am I doing here?" I mutter under my breath. The brisk, late-March wind floats across my cheeks as I glance down the sidewalk in both directions, hoping to catch a glimpse of my best friend. I stamp the bottom of my stiletto onto the concrete and tug my phone from the front pocket of my coat just as I see

Julianna's name flash across the screen. I quickly slide the green button and press the warm device to my icy cheek.

"Julianna—thank God. Are you almost here?" My chin quivers against the cold breeze as I tuck a stray strand of hair behind my ear.

"Hey, Charleigh. Are you already at the bar?" Her voice sounds weak and distant.

Why does she sound like she's anywhere else but here?

"I've been standing out here for the past ten minutes. Are you inside?" I spin on my heel, and peer through the window, searching the crowd. "I don't see you."

The bar is small, each wall covered in faded red bricks that must be as old as New York City itself. Despite its rough appearance, I'm impressed. String lights are strung across the ceiling, giving the bar a warm, cozy glow. Just like the sidewalk where I'm standing, the bar is packed to the brim with patrons both seated at the small tables in the middle and at the long, glossed walnut bar that runs the length of the building. The wall-to-wall packed bar is the reason I happen to be standing outside instead of enjoying what I'm sure is the opposite of this frigid weather.

"This place is insanely packed," I tell her. "What are you wearing?" I narrow my eyes even more, trying to get a better view of who is inside and catch a glimpse of Julianna's signature fire-red hair. Perhaps I missed her as she walked in, or maybe she's sitting at a table in the back.

"I'm not there," Julianna finally answers, her voice growing smaller and shakier. "I think I came down with a bad case of food poisoning."

"What?" I ask, breathless as a white cloud of hot air bursts from my mouth. Seriously, it's ridiculous how cold it is in March. However, I'm used to this Northeast weather. I already know it doesn't truly feel like spring until the end of April here.

"Yeah," she gulps. "I've been throwing up in the toilet for the past three hours."

"How long have you been feeling like this?"

"My stomach has felt off since last night after I left dinner." She sighs. "Taron and I tried that new Italian place in Uptown."

"Oh." I scrunch my nose. "Do you want me to come over? Do you need anything?"

"No." Julianna swallows. The flushing sound from the toilet echoes through the phone. I picture her slipping to the bathroom floor, refusing to leave her safe spot in front of the toilet. "Taron's coming by later to bring me crackers and ginger ale."

My teeth cut through the tip of my tongue, holding back my reaction to my best friend's shitty boyfriend offering to come over and help. Over the years, I've voiced my opinion about Julianna's on and off again relationship with Taron to no avail. Why Julianna has put up with him is beyond me. I don't trust Taron to follow through on his promise to come over, but I can't say much. I've learned it's best to stay out of it. At least for tonight.

"I'm not sure crackers and ginger ale are what you need right now," I mutter, bitterness souring the tip of my tongue.

"I don't know, either." She sighs. "I haven't Googled food poisoning remedies, but it's the thought that counts, right? At least Taron is trying."

I don't know why my best friend feels this is the type of love she deserves.

"Are you sure I can't come by?" I offer once again, keeping my thoughts to myself.

"You need this meeting, Charleigh," Julianna insists. "I'll be fine."

I close my mouth and nod. She's right; I do need this meeting, but is it so pressing that we couldn't possibly reschedule?

"You're right." I mutter.

Julianna sighs again, the lightness in her voice waning. "I'm really sorry I can't make it."

"It's okay. I'm sorry you aren't feeling well." I know if she could be here she would. My best friend has never abandoned me when I need her the most.

"No." She disagrees. "I'm sorry you're going to have to meet Holt's friend without me."

"Okay, we need to quit apologizing to each other." We both giggle but my smile slowly fades. I wince, then tuck my lip nervously between my teeth. "But maybe we can try to meet up another night. When you can be here."

"Stop, Charleigh."

"What?" I ask, pretending not to know what she's getting at when I know exactly what she's thinking.

I'm terribly shy and won't hesitate to leave if it'll help me avoid a night full of uncomfortable conversation and stretches of awkward silence. I don't do well with blind meetings, especially when it's just me, but the longer I stand here, the more I realize it isn't simply because I'm an introvert to my core. Anxiety about what tonight means settles into my bones. This night is big. Big for my business, and an important step in achieving a dream since I plucked my first flower at three years old and pressed it between the pages of my favorite book.

"You're not getting out of this one," Julianna argues.

I shrug, even though I know she can't see me. "I'm not trying to get out of anything, just postponing. This meeting will be awkward without you. I already think it's strange that Holt won't be here since he's his friend. What am I supposed to say to him?"

"Charleigh..." Julianna sighs for the third or fourth time. "You're there to talk to him about your business plans. It's important you meet with him. Expanding your business has been something you've been wanting for years, and now that opportunity is within reach. And what, you're going to pull out now because Holt and I won't be there? No way."

My silence allows her to continue, though.

"He's one of the biggest real estate agents in the country, Charleigh. If you want the best shot at expanding your floral business, he's your guy. He'll probably be more inclined to help you since he's friends with Holt."

Holt is Julianna's older brother. He also happens to be running the largest publication company in the world and has connections deep within the glitzy, glamorous lifestyle of New York City. Despite Julianna and Holt's endless wealth that's inception runs as far back as the previous century, Julianna is one of the most down to earth people I've ever met. Her older brother included.

But something tells me that isn't the life they project to just anyone. Only a select few, me included. And, considering I come from a similar background but have dedicated the past several years of my life keeping my head down by living as unassuming as possible, I relate to them probably more than they realize.

"I get it." I shiver. "But it feels kind of odd that it'll be just the two of us. Suddenly, this feels like a blind date."

Silence. Silence so loud, the background noise of the city is drowned out, and I can hear every breath passing Julianna's mouth.

"Wait. Jules...?" A knot forms in my chest.

"Hang on, Charleigh. Let me explain," Julianna is quick to defend.

"You've got to be kidding me." I groan and blow out a heavy breath while I quickly glance up and down the street, hoping to spot a cab to flag down before my toes snap off. That's it. I wave the white flag. There's no way I'm continuing this meeting now. "I'm not doing this. I should've known."

"Should've known what?" Julianna pretends to be clueless, her voice meek and cautious.

"You setting me up," I huff, wrapping my arm around my middle, tucking my frozen hand under my armpit. "This isn't just a business meeting, is it?"

"No." I can imagine the wince on her face.

"Julianna," I groan. "I can't believe you set me up. Are you truly sick, or was this part of your plan?"

"No! I really am sick. I wouldn't lie about that." She pauses, the sound of her heavy, weighted breath hitting my ear. "I do believe he can help you with your business, but I won't deny there's a part of me that's maybe thinking this could be an opportunity."

"Opportunity for what?" I ask, shock settling in. I can't believe Julianna went this far.

"We've been friends a long time, and you've barely dated in the time we've known each other."

My stomach flips. I haven't thought about my love life in a long time.

For a reason.

I'm surprised to hear my best friend is more invested in it than I've been, or that she's even noticed. Have I truly been that obvious in avoiding my love life like it's the bubonic plague?

"I didn't realize I needed to date someone to be happy, Jules," I mutter, ready to throw this night in the nearest back-alley dumpster.

"You don't," she agrees, her voice softening. "But I'm not going to pretend I don't see the sadness and loneliness in your eyes, wishing you had someone other than your best friends to share your life with."

My throat swells, and I swallow around the lump building, unwelcome tears pricking the back of my eyes. I did have someone before, when my heart hadn't been expecting it.

Someone who shared the same hopes and dreams. Someone who lied next to me, staring up at the stars that mapped out the life we had planned on sharing together.

"Dating isn't a priority for me, Jules," I tell my best friend, not wanting my emotion to pour out with my voice. "My business is."

"Both can be true at the same time."

My best friend's argument knocks me in my chest like a heavy rock. I nervously chew on the inside of my cheek, taking credence with her words. She has a point, even if I'm reluctant to admit it. I stare at the wad of gum stuck to the side of the curb before swinging my gaze back over my shoulder at the bar.

"Is he even single?" I think back to the last time I went on an actual date. It's not that I'm against the idea of dating; I just haven't found anyone who sees me for more than who I am on the surface. It's hard to find an all-consuming kind of love when you've already experienced it once before. Mine just happened to be when I was seventeen. Sometimes I wonder if we're only meant to find that kind of love once in our lifetime, and my chance has already come and gone. It's part of the reason why I've abandoned my dating life to collect dust and cobwebs.

"As far as I know, he is." Julianna inhales deeply. Her voice perks, picking up on my very slight interest.

"That's reassuring," I mutter unenthusiastically.

"Come on." Julianna shamelessly begs. "I'm almost certain he's single. Holt told me he hasn't seen or heard him talk about any other women for a long time. Just sit down and have one drink with him. For me?"

I swallow and look down at my feet again. My bare legs have practically turned into two sticks of ice at this point. I'm surprised my best friend is so focused on my love life. Maybe it's easier for her to look at mine with hope and possibility rather than her struggling relationship with Taron.

Finally, a cab pulls alongside the curb in front of me. I stare at my reflection in its window, watching the white puff of air leaving my mouth with every breath I exhale. Swallowing the doubt I have about Julianna's not-so-subtle set up with this stranger, I think of my business. I've worked so hard these past five years to get where I am, and I can't pass up the opportunity to become a bigger success. I don't *have* to walk into this bar and sit with him thinking about this as a blind date. It's a business meeting—one I desperately need.

"I'm still not sure it's a good idea to date the man who is going to potentially help me franchise, *Charleigh's Florals.*" I huff, shoving my hand into the pocket of my peacoat. "But... okay. *One* drink."

"Yes." Julianna squeals. "Perfect."

I roll my eyes and spin on my heel, leaving the waiting cab where the sidewalk meets the street. Swallowing the lump of nervousness in my throat, I fully considering the fact that I'll now be meeting this stranger by myself because Julianna happened to come down with a case of food poisoning.

A blast of heat slams against my face the moment I step through the threshold of the bar, swallowing me whole. Despite my hesitance about meeting this stranger without a clue as to who he is, I'm thankful I'm at least inside now, soaking in the warmth. It's a comfort to my anxiety ridden nerves.

I elbow my way past several of the patrons, who are packed in like sardines, but I keep my phone pressed to my ear, hoping Julianna's voice drowns out the loud chatter surrounding me.

"So, how am I supposed to know who I'm looking for?"

"Oh..." Julianna pauses. "Um, hang on. I'll search him up and send you a screenshot of his picture."

"What's his name?" I ask, but she must have already pulled her phone away from her ear.

While I wait for Julianna to get back on the phone, my

stomach twists into tighter knots, anxiety and nerves taking over. I'm tempted to sneak my way over to the bar and flag down a bartender. A shot of tequila would make a quick cure for the nerves.

My shoulders fall when I don't spot an opening within the crowd. There must be at least two rows of people blocking the bar. Deciding to just grab a drink when I sit down, I continue making my way farther inside.

"Okay," Julianna breathes back into the speaker. "I just sent you his picture."

I pull my phone away from my ear and look at the screen. No new texts or messages. "No picture. It must not have come through yet. What's his name?"

"Oh, no," Julianna's voice garbles. A loud crash followed by the sound of her hurling fills my ear. I stop where I am and scrunch my nose. Instinctively, I lift my phone away from my ear until it stops.

Julianna groans in the background. "Ew. There's nothing worse than vomiting into a toilet. I'm almost certain."

The corner of my mouth lifts into a meek smile. "Jules?"

"I'm here," she whines. "I should get off the phone. I feel another round coming on."

My shoulders sink again. "Okay." Although she isn't physically here with me, her support over the phone has been helpful. "I love you, Jules. Feel better and keep me updated."

"Thanks," she grumbles. "And keep me updated about your meeting."

"I'd say I'll call you afterward, but something tells me you won't be up to it."

"Probably not." She burps. "Oh, no, it's happening again. I've got to go, Char."

I hang up with my best friend, inhale a deep, resolving breath, and brush my hair away from my face, threading my fingers through my loose waves. I put Julianna's suggestion of turning this into a date out of my mind. It's only making me more nervous. Instead, I focus on the expansion of my business.

After all, that's the reason I agreed to this meeting.

I steel my chest and square my shoulders as I stand in the sea of people surrounding me, unsure of what to do or who to look for. My conversation with Julianna plays through my mind, and I'm unable to move on from her comment about the sadness in my eyes.

I've fought for years to put my previous life behind me. And I hate that it's followed me like an unrelenting shadow. The air around me is stifling, thick and heavy. It feels like men and women are closing in on all sides. Pushing through the crowd, I make my way to the other side, gasping for air once I break free.

I take a deep breath and look around as tears prick my eyes. I hate that I feel this way.

After shoving it back down, my phone pings in my hand with a message from Julianna.

Quickly swiping my thumb across the screen, I unlock Julianna's message. The picture she sent of the man I'm supposed to be meeting has finally come through.

Just when I think I've regained my bearings and gifted the oxygen to my lungs, it's sucked from my chest all over again. The blood drains from my head to my toes. My heart races, and I blink several times, convinced I'm not seeing him correctly. I must be mistaken.

But the name under his picture confirms he's the man I'm seeing. Those same golden flecks in his green eyes. A smile that makes me go weak in the knees. A face that's now matured and sharpened, compared to the boyish, unkempt version I once knew.

A breath hits the back of my throat when I look up from my phone. My hand is shaking, and my heartbeat is erratic, anticipating the moment when my eyes land on the *him* in this bar. The man I haven't laid eyes on since I was seventeen.

The back of the space has several small tables lining each wall, with rustic-style benches set in front of each one. I scan the area until my gaze lands on the back of a stranger sitting at a table alone.

His attention isn't on the crowd around him as he shields his face by keeping his focus trained on the phone resting in his hand.

I step closer, and the closer I get, the more my stomach sinks. I feel it in the way the hair on the back of my neck stands up. Suddenly, memories of my past life come flooding back.

Secret notes and pressed flowers.

A whisper across my skin.

A life that feels a thousand solar systems away, lost in the stars that once mapped our future. A future lost to cataclysmic events that changed us forever.

The chatter and conversation around me is muffled and garbled, like I'm submerged under water.

I stop a small distance from the table, unable to allow my sore feet to carry me farther.

His black coat is draped over the back of his wooden chair, and his red scarf is folded neatly on top of the table.

I watch as he rests the tips of his fingers around his small glass. He still hasn't looked away from his phone as he slides the glass closer to him. He doesn't look up or bring his drink to his lips. Instead, he slowly spins it around, never once lifting it off the table.

I study his profile, from the sharp plane of his nose to his smooth mouth. The lights of the bar aren't as bright here as they were at the front without any string lights hanging from the ceiling on this side of the space. His face is covered with shadows, hiding the tiniest of his features.

Despite the span of time since the last time I laid eyes on him, I know exactly who he is.

My stomach takes an even deeper plunge when he finally looks up.

His face doesn't change at the sight of me. Unlike mine.

An audible gasp escapes the small space between my lips.

"Asher?" His name falling from my mouth is like opening an old chest. The dusty remnants and memories of a past life surround me like a dark cloud. At first, saying his name feels foreign, but the more I let it linger in the air between us, the more familiar it becomes. I haven't uttered his name in almost ten years, yet it somehow feels so normal leaving my lips. He's changed, and if it weren't for the confirmation in Julianna's text, I would second guess whether this was him or not.

But even now, I have my doubts. A love like the one we had isn't easily forgotten. A touch like his. A kiss like his. A voice like his. A love so powerful, it took years to repair the cracks he'd cut into my heart.

"Charleigh?"

That voice. It's deeper... smoother than what I remember.

I inhale a sharp breath, unsure of the man sitting before me. My mind tells me it's Asher, but my heart doesn't want to believe it. It *can't* believe it.

"I'm sorry, I, um..." I nervously tuck a strand of hair behind my ear while I try to wrap my head around what's happening.

Asher is here.

In New York City.

In this bar.

Sitting at a table with a drink and his perfectly folded red scarf.

I instinctively take a step back, convinced this is a mistake. Holt's friend must be someone else. Julianna must have sent me

Asher's picture by error. Her sending him to me is a mere coincidence.

"Are you okay?" he asks, his perfect eyebrows raised, revealing his familiar, kind eyes. Everything about him has changed since the last time I've seen him. Everything but those.

"Oh, um, I'm supposed to be meeting someone."

"Huh." His eyes narrow. The corner of his mouth twitches. "Like a date?"

Again with that voice.

I hate the way it makes my heart race and my thighs clench in response.

But his words quickly register, and my cheeks redden. I cut him a glare. "No, not a date."

"Okay." He nods, looking from the top of my head down to my toes before meeting my gaze again.

His stare is intense but, for the most part, unaffected. His lips press together, with three lines creasing his forehead. He's the same man I knew at eighteen, only he isn't. His features are more prominent, fuller, and more defined. He looks his age—closer to thirty than twenty. A sharp nose is set between two piercing eyes, filled with years of silence, and the echo of a life we both once lived.

My nostrils flare from the anger bubbling inside me as he continues to size me up. The arrogance dripping from him is suddenly so blindingly obvious.

I cross my arms over my chest. "What is that supposed to mean?"

He shrugs. "Nothing. I didn't mean anything by it."

"Well, you were looking at me in a way that suggests something."

"I wasn't suggesting anything." He frowns.

I tighten my arms around myself to keep me grounded. Slowly, pieces of my previous life in Connecticut begin to resurface, chipping away at the new life I've built around it to protect myself. I feel vulnerable and exposed, as if Asher can read every thought creeping in my mind.

By this point, I'm thoroughly convinced Julianna has made a mistake. In her delirious, food poisoned state, it's completely plausible for her to have sent me Asher's picture by mistake.

"Well..." I nervously unravel my arms and clap my hands together. "This has been fun, but I'm going to get going."

His stare burns a hole in my chest, and I want to rewind to thirty minutes ago before I allowed myself to step out of my apartment. No business deal is worth spending time with Asher when it's clear we're not happy with seeing each other.

I wouldn't expect it to be, considering how our relationship ended years ago.

But I can't ignore the prick to my chest when realizing how he's treating me in this moment. As if I were the one who hurt him. As if he weren't the one who tore my heart out and disappeared as though he'd never existed.

He lifts the glass to his mouth, his lips uncurling, then he shrugs before swallowing the rest of whatever liquid remained. He slams the empty glass down on the table, making the half-melted ice rattle against the sides.

I'm fully prepared to walk away, but something in the way he moves makes me stay.

For nearly a year since the last time I saw Asher, I imagined what it would be like if I ever saw him again, but never did I imagine a moment like this one. I can't pinpoint the way I feel. Seeing your first love after ten years is surreal, but seeing Asher has also opened a chest I locked and shoved in a corner a long time ago.

I bite the inside of my cheek. The remnants of ash left behind from all those years ago are nothing but a ghost of a memory.

Now, we're simply two strangers standing in the middle of a bar in New York City.

I watch him carefully as he walks around the table to move past me. He's taller than I remember—or maybe he isn't. The faded memory I have of the boy who stole my heart before burning it to nothing more than a pile of ash rests in the back of my mind. I also can't ignore how good he smells or how expensive his clothes look. His hair is longer on top, cut shorter on the sides. What used to be hints of dull blond in his hair have now faded to a light brown.

Even if I let him go all those years ago and moved on, creating a life of my own, I can't help but remember how it was back then. How, in the end, *he* was the one who chose to leave *me*.

"I was supposed to be meeting someone, too," he finally says, pulling me out of my thoughts as he shakes his head, glancing at the gold-plated watch wrapped around his wrist.

"Oh." I smack my lips together. "What? Like a date?"

He snaps his head in my direction, cutting me a glare with a hint of amusement. "Possibly." He gives me a smug grin, picks up his red, cashmere scarf, and wraps it around his neck, his gold watch clanking with the motion. He's polished and clean. Vastly different. "But time is money, and I've wasted enough of it."

I'm ready to throw this night in the garbage and leave Asher behind—chalk it up to a loss and find another real estate agent to help me—but I need this. Whether I'm a glutton for punishment, my curiosity gets the better of me, or maybe it's because my love for my business is stronger than anything else, I reach out and stop Asher before he gets too far ahead of me.

"Wait." My hand lands on the sleeve of his black, wool coat —a hand that once touched Asher in a much different way than I am doing now. The way my fingers used to thread with his to remind us that our love would withstand anything thrown our way.

Teenage love can be grossly delusional. A fact I quickly learned the night he left.

Now, though, his coat is smooth against my palm. His eyes fall to my hand before he slowly lifts his gaze that's burning with an intensity that shoots straight to my chest.

I jerk my hand back, realizing I'm still touching him. "Are you the real estate agent I was supposed to meet?

He considers me for a moment, avoiding my stare before looking back at me. "No. I don't think so." Short and to the point.

He moves to continue leaving the bar, but I stop him again. All the pieces of the Asher standing in front of me fall into place. The expensive watch and coat. The way his brown hair is impeccably groomed. The way his arrogance drips from him like all the men who hold offices on Wall Street.

"I think you are," I tell him. "Do you know a Holt Capuleti?"

Asher's gaze hardens, his eyes narrowing into two small slits.

A long time ago, those same eyes took my breath away. Now, they belong to a stranger. The once soft features of the boy I used to know are the hardened ones of the man standing in front of me. He backs away, and my hand falls from his arm.

He sighs, pressing his mouth into a tight line. "Nope. Can't say I do."

With those few words, he disappears into the crowd, and this time I don't stop him.

I don't believe him for one second. He knows Holt, and he *was* the man I was supposed to meet. Julianna's text wasn't a mistake.

Even so, there's no way in hell I can hire him. The past doesn't easily forget. It may forgive for a time, but the moments that shape our futures are always dictated by the past, no matter how far we attempt to put it behind us.

Because my business isn't worth re-opening the pain caused by Asher.

I'll just have to figure out another way to expand my business.

THREE

ASHER

"Janette?"

"Yes, Mr. Egan?"

My assistant Janette shuffles into my office, her tight pencil skirt shifting against her thighs with every step. She stands in the doorway, with her phone resting in her hand, ready to jot down any notes I give her. She blows out a quick breath and stiffens her spine as I lean back in my chair before turning my attention to the city outside my window.

"I thought you were going to email me the details for the Knight account," I say between gritted teeth. My head pounds as I loosen my tie around my neck.

"I was just going to, sir." I hear Janette's long nails tapping on her screen. "Mr. Knight sent an email yesterday afternoon with all the information you requested. Once I'm at my computer, I'll forward it over."

"Why didn't you send them over immediately?" I ask in a tight voice, curling my fingers. I can't help it; I'm tense as fuck this morning. I also know why, but I'm trying to push the reason to the back of my mind. I'm trying to pretend the life I've built over the past ten years didn't come barreling into me, knocking me on my fucking ass.

Ever since last night, I've been out of sorts. Despite my efforts, I'm failing miserably at not letting it affect my work.

I spin in my chair and stare at Janette, waiting for her answer as I raise my eyebrows in anticipation, my nerves getting the better of me. I realize I'm not always the best when it comes to cordial interactions when it comes to matters of business, but deep down I know Janette doesn't deserve the mood I'm giving her.

"Well?"

"I'm sorry, Mr. Egan." She blinks several times, and her neck bobs dramatically as she swallows. "The email didn't come through until after I left yesterday. I'd only just come by it after I'd arrived this morning and was sifting through my emails."

"Fine." I hold my hand up.

She gives me a curt nod. "Is there anything else you need me to do?" Her soft voice fills the large office. Her dedication to working for me stems from years of proving she can handle my mood swings and tough work ethic.

When I first established my firm back in Los Angeles six years ago, my first assistant Francine rushed out of my office in tears after I told her the one appointment she'd failed to put in my calendar cost me a ten-million-dollar sale. I'd never seen her after that day, and I swore I would never hire another assistant as incompetent as her again.

So far, Janette has proven to be better than Francine. She's testing my patience today with her lack of hustle regarding Weston Knight's email, though. It's a well-known fact that New York real estate is a dog-eat-dog world, and landing Weston Knight as a client has been a goal of mine ever since I arrived in the city all those months ago.

But despite my frustration with Janette, I know it's something else entirely that has me bothered. One woman in particular has been on my mind since I saw her last night. The only woman I've ever allowed to see what's beyond the surface. Although letting her in burned both of us, it's clear after last night that the scars of our past lives are still very evident.

I knew coming to New York City was risky. I knew Charleigh was here, wedged in among the millions of people packed between steel and concrete, but I figured the chances of my past catching up to me were slim to none in a city of over eight million. Last night, however, proved me wrong.

Now, I can't get her out of my head. The way her body has clearly changed since the last time I touched her. Her curves have widened, and her eyes have somehow brightened. Her gaze shot straight to places that have sat dormant for years. Places I've refused to acknowledge. It seems I'm now caught between the man I've become and the boy I used to be when it comes to Charleigh. I'm all sorts of fucked up this morning.

"Sir?" Janette asks.

I snap my head up to focus on the New York skyline on display for me through my floor to ceiling office window after realizing I zoned out.

"No, I don't need anything else." I take a deep breath and turn my attention back to my computer. "But I'll need that email within the hour. I'm supposed to be meeting Holt for lunch, and I want it sent to me before then." I click on my internet tab, pulling up a search engine.

"Of course." Janette dips her head and shuffles across the tile floor without another word.

My fingers hover over the keyboard. I'm ready to type in Weston's name, but the piece of my brain I've been fighting against all morning urges me to type a certain name starting with a 'C' instead.

Deciding on neither name, I open the listing database for

the city. When I'm stressed, it's the perfect place for a distraction.

I immediately begin sifting through the hundreds of available listings in the area. Every few photos, I find myself raising my eyebrows, scrutinizing every little detail of each one. New York's real estate is quite different from southern California's. Every building seems cold and dark. Some pictures are even shrouded in a backdrop of deep gray clouds and rain. I take note of several properties that catch my eye. I may not know exactly what Weston Knight is looking for, but I can at least tab a few just in case.

I've flagged nearly ten properties when I come across one unlike any other. The description says the building is in Lower Manhattan, opposite to where my office is. I'm not sure what pulls me to it. Maybe it's because it doesn't look like any of the other listings I see in the price range I've chosen. It's in a neighborhood I'm unfamiliar with, too, and the price is outrageous, even for New York City.

I open a separate window and Google the address to see what the surrounding area looks like.

My eyes widen when I see it's in a less-than-stellar neighborhood. Everything about it is run down. Most of the buildings look vacant and abandoned, at least in the immediate vicinity. Beside the vacant office space for sale, there's a tall, brick building at least twenty stories high. It looks as if it's a dilapidated apartment building. For a moment, I think it's just another forgotten piece of the city left behind to fall apart by the more up-and-coming surrounding districts, but it isn't. The picture captures a moment in time—one where a woman is walking out the thick black door, with a little boy latched onto her hand. I'm staring at the boy and his mother, wondering what their story is. How did they end up living in a place like that? Clicking on the image, I swivel it back around to the office space and narrow my eyes, studying the neighborhood even more. In the distance I can see bright lights and cleaner streets. It's not pretty, but it's workable.

I go back to the listing on my other open tab. The agent definitely has this place way overpriced.

"Oh," my best friend's voice booms from my open office door. "Don't tell me I caught you *actually* working."

I look up to find Holt standing in the doorway, leaning against the doorframe, with his arms crossed, the sleeves of his suit jacket stretched.

I laugh and close out my screen, relaxing back into my chair. "Only every now and then."

"Are you kidding?" His eyebrows shoot into his forehead. "I don't think I've ever seen you *not* working."

I shrug off Holt's comment, not wanting to dig into it any further. He isn't my therapist, and I don't want to dive into that one.

I run my fingers through my hair and stand before grabbing my suit jacket from where it's draped across the back of my chair and tossing it on. For the past few years, I've grown accustomed to wearing suits every day. At times, it feels foreign. It's hard to believe there were days I only had three different shirts to wear, nearly every single one littered with holes. The suit glides onto my body effortlessly as I slide each arm into the sleeves. It fits me perfectly, just how I like it. I adjust the cuff links and glance up at my best friend.

"We're still on for lunch, right?" I ask, desperately needing to put as much distance between me and my computer as possible. The temptation to dig into Charleigh's life since our split is eating away at me.

"Definitely." He hitches his thumb over his shoulder. "I have a meeting in my board room in about an hour, so we're good as long as we don't go far."

I frown, having hoped Holt would have agreed to a restaurant farther from my office and my damn computer. Maybe then I could shake off the shock of seeing Charleigh or acknowledging how it has had me all fucked up all day.

But I'm a fool in thinking my phone won't be enough temptation to look her up at some point.

"Did you have a chance to speak with Weston Knight? My assistant said he sent her an email and she's forwarding it to me this morning. I'm assuming that means you talked to him." I shift the topic to a more pragmatic, business-minded one. Anything to forget the curves of Charleigh's body and how muscle memory seemed to kick into high fucking gear last night.

"I did." Holt sniffs. "He's the reason I had to bail on our meeting last night."

"Oh?" I raise my eyebrows and give Holt a knowing nod. "I was wondering why you would recommend a client informally without showing up. At least it was for a good reason."

Holt must sense my bitterness. He gives me a quizzical expression as the creases in his forehead deepen. "You still met up with Charleigh, though, right?"

I move past him and head straight for the elevator, ignoring his interrogation. Well, he's asking a simple question, but any conversation on the topic of Charleigh is anything but simple. It's complicated as fuck.

"No." I glance over my shoulder, shooting him a straight lie. "She didn't show." The lie sits like acid on the tip of my tongue, but every aspect of my past burns a piece of my soul. I've learned it's easiest to just ignore.

"That's strange. Julianna told me she was there. She said she was on the phone with her while Charleigh was looking for you. You must have missed her."

"Mm," I hum while passing Janette's desk outside my office. I don't acknowledge her on my way out or tell her I'm leaving for lunch. Instead, I glance at my watch to distract myself, realizing we're leaving for lunch earlier than usual.

"So?" Holt asks once we reach the elevators.

I lean forward and press the call button before shoving my hands in my pockets. I stare up at the light, watching the numbers tick by. "So, what?"

"Did you miss her?"

His question is a heavy weight on my shoulder. I want to shake it off, but I know if I don't answer him, he won't let up, and I won't be able to get my answer about Weston Knight.

I shrug, still unable to look my best friend in the eye. "I guess so."

"Oh, well, I'll message my sister and see if we can set up another meeting." From my peripheral, I watch him tug his phone from his pocket. He's tapping on the screen as the elevator dings and the doors slide open.

"You don't have to do that." I step inside the four golden walls.

Emotion is thick in my throat. The chambers of my heart and lungs seize with the memories of a tragic past that nearly suffocated me. Suddenly, I'm faced with a cold, hard truth as I stare at my reflection in the elevator's mirrored wall.

Charleigh is a reminder of the person I used to be, of a life that no longer exists. A life I walked away from. The Asher who once belonged to Charleigh is no more. I haven't been him for a long time, and I don't want to be.

"It's fine," Holt says. "I'll text Julianna and see what she thinks."

My stomach churns.

I close my eyes and am immediately pulled back to last night.

Charleigh's standing in front of me wearing a bright yellow peacoat and a black skirt. She stood out from the crowd, and if I hadn't been so focused on my phone when she walked up to my table, I would have spotted her from a mile away. That part about Charleigh hasn't changed in ten years—her ability to wear the most obnoxious colors yet still look sexy as hell. Her floral scent surrounded me, making it impossible to concentrate on anything else besides her pink-painted lips and her red, rosy cheeks.

My cock twitches, and I snap my eyes open, forcing myself to shove the memory away.

Fuuuuuuck.

When I look back at my reflection, I see Holt leaning against the back of the elevator.

He's still typing out a message on his phone as the elevator carries us down to the lobby.

Holt has been a friend of mine since I graduated from UCLA with my bachelor's before transferring to Columbia for my graduate degree. We were both completely shit faced at a fundraising gala for the New York City Mayor at the time. The mayor who also happened to be Holt's dad.

Born from generational wealth, Holt is most likely a friend I wouldn't have imagined having before I became the person I am now. Not because we wouldn't have gotten along, but because Holt's world simply never touched the one I had growing up. A world I forced myself to walk away from, even if coping through the trauma of my childhood hasn't exactly been healthy.

Connecticut left me with deep, gaping wounds, and I searched for every piece of thread I could find to stitch myself back together. If I wasn't studying my ass off in business school, I was fucking any woman willing to give me the time of day. I haven't been interested in a relationship in years, and I don't plan on starting now. Holt should know this... I think.

I haven't told him about my past, before I came into the wealth I have now. He's never asked, and I've never willingly offered it up to him. The dark, ugly pieces of the past are easier to deal with when kept to myself.

If Holt thought last night could possibly be anything other than a business meeting, he was wrong. Very, very wrong.

I lean against the wall of the elevator and study him, trying to search for any indication that he knows about mine and Charleigh's past. For all I know, Charleigh could have told Julianna all about me and our sordid past, then Julianna could have told her brother. Is Holt fishing for information, or is he simply curious about how the night went?

I need to fucking stop thinking about Charleigh.

I'm not so lucky when we step out onto the sidewalk, though. The air isn't as cold as it was last night. The sun beats down on my skin, and I wince against the bright light peeking through the enormous buildings surrounding us.

"Done." Holt says, slipping his phone back into his pocket.

"What's done?"

"I asked Julianna if she could talk to Charleigh about scheduling another time to meet."

I roll my eyes, frustration boiling over. "Seriously, man. It's fine."

"Well," Holt continues, annoyed with my stubbornness. "I think you'll find this more than fine when I tell you about my idea for a different time."

I pause, eyeing him in the elevator.

"It has to do with Weston Knight."

My heart jumps. Now he has my attention.

He smirks. "Weston is holding a soft launch of his new beer garden over in SoHo in a couple of days. I thought it would be a good time for you to meet him and establish a rapport outside of a business setting. The man is sort of hard to pin down unless it's on his time."

I swallow my nerves and stare at my best friend as the

elevator stops on the first floor. The doors slide open, and Holt is the first to step out, passing me to head into the lobby. He half turns, waiting for me to catch up before we both head out of the building.

Merrick, the valet, holds the door open for us, nodding in acknowledgement. The cool midday air hits my face as soon as my feet hit the sidewalk.

"Soft launch, huh?" I say to Holt.

"Yep," he says, popping his mouth. "Since this is West's eleventh restaurant opening, he's sort of decided to stop making them a big deal. He likes to fly under the radar like that."

I nod in understanding. Before my life changed, when my world revolved around Charleigh, I used to live mine the same way. Completely in the shadows. Until Charleigh brought me out into the light.

"Well, now that we have Weston Knight nailed down, will you reconsider working with Charleigh?"

I scrunch my nose and stop walking when we reach the café less than a block from mine and Holt's office. I look up at the neon sign, anything to avoid looking at my friend. "I don't know. Maybe she's better off working with another real estate agent."

"Are you joking, man?" Holt asks, forcing me to look at him. "*Fortune* just listed you as number two on their list of top one hundred fastest-growing companies. If it wasn't for that fucker Cyrus Temper, you'd have been number one."

Thinking about Cyrus makes my skin crawl and my blood pressure rise. He is New York's top real estate executives, and my number one rival in this industry.

I shake my head. "Fucking Cyrus."

"Right?" Holt scoffs. "So, what I'm saying is, *you're* the perfect realtor to help Charleigh. If you want to be the best and take that rightful place in *Fortune*, you're going to need every high-profile client you can get."

I raise my eyebrows. Charleigh is considered high-profile? Probably has to do with her family ties and the fact she carries the Keeler name.

Eyeing Holt, I give him a smile. "Well, damn, Holt. With how hard you're selling me clients, you think you want to trade your title as head of that magazine you're running up there and come work for me?"

Holt tips his head back in laughter. "Yeah, right. There's no way I'd give up my job."

I shrug, and his face falls back into a serious expression.

"Besides," he continues, "I thought you never turned clients away."

"I don't, but..." I slide my hands into my pockets, dart my eyes over Holt's shoulder, and zone out, thinking about what to do. On one hand, I don't want to hurt Holt by telling him no. On the other, I'm not sure I want to see Charleigh again. I'm not sure I can handle it. Walking away from her the first time was difficult, and I've moved on. Seeing her drags up old feelings and the promise I made to myself the day I left. Seeing Charleigh again would jeopardize it all.

How do you go back on a promise you made ten years ago?

A broken heart never fully mends itself. Even if I'm the one who caused the wounds in the first place.

"I'll think about it."

FOUR

CHARLEIGH

It feels like embers have been smoldering inside my chest since the night I saw Asher.

I'm staring at my phone on the nightstand. The screen is black, yet there's an invisible thread pulling me toward it. I haven't been able to shut out the endless thoughts. The way my hand felt against the sleeve of his expensive coat. The rich and powerful scent of cedar and pine surrounding me. The flicker of resentment and aloofness in his golden eyes. Unjustified.

Turning onto my side, I pick my phone up and swipe to unlock it.

It's late—nearly three in the morning. The bright lights of the city are blocked out by the blackout curtains of my window that I fitted when I first moved into my apartment three years ago. There's an unread text from my mother, but I ignore it and click on the Google tab.

Asher Egan.

I type his name so fast I surprise myself. I've spent the past ten years working to forget him, yet here I am, lying in my bed in the middle of the night, Googling him. I've thought of it before only once. It was the year I graduated from NYU. I thought of him as I walked across the stage, my degree handed to me. I mostly thought of him because it had once been a dream of ours to go to NYU together. I wondered who he had become. At that point, I hadn't seen him in four years. Had he moved on? Had he met someone else and gotten married? Was he better off without me? Later that night, after graduation, I considered seeking Asher out through social media but decided against it. He'd had been strong enough to break our relationship off when he moved to California. I knew I needed to do the same.

It was also the time when I learned dreams are fleeting. One minute, you believe you have everything you've ever wanted, and the next, it's ripped away, and you're left with nothing. You're forced to build a new dream, a new way to move on. That's what the night of my graduation had transformed into: a new dream. One Asher was no longer a part of.

Once my phone has brought up the list of results for Asher's name, I rest my head back down on my pillow and place my phone beside me. I take a few breaths and stare at the wall, reconsidering. Why do I even care enough to search his name?

He probably hasn't thought about me even once. Not until he saw me standing in front of him last night.

A knot forms in my chest when I realize I do care, and I hate that I do.

Curiosity gets the better of me. I pick up my phone again. The light casts a bright blue beam across my face.

The first result is a link to his Instagram account. I ignore that one and continue down the list. The second link is an article for *Fortune* Magazine's *Top 100 Fastest-Growing Companies.* My eyes widen when I read the small paragraph beneath the link.

#2: Egan Realty—Asher Egan, 29, Los Angeles-based real estate executive. Up 93% due to organic growth and marketable investments.

I don't click on the article. Instead, I stare at the text, dissecting each word letter by letter. I'm happy Asher became successful in his career. There's an ache in the pit of my stomach, though, and I can't quite shake this uneasy feeling. Why would it matter to me that Asher was satisfied and fulfilled in a career I knew he'd always wanted?

Because even with all of Asher's faults, his ambitions to dive into high value real estate never wavered.

My thumb hovers over the link to his Instagram account. With my other hand, I bite down on my thumbnail and roll onto my back. I raise the phone in the air and suck in a sharp breath between my teeth before I click on the link, unsure of what I'll find. I expect to see a page full of Asher and a woman—possibly his wife—or maybe several women. My shoulders drop, and all the air in my chest deflates. I don't realize I was holding my breath until I feel my lungs filling with air again.

His account is set to private. It surprises me, yet it doesn't. Maybe it's for the best that I can't see the kind of pictures I assume he has on his profile anyway. I roll onto my other side and open the text from my mother.

> Mom: Are you coming down for Memorial Day weekend? Your father would love to see you.

I sigh, closing out her text without responding and dropping my phone back onto my nightstand. This time, I don't feel that invisible pull anymore.

"HEY, Selene. How's today going so far?" I walk through the front door of my flower shop to find my best friend Selene. The one who also happens to work for me. At least temporarily, according to her.

We've been best friends since the day she stumbled into my shop, looking for a job but insisted it was only temporary until she could find one in her field of work: writing.

But it's been years since that day, and she still hasn't left me.

Selene is finishing up typing something on the computer when I finally make it to the counter. Her fingers frantically dance across the keyboard. She waits until she's finished before she finally answers me.

"Charleigh." She sighs, looking exhausted already. It's only nine in the morning. "I'm so glad you're here." Her mouth dips into a frown.

I slide her one of the coffees I picked up on the way over. I may have taken a few extra minutes to soak up the warm, spring sun, hoping to start my day fresh, free of thoughts about Asher.

Finally, it's starting to feel like spring. My favorite season.

Selene's shoulders sag in relief as her eyes drop to the paper cup in front of her. Quickly, she wraps her hand around it and immediately brings it to her mouth. She takes a sip, then places it next to the computer.

"What's going on?" I ask.

"We are completely booked up for the next two months. Like, *completely*."

I bite back a laugh. Being completely booked is a great thing, but something in the way Selene's voice is laced with panic tells me there's a 'but' coming.

"That's great," I say cautiously. "But..."

Her emerald eyes search around the room before landing on me again. "I'm not sure we have enough stock to hold on to the orders. We have the wedding coming up for the Motleys, then the week after, we have the gala for the art museum. Maybe we overbooked?" She flips through the open calendar on the front desk. "Every single day is taken."

"Oh, no." I place my palm against my forehead and look

around my flower shop. My hands grow clammy as panic sets in. "I don't think we overbooked, but you're right. We should be happy that every day is filled, but this isn't good." This place is too small, and as more time passes, I'm finding more and more reasons why I need a larger shop. This place was inexpensive when I first bought it. At first, business was slow, but it seemed to take only months for me to have an event nearly every few weeks. Now, Selene and I are struggling to keep up with the demand.

The problem is, I want the large events. I want to be the florist who works for high-end clients. But I know I can't do that if I'm stuck within the limited confines of these four walls.

I sigh and press my palms flat onto the desk, eager for a solution. "Do we have any room in the refrigerators in the back?" There are only three small commercial refrigerators located in the front of the store, but those are reserved for clients who come in on the spur of the moment, not for large catering events.

"Not if we're going to store flowers for both events," Selene answers, tucking her wavy, blonde hair behind her ears. She sounds just as worried as I feel.

"I'm sure we'll figure it out." I place my hand on her arm, hoping to reassure her. I'm projecting far less worry than I feel, but it's the only response I have in me before completely melting down. "Don't worry."

As if on cue, Julianna walks in through the front door. The bell above it clinks several times as her heels click across the floor. She's the CEO of her own interior design firm, and her office is only a few blocks away from mine, so I'm not entirely surprised to see her. But I do wonder where she finds the time to stop by a few days a week to help trim some of the flowers or refill their water.

"Julianna." I smile, hoping Selene and I can dissolve the fear lingering in the air. "Feeling better?"

"Better?" Selene asks, her attention darting to Julianna.

She waves her hand, scrunching her nose. "I had a bout of food poisoning last night, but I'm all better now."

"Gross." Selene makes a disgusted expression before fussing with the single-wrapped roses we have for sale on the counter next to the register.

"It was awful," Julianna says.

"Did Taron come over like he promised?" I ask, anticipating her response. I keep waiting for the moment she'll give up on him and realize he's a complete and utter dick. So far, no luck.

"No." She frowns before shooting me a pointed look. "And before either of you say anything about him bailing, he didn't *promise* he would come over."

"Ok*ay*." Selene sighs, resting her elbows on the counter. She's still fussing with the twine wrapped around a rose. "But when your boyfriend says he's going to bring you stuff to make you feel better, I think it's safe to assume he'll actually go through with it. Just because he didn't use the word 'promise' doesn't mean you should give him a pass."

Julianna waves her hand in the air as if the room suddenly smells foul. "I know, I know. I still need to figure out what's going on between Taron and me, but I didn't come down here to talk about me."

The glimmer in her blue eyes shifts toward me. Her mouth curls into a grin, and I can tell she's wanting me to dish what happened between Asher and me. So far, I've ignored her prying texts about our meeting.

I smirk, avoiding the topic of Asher just as hard as she's avoiding the topic of her doomed relationship. "We're actually kind of swamped at the moment."

"Oh." Julianna's eyes fall to Selene's hands picking at the heart tag cut out of paper. My signature for every bouquet. "Anything I can help you with?"

I open my mouth to answer her, but Selene beats me to it.

"I was just filling Charleigh in on the next few months. We're completely booked, and I'm afraid we don't have enough space to hold the inventory."

I nervously bite the inside of my cheek.

"I think Charleigh is afraid to admit we're in over our heads."

I gape at Selene before turning to Julianna. "We are *not* in over our heads."

From the corner of my eye, Selene mouths, *"We are,"* to Julianna, giving her a small nod.

Julianna giggles before shifting her attention to me.

"Really, Charleigh?" She raises her eyebrows with a satisfied smirk. "You didn't tell me how last night went. How did it go with Asher? Did he agree to find you a new building?" The words spill from her mouth faster than water rushing from a broken dam.

"What?" Selene perks up. "You're looking for a bigger store? That's great." She blows out a large breath of relief. "That'll solve so many problems."

I trade glances between Julianna and Selene. *Shit.* "Not exactly." I wince, ready to hear Julianna start spouting off about how she thinks I chickened out from my meeting and so-called blind date.

"What do you mean?" Selene asks, her face immediately slipping into disappointment.

"Yeah, Charleigh. What *do* you mean?" I have a feeling Julianna knows more than she's letting on. Maybe Asher told Holt about our run in, then Holt told Julianna.

Word can travel fast in situations like this.

Thankfully, a customer walks in. The bell jingles over the front door, and Selene is quick to assist her, leaving Julianna and me at the desk. But not before Selene spins around and wags her pointed finger between us. "I'm going to help this customer and then I want a full play by play of this conversation when I'm done. Leave nothing out."

Julianna giggles again, and I internally groan.

Selene spins around.

I snatch my coffee off the counter and head for my office. If I'm going to talk to Julianna about Asher, I need plenty of caffeine coursing through my veins.

She follows me and immediately sits in the chair across from my desk.

I sit down in mine and place my elbows on the dark oak top. I rest my head in my hands and run my fingers through my hair, pushing it back off my face. I'm still looking down when Julianna breaks the silence.

"So, what happened?"

I release my hands from my head and sit back in my chair. "Do we have to talk about it? I decided to go with a different realtor."

"Bullshit." Julianna places her hands in her lap and sits back in her chair. She's so sure of herself. She's also right. "Holt texted me and said Asher told him you didn't show up, which I know isn't true. Asher is lying, and so are you."

"What are we, in high school? It's like a game of telephone."

"You're keeping something from me, Charleigh Keeler, and I want to know about it." She pauses, then flicks her gaze up, nodding back to the front of the store. "Selene, too."

"You suck, you know that?" I scrunch my nose, but then follow it up with a grunt. "Uh, fine."

In the five years I've known Julianna, I've never once mentioned Asher. I guess now is the time. The words bounce around in my chest, dancing with the embers of a life I used to live. A life completely different from the one I've built and from the one Julianna knows.

I stare off at the pile of papers sitting on my desk. "If I had known it was Asher I was meeting, I wouldn't have gone in the first place."

Julianna leans forward, resting her elbows on the edge of my desk and her chin in her petite hands. "I'm listening," she croons happily.

I look into Julianna's eyes, feeling the heat in my chest starting to simmer. I sigh and pick up a paper clip, sliding my fingers across the thin metal. "Asher and I knew each other back in Connecticut. In high school."

"Oh." My best friend's eyes widen, her pink links forming a perfect circle. Her back turns straight as a pin as she sits up, curiosity piqued.

I take her silence as her wanting me to elaborate a bit more. I'm just not sure exactly how much I'm willing to divulge right now but I know I need to start somewhere. Maybe it'll help get all the stress and shock of seeing Asher out of my system.

"We started dating when we were seventeen. He moved to California the night of our graduation. It didn't exactly end well between us. And by end well, I mean him disappearing in the middle of the night, leaving only a note taped to my windowsill." I leave out the details surrounding Asher's move to California. As the words sift through the embers and make their way out of my mouth, I'm realizing I'm not ready to tell Julianna everything yet. The sting of the wounds worn around my heart is still there. I swallow it down, willing it to fade.

"I'm sorry, Charleigh. If I had known..." Her voice trails off, and I'm thankful she doesn't interrogate me any further.

"It's not your fault. There's no way you could have known. Why would you?" I tilt my head, reading the unwarranted guilt all over Julianna's face.

I rest my palms on my desk and move to organize the loose papers scattered across it. "Anyway, he basically treated me like a stranger when he saw me. He made up some shit about not knowing Holt, claiming he wasn't the one I was supposed to meet. I took his lie as an affirmation that things between us haven't changed in ten years. He obviously still harbors some resentment toward me for whatever reason. I don't even know why when he was the one who left and ended things between us." I sigh. "It's fine, though. I'll keep looking online for a new place, and I'll research other real estate agents. I'll find someone else."

"That's good. Pick yourself up and keep moving on." Julianna nods, but I can tell from the way her eyes dim that she's saddened by my background with Asher.

"Thanks." I give her a warm smile.

"I have an idea." She perks, changing the subject.

I'm not as quick to pull out of my nostalgic mood. "What's your idea?" I begrudgingly ask, scared for the answer. Julianna's ideas don't always turn out for the best.

"Holt has a friend opening a bar this weekend." Her grin stretches from ear to ear, and her eyes sparkle. "It's marketed as a soft opening, but everyone knows all the elites will be there. We can score a few drinks and forget our relationship disasters while plotting your expansion."

I shake my head, blowing out a heavy breath. "I don't know."

"Come on, Charleigh." She taps her fingers on the edge of my desk. "I could really use a night out with my girls, and you could use a night out from the solitary confinement of your apartment."

"My apartment is *not* solitary confinement."

"May as well be."

Despite the knots of sadness tightening in my chest, I cave. "Fine."

Her spine straightens, and she squeals, clapping her hands. "Yay! I can't wait."

She stands in front of my desk and hitches her thumb over her shoulder. "I'll give you a few minutes, and I'll catch Selene up on everything. As long as she's done helping that customer."

I chuckle. "Thanks. She'd probably kill us both if we don't fill her in about Asher as soon as possible... or tell her about your scheme to get us all to go out this weekend."

"She's going to love the idea, and you've got to love her." Julianna beams.

"I do, and I love you, too."

Even if the past has come back to hang over me like a dark cloud, my best friends have come through, carrying the sun with them.

Once Julianna leaves my office, I close the door to think. Selene can handle the front desk for a few more minutes while I figure out what to do about finding a new store.

I open my computer and start browsing the internet for real estate agents who specialize in business spaces as opposed to residential. I need a knowledgeable agent who's familiar with the ins and outs of both the city and accommodating a flower shop's needs. The clock is ticking.

After an hour of research, I finally find someone with credentials close to what I'm looking for: Cyrus Temper.

I type in the address to his office and grin when I notice it's the same building Holt works in. Maybe he knows him, too. I call and set up an appointment for tomorrow.

For the first time since seeing Asher, I see the light at the end of the tunnel. Hopefully, this new realtor will find me the second storefront I so desperately need.

FIVE

ASHER

I manage to sit through all of lunch with Holt without another mention of Charleigh. I guess my compromise of rethinking working with her was enough to suppress his need to pry any further.

Although, I was lying. The way she has my mind all jumbled, there's no conceivable way we can work together without letting the past get in the way.

With my stomach full of lunch and unsettled thoughts of Charleigh, I have my web browser open again, with her name typed into the search bar, when an email comes through. My computer dings, and I open the email as soon as I see Allen Simon's name. A long-time client of mine, Allen has bought several of my listings. I nearly leaped out of my chair when he emailed me saying he was in the market again, looking to buy an apartment building out in Brooklyn. With only a handful of locations, I sent them over for him to consider and have yet to hear back. Until now.

But my vision fades, and my blood pressure rises as I read the text.

"Janette!" I yell.

Within seconds, my assistant quickly shuffles into my office, pushing through the large wooden door. "Yes, Mr. Egan?" she asks on a breath.

"I just received an email from Allen Simon." I shoot her a glare over my computer. "Did he try calling?"

She furrows her brow. "No, sir."

"What the fuck?" I seethe, sitting back in my leather chair as I run a frustrated hand through my hair.

"Is there anything I can do for you?" Janette asks.

I keep my eyes trained on the email. This day has turned into an absolute dumpster fire.

"Allen just emailed me to tell me he's found a better property with Cyrus Temper, and he's going to close on it next week. Faster than I was able to secure for him with the listings I proposed."

"Oh." It's the only word to fall from Janette's mouth before her expression slips into a frown. Her eyes shift to the side, avoiding my stare.

"What is it?" I ask.

"Well," Janette says quietly, her eyes making their way back to me. "On my lunch break, I overheard one of the secretaries for Cyrus Temper talking about Mr. Simon. She mentioned that Mr. Temper told Allen Simon you were increasing your realtor fee and commission by more than fifty percent."

Heat blazes from my neck to my ears. "What the fuck?" I seethe, standing from my chair. "Did you tell her that was wrong?"

"Of course, I did, but she didn't believe me," Janette explains. "I doubt she has little sway persuading Cyrus with the truth since she's just his secretary."

"Fuck," I mutter, raking my fingers through my hair before I slide my palm down my face. "I wish you'd told me this before."

The idea of losing a client to Cyrus has my anger at an all-time high. Panic sets in, and maybe it's because I can't stand losing. I can't stand the thought of returning to the person who lived out of a fifteen-foot trailer with nothing but the hole-laced shirt on his back.

Cyrus threatens everything I've built.

"I'm sorry," Janette apologizes. "I should have told you."

"It's fine," I mutter, waving her off. "I'll figure it out."

She gives me a sympathetic look before turning on her heel and leaving me in the heavy silence of my office.

I'm staring out my window and out at the city. Every day, it looks the same, yet every day is different—much like my job. I didn't get to where I am now by letting clients slip through my fingers. Especially when it comes to competition such as Cyrus Temper.

He's well regarded in the real estate world, and one of the top executives in New York. He's old enough to be my father. Hell, probably even my grandpa. And I know Cyrus doesn't back down from a client, but neither do I. Liquid heat courses through my veins.

With fear of losing Allen setting in, I dial his number, hoping to straighten out any misinformation. The last thing I need is losing out on a multi-million-dollar deal because Cyrus can't keep his greedy fucking mouth shut from all the lies he spews. When Allen doesn't answer, I leave him a message to call me back.

Nothing is a done deal until he signs a contract.

I grab my suit jacket from the back of my chair and stride out of my office, heading straight for the elevators, knowing full well where Cyrus's main office is located. If I can't talk with Allen, I'll go straight to the source.

"I'll be back in a few," I call out to Janette over my shoulder as I stride past her." Cancel all my meetings for the rest of the afternoon."

"Of course," she answers.

Once inside the elevator, I press the button for the top floor. The ride isn't as long as it would be if I were going down to the main lobby. Soon enough, the shiny metal doors slide open effortlessly, then suddenly, I find myself standing in the front lobby of Cyrus's office, where every surface is made of white marble. I straighten my tie and walk up to the desk. The reception area looks so different from the one on my floor, which is covered in hardwood, with tall, glass walls separating the offices. This room is white—stark white.

I clear my throat. "Excuse me."

"How may I help you?" the man behind the desk asks. The name *Travis* is etched into the gold name tag pinned to his chest. His smile is just as white as the floor and walls of this place.

"Yes, I'm Asher Egan. I was hoping to see Mr. Temper. Is he available?"

"I'm sorry, he's with a client at the moment. Would you like to leave him a message or set an appointment to see him?"

"Shit." I rest my hands on my hips. "No, that's okay. Thanks." I scratch the light scruff on my chin and spin on my heel. I may lose a client to Cyrus Temper after all. And not just any client, but one I've worked with in the past. Losing Allen is personal and cuts deep to my core.

I'm tempted to interrogate the secretary by demanding to know which client Cyrus is with, but I bite my tongue and concede instead. For now.

Reluctantly, I head back to the elevators, only to screech to a halt when I hear a familiar voice behind me. It slides down the back of my neck like smooth velvet, warming me in places that have frozen over.

"Have a nice day, Travis. It was nice meeting you." Her

heels click across the marble floor, the sound growing louder as she approaches the elevators.

I keep my back turned to her and look up to see the indicator for the elevator light switch on.

"Asher?"

I twist my head to the side, finding her wide, hazel eyes staring back at me. The expression on her face is almost an exact copy of the one she had the other night at the bar, filled with surprise. Only this time, Charleigh's dressed a bit more modestly. Her skirt isn't as short as the one she wore the night we were supposed to meet. This time, she's wearing a dress, minus the coat. Every inch of her silhouette is on full display, showcasing the curves I haven't been able to kick from my mind. Although the hem of her dress stops just above her knees, the dark purple fabric clings to her body. My gaze travels down to her feet. The image that remained in my mind after I left Connecticut was of the younger version of Charleigh. This Charleigh is full woman. Her hair is a little longer now, her brown waves cascading down below her shoulders. Charleigh's always had curves in her hips and all the places that drive me wild, but somehow, in the past ten years, they've become even more accentuated.

She catches me staring at her and crosses her arms over her chest, pushing her breasts up. Her cleavage is exaggerated, pressing out of the V-cut neckline of her dress.

"Asher," she says again, straightening her back.

"What are you doing here?" I find her eyes.

"I could ask you the same."

I give her an amused grin. "I asked first."

Her left shoulder drops. "You've always liked to play games."

Okay. Not sure what that's supposed to mean.

Her comment adds salt to the wound of possibly losing Allen to Cyrus.

"I guess I'll play your little game," she mutters. My eyes fall to her tongue slipping between her lips to sweep across her pink-glossed mouth. She tosses me a smug grin. "I'm hiring Cyrus to help me find a new location for my business."

The elevator doors slide open, and she glides inside, leaving me to follow and stand beside her before watching the doors close us in. I don't press the button for my floor. Instead, I let Charleigh select the first floor. I clench my hands inside my pockets, and I'm not sure why. It's as if every nerve in my body is on alert around her, every feeling heightened. She knows how to get under my skin, but the sensation it gives me has me wanting to feel it a little longer. Back when we were teenagers, she was the addiction I couldn't break. Seeing her now, I'm realizing she can make that a possibility once again. I already feel it seeping its way into my bones. It's a dangerous feeling—one I've fought to keep away for nearly a decade.

Now I'm stuck inside this small ass elevator with her. My dick twitches, and heat pools in my lower belly from watching the fabric of her skirt stretch and strain around her full, round ass. Her floral scent surrounds me, and her body heat seems to radiate off the metal walls. It's suffocating.

I lean against the wall, putting as much distance as possible between us.

"You're really hiring him?" I choke out.

"Is that so hard to believe?" She arches an eyebrow, mimicking my stance on the opposite wall. "I needed a realtor for my business, and I found Cyrus. He has a great track record of helping business owners like me. He's been around for decades, and he actually wants to help me, unlike other real estate executives I've previously met."

Her usual gorgeous, round eyes narrow into two thin slits.

I resist the urge to roll my eyes at her small dig at me. Cyrus has already sunk his money-hungry claws into her. Just like Allen. Fuck.

I shrug. "It isn't hard to believe. I just hope Cyrus doesn't try to rip you off." I stare up at the ceiling and rock back on my heels. Teasing her used to be a part of who we were. Now, I wonder if I'm just coming off as an arrogant asshole.

By the expression on Charleigh's face, she isn't surprised.

"Why did you lie?" she asks.

"Lie about what?" I ask, confused.

She clenches one hand into a fist and tightens the other on the handle of the purse by her side. "I'm talking about knowing Holt. You said you didn't know him, but you were lying."

"What makes you so sure I was lying? What would I gain from that?" I bite the inside of my cheek. The air inside the elevator swells as Charleigh's shoulders rise. The ends of her dark hair lift with the motion.

"Holt's sister, Julianna, happens to be my best friend. Plus, you're a terrible liar." She shifts her gaze back to the doors, refusing to face me now as she mutters under her breath, "You always have been."

Ouch. Why did that last jab hurt more than it should?

"Fine. I lied. Holt and I have been friends since college."

She scoffs, shaking her head in disbelief. "I knew it. What are the odds?" She looks over her shoulder. "What are the odds of both our best friends being siblings, yet they never mentioned us to each other?"

"Hmm. Seems the Capuletis keep a whole closet stuffed with secrets."

"Possibly." She quickly spins on her heel, turning her whole body toward me as she crosses her arms over her chest and cuts me a glare. "But how do you think your friend feels knowing you lied about not knowing him?"

"How do you think Julianna feels knowing you never told her about me?" I bite back.

The anger in Charleigh's face transforms to one of hurt. The bottoms of her eyes line with liquid, and the colors in them change like a kaleidoscope. Her full lips thin as she inhales a hot breath.

I step forward, closing the space between us. It's the closest I've been to her in ten years.

She steps backward, her spine hitting the wall behind her. Her scent fills the air around us; a mixture of vanilla and flowers. Even with her heels, the top of her head still doesn't meet my chin. I'm hovering over her, looking down at her as she tips her chin up. I take a quick glance at how many floors we still have to go—only ten more left— and her whole body turns rigid with mine pressed against hers.

"Yeah," I practically growl. "Something tells me that if she would have told you it was me you were meeting, you wouldn't have shown up. She didn't know she was setting you up with me, did she?"

Her bottom lip quivers as she inhales a shaky breath. Her face is close to mine. Too close, but she doesn't back down.

"I don't think you want to start comparing relationships and trust."

"What are you implying?" I tighten my jaw, the air swelling once again. Charleigh's expression is full of tension. I can't decide what has her more annoyed: my lie to Holt or the fact I didn't agree to take her on as a client, leaving her to resort to working with Cyrus Temper.

She presses her lips together and swallows, her attention dancing between my mouth and my eyes. She doesn't answer my question.

"What bothers you more, Charleigh?" I ask. "The fact I

didn't want to work with you, or that you think I'm a shit friend? Because it seems to me it might be both."

She bites down on her bottom lip, pulling it between her perfect teeth.

Fuck.

Suddenly, I'm remembering how those lips were once mine to kiss whenever I wanted to.

But things are different now. Vastly different.

Standing this close to her is a mistake. My cock swells, and I have to consciously tell myself this is a bad idea. The elevator can't reach the lobby soon enough.

I'm drawn to Charleigh as quickly and as strongly as the first time I spotted her watching me from beneath her favorite tree.

Despite my interrogation, she remains silent, so I continue. "And don't pretend to be shocked by my question. We both know the truth behind how you really feel about me."

Her bottom lip pops out from between her teeth, the flesh pink from the pressure she placed there. "Wow." The word slowly seeps out of her mouth. Her eyes narrow, once again, and it's as if she's pierced me straight in the chest. "How arrogant you must be to feel hurt for the way I'm treating you now. Doesn't feel good, does it, Asher? Maybe I'm giving you a dose of your own medicine."

I've struck a nerve. Fury and anger have returned to her gaze.

"Ten years. Ten years of dead silence," she forces out. "Silence *you* chose. So, don't act like you're the victim here. You were the one who left. And the thing is, I moved on and made *my* choices."

It took nearly ten years to get Charleigh out of my mind. The pain of what happened, her forcing me to make the decision to leave, is still fresh, even after all this time. We both lost something the night I left, but in a way, I feel I lost more than Charleigh did: my mother *and* Charleigh.

I thought I was doing what was best for the both of us, but the differences between her and me couldn't be more apparent now.

The elevator finally stops. An ear-piercing ding fills the space between us before the doors slide open. I'm still standing in front of Charleigh, pressing her body against the wall for everyone to see.

Pinning me with a sharp glare, she shoves her hands to my chest and quickly walks out. I hold my breath, knowing I should let her go... but like the fool I've always been, I don't.

Charleigh's feet have already carried her out of the main lobby by the time I catch up to her. She pushes against the large, glass door with force and stands on the curb, waiting for a cab. Clearly ignoring me, she raises her hand in the air.

I stare at her for several seconds before she finally speaks again. "What more do you want from me, Asher? At this point, I think it's best if we don't interact with each other."

I keep staring at her, watching her hail a cab. There isn't one for at least another block, but she keeps her hand raised anyway.

"The city really grew on you, didn't it?" I ask quietly.

My question softens her anger. She turns her head, still refusing to lower her hand. The wind blows her hair across her face—a strand getting caught in the corner of her mouth. I itch to reach out and push it back.

"I'm happy," she tells me. "It was always my dream to live here. It was yours once, too, you know. But I guess we both made it. Just not in the way we envisioned."

A pit forms in the center of my chest. I don't like how Charleigh's comments keep finding their way into some deep, hidden part of myself I buried long ago. It's effortless to her. It's effortless for her to tear me apart.

"I'm not the same person I was back then."

"No, you definitely aren't. I'm learning that." She swallows, her eyes flicking back to the building behind us before her gaze swings back to mine. "But neither am I, so..."

The pit in my stomach transforms into a feeling I'm unfamiliar with. I want to change the subject. "Are you sure Cyrus is the right person to help you?"

Her shoulder falls as a cab pulls up alongside us both. She lowers her arm and opens the door, clearly exhausted by our conversation. "What do you care, Asher? You clearly don't want to help me, and my business needs this, so I'll do whatever it takes to make sure I get where I need to go—with or without your help." She glances up at the building again, all the way to the top, where Cyrus's office is. "If Cyrus is that person, so be it."

"Cyrus is a shark in this real estate game. Are you sure you want to risk swimming in those waters?"

Business. It's easier to talk to Charleigh when it's about business.

"He's my only shot..." Her sentence trails off. She shrugs her shoulders and moves to sit in the cab. "What choice do I have?"

I step forward, catching the door before she slams it shut. My fingers grip the top. She sits inside; her chin tipped up as she looks at me.

"Don't hire him. Let me help you find a place." The offer leaves my mouth before I've even comprehended what I'm saying. Call it desperation. Call it ego. Either way, I know money isn't the only force pulling me to Charleigh. There's something more. Something I can't, won't, acknowledge just yet.

"What?" she asks. "That sounds like a terrible idea."

"Come on," I tell her. At first, I'm not entirely sure why I'm offering to work with her. I've been trying to stay away from Charleigh, but then Allen Simon quickly comes to mind. The potential of Allen falling through leaves me desperate. I can't lose the chance to work with Charleigh, either. "I can find you a better place than that asshole upstairs."

"Asshole?" She laughs. "He didn't seem so bad to me."

"Yeah... But that's what you thought about me when we first met."

My comment clearly hits at another place deep inside her. Her mouth twitches, and her smile fades, the memory of me swiftly breaking her heart clear as fucking day. Silence swells between us before she asks, "Why would you want to help me?"

I avoid her stare, looking out at the traffic-riddled street before looking at her again. "Because I can't lose to someone like Cyrus."

"Wrong answer." My hand falls from the door as Charleigh pulls it toward her, closing it. "That was a test question, and you failed."

"You're joking?"

"Nope." Once she closes the door, she rolls down the window and dips her head, looking up at me through the opening. "See? You aren't the same Asher I used to know."

When the cab pulls away, I can't figure out what bothers me more: losing Charleigh to Cyrus, or Charleigh's constant jabs about what a horrible person I've become.

Deep down, I know Charleigh's feelings toward me have merit.

I *have* become an asshole.

SIX

CHARLEIGH

September 24, 2014

The lined paper crinkles under my fingers as I clutch onto it for dear life.

I'm staring out at my twenty other classmates but can only concentrate on one pair of golden-brown eyes staring back at me. My cheeks redden, and heat spreads across my body. Suddenly, I'm aware of everything. The way my jeans sit on my hips. The way my hair is curled. The way my jacket hangs loose over my shoulder.

I nervously run my fingers through my hair and lick my lips.

"Ms. Keeler?" Mr. Jorgeson says beside me.

"Yes." I snap my head to the right.

"You may return to your seat now." His eyebrows rise over his thick, black-rimmed glasses. "Unless you have more to your report on how the Declaration of Independence was drafted?"

I blink, swallowing the lump in my throat. Today isn't my day.

Between the snickering and hushed giggles from the rest of my classmates, my cheeks engulf into flames. "No, sir," I mutter, before shuffling back to my desk in the third row, directly in front of the boy I haven't been able to stop thinking about.

He's wearing the same clothes he's worn every day that I've seen him, but I can't help the thoughts running through my mind. It's as if there's this secret between us—one only either of us know—and every time he looks at me, my heart skips a beat. He still hasn't spoken to me. I've never heard his voice, and while it's three weeks into the start of our senior year, this is the first time I've seen him at school.

I take my seat in front of Asher, only knowing his name from when our teacher introduced him to the entire class less than an hour ago before directing him to take the empty desk behind me. I rest my head in my hand, shielding myself from the rest of the class.

While staring at the pressed flower between the pages of my history textbook, I hear Miranda giggle beside me. "Not only is her family an embarrassment, but she is, too."

"I know," I hear Courtney whisper back. "Can you believe she's wearing that fuzzy jacket? What animal had to die so she could look that stupid?"

"Right?" Miranda croons. "She's just screaming for attention. She's so lame."

Tears sting the back of my eyes, and I inhale a shaky breath. They both continue in a fit of hushed laughter as Mr. Jorgeson calls another student up to give their report. A tear slips from my eye, and I shudder when I feel a tap on my shoulder.

Sniffing, I wipe the tear away and quickly glance behind me. My eyes meet his golden browns before falling to the piece of folded paper in his hand.

I grab it swiftly before twisting back around to unfold it under the shield of my wooden desktop.

My hands are still shaking when I read the five words written on his note.

I thought it was beautiful.

I stare at them before looking back up. Mr. Jorgeson's attention is on Trey reading out his report. I flatten the paper on my desk and scribble out my response.

Beautiful? I wouldn't exactly call the drafting of the Declaration of Independence beautiful.

When I'm finished, I refold the paper and twist back in my seat, hastily dropping the note on the top corner of Asher's desk before anyone notices.

I swear my heart beats loud enough for the entire class to hear. I bite my lip, expecting Mr. Jorgeson to look up and tell me to quiet it down, but he doesn't.

I wait impatiently for Asher to read my reply, knowing I'm already falling for the boy I've never even spoken to.

What is happening?

My mind in spinning in circles, and my stomach flutters, when there's another tap on my shoulder. The folded piece of paper slips down the front of my chest and into my lap. My cheeks are sore from grinning so much when I pick up the paper and unfold it again.

No, not that. Your voice.

I'm fixated on the last two words. Forcing my giddy heart to calm down, I stuff the note in my bag and pretend to focus on the rest of Trey's presentation.

But the truth is, I can't stop thinking about Asher's note both burning a hole in my bag and on my heart.

SEVEN

CHARLEIGH

I was tempted to bail on Julianna's plan to go out tonight, but I changed my mind last minute because I need a night with my girls.

Sitting in my apartment, alone, was only asking for me to think about Asher. Every breath inside the four walls for the past few days has been a hollow reminder of the life we used to have together. Every memory on repeat like a silent movie. The flickering of black and white. The kisses. The tears. The fevered touches. His finger tracing my collarbone. All of it silent but full of meaning.

But unfortunately, along with the pain comes the reminder of how my love for him blossomed. His adoration used to feel like the warm sun beating against my skin on a sticky summer's afternoon. I can't deny the haunting memories of how strong his touch used to be, or how the taste of his tongue used to light my entire body into flames. Over time I thought the memories would become foggy, but ever since seeing him again at the bar, I've been proven wrong. Every memory of Asher is crystal clear, and I hate it.

His arrogance about me working with Cyrus has chiseled its

way under my skin. Why, if he doesn't want to be around me, would *he* want to work with me? I've tried not to think about it since seeing him the other day, remembering that Asher is the one who left me all those years ago. He chose this. Now I need to remember what it took to let him go. I need to remember what it took to forget what he did.

Shoving thoughts of Asher aside, I knock on Julianna's door three times in a row and rock back on my heels. I'm wearing my favorite knee-high, sequined boots, paired with my favorite black sequined dress. The cleavage dips lower than most of my other dresses, and the back is open down to the tailbone. I can't remember where Julianna said we were going. I didn't care as long as it got me out of my apartment and away from thoughts of the boy who stole my heart ten years ago.

I'm doublechecking my outfit when Julianna opens the door.

"Oh, good. You're here." She swiftly wraps her hand around mine before tugging me inside. "Almost ready," she says, leaving me by the front door and disappearing back to her bedroom at the other end of her penthouse apartment.

I glance around the open living room and kitchen. Julianna's clothes are draped over every surface of her living space. Sweaters and dresses are lying across the back of her sofa, and piles of dresses are grouped onto her large, glass coffee table.

"Don't mind the mess!" she yells as if she can read my mind. "I was purging my closet, ready to donate a ton of clothes, and I lost track of time."

"Where's Selene?" I call back from the hall, loving the fact that Julianna thinks to donate her clothes when others of her fortune are quick to throw them out.

She reappears in the doorway at the end of the hall seconds later, stepping into her dress with only her bra and panties on. I didn't even realize she answered the door barely dressed.

"She got caught up writing another chapter in her book, so she's meeting us there."

Selene's true passion doesn't align with mine, as much as I wish it did. She's my best friend, and she's also a killer employee. But I know flowers and plants aren't where her heart lies. Words are more her thing.

"Okay." I nod, inhaling a deep breath. "Is Taron coming?"

Julianna pauses while slipping her dress over her waist. Her eyes harden, and her face stiffens. "No."

I hold my hands up in surrender, sensing her annoyance. "I won't ask for more details."

"Good." She shimmies her hips, and her black dress stretches over her curves before she slips her arms into the sleeves. "Because I don't want this night to be tainted before it's even begun."

"You know..."—I smile—"I find it funny you were relentless when you wanted to hear about Asher, but you won't spill as easily about Taron."

Her face falls, followed by her shoulders. "I promise I'll catch you up on where I'm at after tonight. I just want one night of fun and nothing serious."

My heart aches for my best friend. I love Julianna and just want her to be happy. Despite her immense wealth, I know she hasn't skated through life, and I can't help but agree with her. I don't want to think or talk about Asher tonight.

I smirk. "Pinky promise?"

Her grin reappears. "Pinky promise."

"Great." I clap my hands together. "Now, where are we meeting Holt and Selene at again?"

Julianna disappears from the open doorway to her bedroom before reappearing with a bright purple, metallic handbag. She meets me in the living room. "One of his friends opened this new beer garden over in the Village. It's supposed to be this amazing place with at least a hundred beers on the menu, or something like that."

"But you don't like beer."

"Holt assured me they have cocktails as well." She stands in front of the large, round, gold-framed mirror on the wall near the front door and swipes a fresh layer of lip gloss over her lips. "Apparently this guy owns a million bars in the city and it's what he's known for."

"Nice." I nod.

After Julianna slips on her heels, we head out the door and head toward the front of the building to meet her driver, who is taking us to the Village. Once there, we join the gathering crowd outside.

The red brick exterior of the beer garden is covered in strings of golden lights. Along the front and side of the restaurant, patio tables are scattered across the concrete, with a small votive candle sitting in the middle of each one. A large grand opening sign hangs above the bar's front door, and the place is already beginning to fill up. People stand outside, huddled in groups while others are sitting inside near the main bar.

Julianna and I walk in, quickly spotting Holt sitting at a table on the back patio. The patio isn't nearly as full as the inside; the loud music and chatter quickly drowning out, meaning it's quieter out here. Holt already has a beer flight sitting in front of him. Five small beer glasses sit on top of the wooden board, each beer is a different color.

Julianna slides onto the bench beside her brother while I take the chair across from them and soak in the atmosphere. Bright green bushes are situated in each corner of the area. It takes me a moment to realize we're basically sitting in the back alley of the restaurant. The owner of this place has transformed it into something completely different. Warm, soft guitar music lilts quietly in the background.

"Hello, Charleigh," Holt greets me, pulling my attention away from the musician plucking at his guitar.

I smile. "It's good to see you, Holt. It's been a while."

He shrugs casually, taking a sip of his beer. "I've heard your business is booming, so it's understandable." He picks up one of the leather-bound menus from the end of the table and sets it in front of Julianna and me. "There's the drinks menu." He leans back slightly and glances around the bar. "Weston should be around here somewhere. He said he was going to make a few rounds before heading back over."

I shake my head, having no clue what I want. I know I just need alcohol in my system. I nudge the menu forward and give Holt a shrug. "I don't know what I want. I think I'll just take whatever you're having." I nod to his beer.

Holt smiles, swallowing down what's left in his glass. "We'll make it easy on West by getting us two."

I laugh as Julianna continues to scan the menu, her eyes dancing over the glossed page. "I'm just going to have a Manhattan."

"Of course, you would." Holt nods, his perfectly-styled brown hair unmoving. It's easy to see the similarities between the Capuleti siblings when they're sitting beside each other, despite their age difference. I smile, noticing the way the dimples in their right cheeks deepen with their grins.

"I know what I like." Julianna shrugs. "Can't fault me for that."

Holt frowns. "Debatable."

Julianna's eyes flutter shut. "I refuse to fish for your meaning in that comment. I'm determined to make tonight a good one. Instead, I'll be the better sibling and opt to asking how you're doing. How's the magazine?"

Holt's mouth falls open to answer, but he snaps it shut when his attention is pulled away.

"So sorry I'm late." Selene huffs, coming to a stop behind Holt and Julianna. Her eyes dance between the two, obviously weighing her choices. After noticing Julianna is sitting at the end of her side of the bench, she slowly works her way to Holt's side. Her black leather leggings stretch across her thick, curvy thighs, and her mossy green eyes sparkle in the golden lights. She frantically scans the table before her shoulders fall in disappointment. Perhaps she was hoping there would be a drink waiting for her. "I've been stuck on this one chapter for nearly an entire week, and I finally had a breakthrough. I couldn't stop until I finished. But then my sister London called me."

"How is she?" Julianna asks, leaning around Holt.

"I don't know." Selene swipes a few stray hairs from her face, and her eyes quickly flashing to the man beside her. "She's struggling in Boston. I'm working on convincing her to give New York a chance."

I've met Selene's sister London only once, over a year ago. She was very sweet, but also very reserved. I don't know much about her other than her and Selene have only been sisters since Selene's parents adopted London when she was thirteen. From what I've gathered from Selene, she's fairly close with her sister and loves her as if they were born from the same parents.

"I hope she's okay," I tell Selene. "Moving here can be intimidating at first, but I'm sure she'd love it."

"Yeah." Selene scrunches her nose. "I don't know, though. Her husband doesn't even want to consider it. I don't know too much about him. They've only been married for a few days."

"Oh, well, hopefully he's a good one then if she's willing to stay," I offer up, trying to shove down my thoughts of Asher.

"Who knows?" Selene waves her hand, and I can tell she's wishing she had a drink sitting in front of her. "I've tried growing closer to my sister and getting her to share more of her life, but it's been hard. I wasn't even at the wedding. It was a quick courthouse kind of thing, which is a disservice to her, in my opinion. But if I were to guess, he probably isn't that great. London hasn't exactly had the best track record when it comes to men."

"Have any of us?" I ask, giggling to myself.

Julianna shoots me a glare, but it doesn't last long before her mouth pulls into a smile. "Good question," she practically sings, deviously, swinging her attention on her brother with a cheshire cat grin. "What do you have to say, brother?"

"Oh, no." He shakes his head, refusing to look in Selene's direction. He's noticeably scooted farther away from her on the bench. "We're not talking about me."

"Why not?" Selene asks, not caring that Holt has practically ignored her for the entire five minutes since she sat down. "You seem to be avoiding quite a bit of conversation tonight."

Holt sighs and presses his lips together, his nostrils flaring with a heavy exhale. Silence descends the table, until Julianna's attention is stolen from the two sitting beside her.

"Oh, fuck," she whispers, her eyes moving above me, dragging the attention of the everyone else the same way. The toe of her boot sharply meets my shin under the table.

"Ow." I gape, shocked she had the nerve to kick me. "What did you do that for?" I ask, thinking she's getting me back for my passive comment about her track record of boyfriends. But I know it isn't that when her wide eyes stare at something, or someone, over my shoulder. I twist on the bench and immediately spot Asher emerging from the entrance to step inside the bar, heading in our direction.

I twist back around in my seat and roll my eyes. "Oh, fuck."

"That's what I said," Julianna hisses before turning her attention to her brother. "You didn't tell me you invited him."

I can feel Asher's presence immediately. Like a heavy-weighted shadow, lurking, towering above me. The hairs on the back of my neck prickle, and my body hums, the vibration slithering down my spine to the backs of my legs. The conversation at the table has completely disappeared with Asher's entrance.

"Hi, Asher." Julianna grins. "Good to see you."

"You, too, Julianna." His velvety voice slips over my bare shoulder, meeting my ear.

Julianna's uneasy gaze moves back to me as Asher sits down beside me.

"Charleigh," he says, making himself comfortable. "Nice to see you."

I can practically feel his gaze searing my skin. I whip my head to the side, finally bringing myself to look at him.

"Asher." I utter his name through gritted teeth, putting on a fake smile. I can't ignore how my heart pounds, or how all of our friends are suddenly watching this turn of events unfold. His scent invades my space. Everything about him is shiny and new —a complete contradiction to the man he used to be.

A deep blue jacket is wrapped around his broad shoulders. Beneath it is a plain white T-shirt. It's odd to think this is the first time in recent memory that I've seen him in anything other than an expensive, pressed suit. Despite his informal outfit, he still looks as if he owns half of New York City.

His hair is disheveled, yet every strand stands somewhat remarkably in the right place. A few hang over his forehead, allowing his golden eyes to stand out against the lights. He's wearing a pair of dark jeans, torn at the knee. I'm sure they cost more than an entire floral arrangement from my store.

Fuck.

Asher catches my too-long stare. The corner of his mouth curls. "Everything okay, Charleigh?"

"Of course." Sarcasm drips from my tongue. "Why wouldn't it be?" I lift my chin and turn back to face Julianna. I give her a small, reassuring smile. There is no way in hell I'm going to allow Asher to think the way he looks has any sort of effect on me.

Asher doesn't say another word, but I can still feel his stare burning a hole in me.

"I just didn't know you were going to be here," I mutter, scraping my nail across the table. "That's all."

"Would that have changed your mind about coming tonight?" He smirks, and I hate the way it makes my pussy clench in response. Everything about him is shiny and clean. I feel drawn to him for reasons that have my head, heart, and the space between my legs waging war.

I shoot Asher a glare, refusing to answer his question.

Deep down, I don't know if I would have backed out of tonight if I had known he was going to be here. But now, with him staring at me like this, I *know* I would have cancelled.

Asher grins... but he doesn't just grin. He allows his lips to spread as far as they can, displaying his perfect, white teeth. His grin is as devious as if he were making the winning move in a chess game. *Check. Mate.*

My stomach dips because he knows he's won an argument.

His strong thigh is almost pressed against mine, and I can feel the heat radiating off his body. I try to scoot away from him but come up short. I'm sitting on the edge of the bench already. If I move any farther away from Asher, my ass will be planted on the concrete.

I cross my arms and rest them on the edge of the table. Julianna is staring straight at me with a worried expression. Her eyebrows are knitted together, even though her shoulders are relaxed.

"Sorry I haven't been able to get back around yet. This was meant to be a soft launch, but... you know," says a man, who suddenly appears at the end of our table.

All five of us swivel our heads in his direction. He lifts his hands into the air, but his smile reaches his eyes. He appears around my age—late twenties, maybe thirties. His thick, dark beard is just past the point of being considered unkempt, but aside from that, he's polished and clean. His long hair is slicked back, displaying his crystal blue eyes, and the corded muscles in his arms stretch when he plants his hands on his hips.

"It's all right, man," Holt says. "Asher just got here, so you made perfect timing."

Asher stands and reaches across the table. "Asher Egan. It's nice to finally meet you."

"Weston Knight." He grins. "Same here."

My eyes dance between the two men before Asher sits back down. I look at Julianna, hoping she can give me a clue about what's happening, but she simply shrugs and shakes her head.

"Thanks for coming to my opening." West runs a hand across the top of his head as he keeps talking to Asher. "I'm swamped tonight, but I'll be sure to grab your number before you leave. I definitely want to work with you once I have this place settled."

"Sounds good, man," Asher agrees. "I look forward to it."

"Great." West rubs his hands together. "Now, what can I get you all to drink?" he asks, scanning the group.

We all give him our orders, until Asher is the only one left.

"I'll just have an ice water with lime," he says. "Thanks."

"No problem." West offers us a soft smile before disappearing to get Asher's drink.

"You aren't going to try any of the beer?" I ask Asher. "Kind of rude considering you want West to hire you, no?"

He turns to look at me. His eyes narrow, and his eyebrows dip in annoyance. I don't care. He's the one who sat down with arrogance dripping from his all too perfect mouth. "I don't drink. Is it that strange?"

"Well, no." I swallow. "I mean, if you don't want to drink,

it's not strange. But we are at a beer garden, so naturally, I just thought..."

"You thought wrong." He lifts his arm from under the table and rests it on the edge, his gold watch glinting in the twinkling lights strung above us.

"Oh." My cheeks burn with embarrassment. I suddenly feel like I've stumbled into a topic where I'm forcing Asher to be vulnerable in front of everyone. But curiosity still gets the better of me. "Since when?"

"Second year of college." He sniffs, looking down at the table at nothing. "I drank way too much my freshman year and realized how fucked up I was. I didn't want to fall down that path when I knew exactly where it would lead."

I knew his mother's death influenced him, but I never thought it would drive him to the point of going completely sober.

West returns with our drinks before leaving us again. The group each take a sip of theirs, eyeing each other over the rims of our glasses.

Asher's first year of college was immediately after he left me and Connecticut behind. I should have known better than to assume alcohol hadn't influenced his life in one way or another. His mother was an alcoholic, and the repercussions of her drinking led to where Asher and I are today: perfect enemies and perfect strangers.

The entire table falls silent.

"Oh, well, that's good then," I finally say, because I'm unsure of what else *to* say.

"How's the flower shop?" he asks, catching me off guard.

I'm not entirely certain it's genuine.

"It's good." I nod. "Business is thriving."

Short and to the point. I don't want to give Asher too much

information. Or the truth. I glance over his shoulder to Selene, silently begging her not to spill the truth.

"What part of the city is it in?" Asher swipes his tongue across his smooth lips after he takes a sip of his water.

I arch an eyebrow, unsure of his motive for wanting to know the location of my shop. "Upper West Side."

"Huh," he says, smirking. "Sounds like I might have to stop by some time and check it out."

"Right." I roll my eyes, unconvinced he will ever take the time out of his busy schedule to visit my store. "Don't worry about it. I know my little shop is beneath billionaires like you."

The tip of Julianna's foot taps against mine, and I quickly look up and across the table.

"*Stop it.*" She mouths the words quickly, half turning her face away from Holt and Asher.

"*It's fine,*" I mouth back, giving her another smile before I pick up the lightest beer from the selection in front of me. I take a sip, thankful for the relief it brings. The bubbly liquid coats my tongue, fizzing its way down my throat.

When I place the glass back down on the table, Asher's staring at me again. My breath catches in my throat, and butter-flies erupt inside my stomach. I cross my legs, knowing my lace thong is absolutely drenched at this point.

As they say, old sensations die hard. Or is that habits? Either way, my entire body is running on muscle memory at this point.

"Hey, Ash," Holt interrupts, cutting the tension. "How's it going with Allen Simon?"

Asher looks away from me, closes his mouth, and the muscles in his jaw tighten. He scoffs, clearly frustrated as he runs his hand across his mouth before sighing heavily. "He hasn't returned my calls yet."

"Well, shit," Holt blows out.

"Yeah, I don't know what happened, and I really don't want to talk about it."

"I'm sure you'll be fine," I mutter, the bitterness leaving me before I have the chance to pull it back. "You're in real estate. Isn't your job to negotiate? To manipulate others to cut a deal?"

I regret the words as soon as they leave my mouth. Asher tenses beside me, and the air is thick with our sour history. My cheeks flame red, and I want to run and hide from everyone's constant stares. I can't seem to keep my mouth shut.

Seconds pass with the entire table sitting in silence. A lump forms in my throat, and my heart flutters. Julianna quickly glances at Selene before looking back at me.

"Have you found any promising locations for your shop yet?" Julianna asks me., throwing out a lifeline.

"Oh, um..." I frown, thinking of how to answer her with everyone at the table. Cyrus has yet to send me any listings. For now, I'm at a standstill until he emails me.

Before I can speak, Asher interrupts me.

"Charleigh decided to hire Cyrus Temper to help find her a place," he interjects. "Didn't she tell you?"

"What?" Both Holt and Julianna shift their focus on me, asking the same question at the same time, their voices blending. Holt darts his gaze to Asher, clearly expecting him to have a reaction after just telling us he lost a client to Cyrus. Now I've agreed to work with him.

I'm sure the rejection must sting. Especially to someone as driven as Asher.

"You hired Cyrus?" Holt asks, his eyebrows practically flying off his forehead.

"Yeah," I squeak out, shrinking with the sudden attention. "Cyrus has a good track record for helping business owners like me."

I wish I could smack the smug expression off Asher's face

right now. I can feel his gaze piercing me like a hot branding iron. He was waiting for the perfect opportunity to shine the spotlight on me, and I know he's doing it to get back at me for refusing to hire him, for choosing Cyrus over him.

"He also has a reputation of ripping people off," Holt adds.

"Oh, come on." Julianna leans back, rolling her eyes at her brother. "He does not."

"He does," Holt insists. "I've heard stories from some of his clients."

"What kind of stories?" Selene asks, clearly intrigued with where Holt is going with this. Whereas I am not. I couldn't care less. Anyone is better than working with your ex.

"Holt's telling the truth," Asher chimes in. "Cyrus has a history of inflating his realtor fee. Some of his clients have also complained about his lack of negotiating."

"Okay," Selene says, holding out her hand. "Maybe the fee thing can be debated, but the negotiating? How can anyone prove he could have gotten them a better deal?"

"They can't, and I trust him." I take another gulp of my beer and look at Holt, making sure to direct my attention to him, not Asher. "I have my budget set, so I know he'll find a place that will work for me."

"I hope he will." Holt's eyes soften. I can tell he's still slightly worried about my decision to work with Cyrus, but he doesn't press any further.

Beside me, Asher lifts his glass to his lips, stifling a laugh against the rim, his shoulders bouncing.

"What?" I ask, annoyed. When did he become so arrogant?

"Nothing." He frowns, three lines creasing his forehead. The small dimple in his cheek reappears with his smug grin.

"No," I say. This time I turn my body completely toward him. The one beer I've had has already began to warm my body, emboldening me. "I know you want to say something, Asher. So, just say it."

"My opinion doesn't matter anymore, Charleigh. It hasn't for a long time. Do what you want."

"Fine." I press my mouth firmly shut, clenching my teeth. The pressure I put on them makes my head pound. Asher's words cut through me. This is not the man I knew when I was a teenager. This man is narcissistic and arrogant. "You're right—I can do what I want." I stand up, unwilling to take any more of Asher's bitter words. "I'm sorry, I can't do this." I look at my two best friends with watery eyes, unable to look at Holt. "I'm sorry."

I step out from behind the bench and head toward the exit leading to the street. I've nearly made it there when Asher steps in front of me.

I close my eyes and inhale a deep breath, willing the tears to not spill. "Get out of my way, Asher."

I open them to find he's still standing in front of me. Only this time, he's closer, and I track his body all the way from his feet to his chest.

Dammit. Why does he look so fucking good?

I take a step to my right to walk around him and push through the gate, staying close to the building as I make my way to the sidewalk to hail a cab, since Julianna's driver was the one who dropped us off.

"I know you're an adult and you're smart, Charleigh," Asher yells behind me. "That's the only reason I keep warning you about Cyrus."

"Well, just stop." I spin around. My voice has intensified, rising out of my chest with more force than I intend it to. "It's not helping, and I'm not yours to protect. I've gotten this far without you or your help. You can't just suddenly reappear in my life and pretend to be this white knight coming to rescue me.

I don't need rescuing from some billionaire. And just in these few days since running into you, you're proving to me why it's not a good idea to hire you over Cyrus. It's too complicated and messy. *We're* too complicated and messy."

Asher stares at me with a blank expression, lifting his chin. "Hiring him will be a mistake."

"No, Asher. Hiring *you* would be the mistake." I cross my arms over my chest and narrow my eyes. "Good night."

I keep my firm gaze on him, waiting until he finally decides to turn around and head back to the table full of my friends.

After he disappears around the corner, I finally release a breath. The same breath I've been holding since he shattered my heart, leaving the broken pieces behind without another look back.

EIGHT

CHARLEIGH

Hiring Cyrus Temper was a mistake. Asher was right to say he is a shark in the real estate world. What I don't understand is how he's so successful when it's clear he's trying to squeeze every dime possible out of me. Every single listing he has sent has been nearly twenty percent over my budget. Cyrus is circling me like I am his prey while I just try to keep my head above water.

Knowing Asher was right has my stomach sinking to new depths. It's not that I expected to find a new building in time for the dozen events I have planned over the next two months, but I needed to at least start the process. The longer I waste time on spaces like the ones Cyrus is suggesting, the longer it will take. Time is ticking.

"No," I grumble, even though I'm alone. The shop has been quiet these last thirty minutes since it's still early in the morning. I'm resting my chin on my hand, scrolling through the listings again, hoping my eyes are deceiving me. "Nope, not that one." I groan again, picking up my coffee and feeling more hopeless by the second. I tip the cup back, sucking out any last drops sitting at the bottom—the perfect metaphor for my life. I swallow and slam my cup down, preparing to go back over Cyrus's options.

"Having a bad day?"

I look up from the laptop to find Asher standing on the other side of the counter. I must have been too focused to hear the bell jingle above the front door.

"What are you doing here?" I sigh, my attention falling back to the screen. The last thing I need is to let Asher know he was right about Cyrus. I'm still angry with him about what happened at the beer garden. He always finds a way to get under my skin.

He grins and waves his arm around my store. "I came to see all of this."

"Right." I snort, eyeing him across the counter. "Like you care," I mumble sarcastically against the rim of my cup. Mumbling and groaning seems to be the tone of the day.

"I do care." He rests his elbows on the edge of the counter.

I instinctively pull back, but not before shutting off my computer screen.

Ever since the other night at the beer garden, I've realized the hold he still has on me. In a way, as much as I hate to admit it, Asher's had a hold on me since that day in the elevator, when we were both leaving Cyrus's office. It's been ten years since I've felt his body so close to mine. His scent, the way his tall, sculpted body pressed against me—all of it was risky and reckless. I itched to pull away from the elevator wall and press against him. The muscles of my thighs tingled, remembering the way it felt to have Asher between them. It was a dangerous place to be. Even more so when he sat next to me the other night. From now on, I'm not taking any chances. I'm still standing behind the counter, in awe of Asher stepping foot in my store. He looks out of place, much like the way a square peg would fit into a round hole.

Silence has settled between us. I'm silently cursing the fact I gave Selene the day off. She would have made a great buffer.

Asher steps back and begins making his way around my store. On the other side of the full glass window , a shiny black Mercedes is parked along the curb. A man in a black suit and valet style hat is leaning against it, scrolling through his phone, every few seconds looking up into the store. He must be Asher's driver or bodyguard. Maybe both.

I watch Asher carefully while he explores the space, stopping every few feet to inspect several bouquets. I bite my bottom lip as he removes his hand from his pocket and runs his thumb across the petal of a white lily. He's wearing a smooth, black suit, with a white collared shirt underneath. His polished shoes stand out against the dull white floor. He runs his hand through his hair, pushing it away from his forehead. My mind wanders, remembering that he's the same person who used to wear the same clothes three days in a row.

He glances at me from across the room, catching me staring. His face remains still, but his eyes are swimming with thoughts. A piece of me aches, wanting to know what thoughts are swirling inside that gorgeous head of his. He stares at me for several seconds before finally moving on. He makes it to the other side of the room and picks up a bag of dried rose petals before bringing them to his nose. He makes a face then puts it down.

Curiosity gets the better of me, and I move out from behind the counter.

"So, really... what are you doing here?"

I've always wanted to trust Asher, and at one point in time, I did. Now though, I don't. History has taught me to think twice before handing it back to him.

"I'm serious, Charleigh." He laughs. "I came down here to see your shop."

"Forgive me if I have my doubts. You're different than before, so it's a little hard to trust."

He nods, and I can see the twinge of hurt flicker in his eyes.

I don't trust him. At least not yet.

The flicker of hurt vanishes quickly. I can't tell if he's trying to avoid examining my statement deeper or if he simply doesn't care enough to.

His eyes wander across the glass windows, then back to the flowers. "You were always obsessed with flowers," he says. "I used to find them wedged and pressed between the pages of your books. Do you still do that, or did you stop once you opened this place?"

I walk over to the small table of empty vases I have set out and straighten one that's out of place, with Asher only few feet away from me. "No, I still do it. But wildflowers are kind of hard to find in the city, so I really only pick them when I go to visit my parents."

"Right." Asher nods, pressing his mouth into a straight line. His jaw ticks. Bringing up my parents has clearly triggered something inside him, like striking a match in a pitch-black room.

The mention of my parents even catches me off guard. Though they live only two hours away, I haven't seen them for a few months. I like to keep it that way.

He walks closer to me, reaching out to touch another bouquet. This time, his fingers grasp the paper heart tag tied to the ribbon. He holds his breath, then quickly drops his hand and turns to me.

"How's it going with Cyrus?"

"I knew it." I point at him and spin on my heel, shaking my head. "I knew that was the real reason for you coming down here."

"Look," Asher says defensively. "I know you think I

suddenly have this dark, cold heart made of ice, but I don't. Yes, I want to know how it's going with Cyrus, but I also wanted to check out your store, see how all of this is doing, and understand why you need a bigger place."

"Is my store what you expected?"

"It's pretty good, but I can see why you need a new location. This place is small and clearly unequipped to handle your level of inventory." He twists his mouth in thought. "Back to my original question. How is it going with Cyrus?"

I bite the inside of my cheek, trying to contain the frustration boiling over. I don't want Asher to see how desperate I am for his help. I don't want him to know that Cyrus has hardly put any effort into finding me the perfect place. I don't want him to know that I refuse to ask my father for any help. I straighten my back and cross my arms.

"It's working out great." *Lie.* "Cyrus is sending me plenty of great listings." *Another lie.*

Asher stands on the other side of the counter and grips the edge, leaning forward. Again, he's invaded my space, but this time I don't pull back.

"Remember that bullshit you spouted off the other day about me being a terrible liar?" he asks, tilting his head.

"Yes, and it wasn't bullshit. It's true."

"Hate to break it to you, Charleigh Keeler"—he clicks his tongue—"but you're a terrible liar, too. Always have been."

"I'm not lying."

"Listen, I figured it might not be going well with Cyrus. Yes, he's successful and has a great reputation in the city, but I also know he plays hardball with his clients. You give him a budget, and he sends you listings thousands of dollars over what you originally told him. Trust me, after you call him out on it, he's going to tell you there aren't any locations in your price range."

"I don't get it. How is he successful if he's lying to all his clients?"

"He counts on clients not questioning him. He knows New York is a tough place to sell unless it's to the super wealthy."

I allow my eyes to wander around my store. Part of me wants to believe Asher—a very tiny part—and at some point, I may have to consider the possibility that he's telling the truth. I can't allow my pride to stand in the way of my business. Asher isn't worth it. Every possible scenario runs through my mind. I figure I have three options: continue working with Cyrus, hoping he'll show me a listing within reason, work with Asher and see if he lives up to the hype *Fortune* put out about him, or give up on the idea of expanding and scale back on clients. I already know the last option isn't an option at all. I've already lost one dream before. I'm not about to lose another one.

I'm starting to consider my worst-case scenario when Asher cuts into my thoughts. "What if I offered you a deal?"

"What kind of deal?" I narrow my eyes with suspicion.

"You don't officially have to take me on as your realtor, and you don't need to fire Cyrus just yet. I'll send you plenty of options within your budget, and if you don't find a better offer with me, you can go right ahead with what Cyrus has to offer you."

I twist my mouth with uncertainty. "You must be pretty confident if you think you can find me a better place than Cyrus."

"I am confident, and that's because I know I can do better than him." This time, he doesn't grin. He pulls his shoulders back, and slides his hands into his pockets. "What do you say? Do we have a deal?"

The idea of Asher finding me a better place than Cyrus is intriguing. Half of my heart wants to jump on his offer. The other half is still battered and bruised from losing faith in him when he left me ten years ago, then again the other day when he said he didn't want to lose to Cyrus. Hiring Asher on a trial basis would require me to be around him for more than a matter of five minutes, and I've already struggled with the few times I've seen him since that night at the bar.

I inhale a deep breath, knowing just how to keep myself in check with Asher while still working toward doing what is right for my business. "Okay."

His dark eyebrows rise. "Okay?"

"Yes." I cross my arms. "I'll work with you on this trial basis."

"Great." His grin of satisfaction makes my heart perform jumping jacks.

"On one condition..."

His grin drops. "What condition?"

"My store is important to me, Asher. Don't make me regret trusting you again."

Suddenly, the confidence he walked in here with is gone, and I see the boy I met at seventeen standing in front of me. Maybe the old Asher still exists.

I lean forward on the counter and cross my arms on the cool, hard top. I cock my head to the side and stare up into Asher's golden eyes. His movement is subtle, but nonetheless, I do notice him shifting closer to me, slow and deliberate. Calculated, much like the way he runs business. Asher is a bad habit I need to drop quickly.

"Do we have a deal?" I whisper, refusing to listen to the tiny voice in my head screaming for me not to do this. I've never listened to her, despite what the consequences were.

He spreads his arms out and grips the edge of the counter, lowering his head until it's level with mine. "We have a deal."

Asher's lips part as he sucks in a sharp breath.

My heart races in my chest, and for a moment, I wonder what mess I've gotten myself into.

He doesn't give me time to think on it for too long before he pulls away, snapping us out of the vacuum we've found ourselves in. He holds out his hand. "Give me your phone."

"What? No," I say quickly, knowing why he wants it. I'm already heading down a dangerous path. Giving him my phone to put his number in would be a bad idea. It opens us up to talking to each other more than during business hours.

"This is ridiculous, Charleigh." He sighs. "You're my client now. I kind of need to have your phone number."

"Can't you just email me the listings?"

His eyes narrow. "No. I check my phone more than I do my emails. This will be more convenient."

My thighs tingle again with his heated stare, the same way they did in the elevator. I need to figure out how I'm going to work with Asher without finding myself wishing he'd satisfy the need my body clearly wants him to rectify.

"Fine." I grab a blank paper heart tag from behind my desk and scribble my phone number down before handing it to Asher.

He eyes it for several seconds before slipping it into the front pocket of his suit. "I'll send you a text with what time we're meeting tomorrow."

"Meeting?" I ask, already regretting my decision to let Asher back into my life. I should have taken baby steps, not giant-sized ones. "I thought you were just going to send me the listings."

"Is that what Cyrus did? Just send you listings?"

"Yeah." I point to my laptop. "He just had me look over them and go scope them out for myself."

"See, this is another reason why you should hire me instead of Cyrus. We're going sightseeing."

He's already to the door, making his way out. Three lines crease each of his cheeks when he grins. "See you tomorrow."

I watch in stunned silence as his driver holds the car door open for him, and Asher slips inside.

Once the car pulls away, I'm questioning the deal I've just made with him.

Because when it comes to Asher, I'm always left playing with fire.

NINE

CHARLEIGH

October 29, 2014

I'm clutching my phone, pressing it against my chest, still buried under the covers of my queen-sized bed. My house is large enough that my parents shouldn't hear me, but when it comes to Asher I try not to take any chances. I've only introduced him to them once, but that one time was all it took for me to know they didn't and don't approve of him. In any universe or under any circumstances.

My father looked at him with disdain, my mother with disgust. They played their parts well until Asher left, but behind closed doors they didn't shy away from making their feelings known.

So, for the past three weeks, when Asher has been climbing the trellis outside my bedroom window once they've gone to sleep, we've tried to be as quiet as possible.

Every night while I impatiently wait for him, my heart rate accelerates and my neck tingles. The anticipation of knowing how it feels when I'm with him circles around me every night he comes over. It's my favorite part of the day. Even if all we are is friends. For now.

My phone vibrates against my chest, the screen casting a blue glow against my skin. With shaky fingers, I unlock his message.

Asher: Coming up.

I scramble out of my bed, tossing my down comforter to the side. I tiptoe to my window and look out to see Asher climbing the trellis. I pinch my bottom lip between my teeth and glance over my shoulder, making sure my father hasn't woken up. The hallway is still dark, with no light filtering in through the gap beneath my door. Turning my attention back to the window, I see Asher grip the edge of the window before he hoists himself through the opening.

He swings one leg over, but the other gets caught on the lip of the windowsill, and he stumbles forward, his hands shooting out to catch his fall on the plush carpet of my bedroom.

I cover my mouth with the palm of my hand, stifling my giggle.

"Oh, my God," I gasp, muffling my laughter as I step back but hold my hand out to help Asher up off my floor. "Are you okay?"

He nods, keeping quiet while he pulls himself to a stand. When he looks up, he's grinning. My heart races with the way he's smiling at me, as it has since the first time I saw him standing in the middle of my street.

I giggle again, pinching my lip under my teeth to stifle myself.

"Shh," Asher whispers, closing the space between us. His eyes nervously move to my bedroom door behind me before he places his finger to my mouth. "If your dad comes in here and finds me with you, he'll kill me."

Asher's shadowed figure towers over me. He's at least a foot taller than me, and even in the subtle glow of my bedside lamp, his eyes flicker with warmth.

My smile wanes under his touch, alarm bells screaming inside me, focusing on his touch. My heart somersaults in my chest, the echoes of the pounding vibrating up my throat to the place where his finger meets my mouth. We haven't kissed yet, and I play it off as though I haven't spent every minute of the last three weeks wishing we had. Even if he hasn't kissed me or voiced his feelings for me out loud, I know I'm, without a doubt, in love with him.

Asher's gaze constantly dances between my eyes and my mouth, never knowing where to stop. My breath dances across his skin, and I grip onto his shirt to pull him closer. He follows my lead, not breaking the trance we've pulled ourselves in to.

I don't want this to stop. I don't want *him* to stop.

My fingers tighten on the familiar fabric of Asher's shirt. He's wearing the same clothes he did two days ago, but I don't say a word, knowing why. Asher only owns three different T-shirts and two pairs of jeans, but that doesn't bother me.

Unlike everyone else at school.

Apparently.

Though they don't like me, either. I think it's another reason why Asher and I clicked effortlessly. We're outcasts. Two sides of the same coin.

Asher changed my perspective on life that day he told me my voice was beautiful, and I haven't looked back since.

"Can I tell you something?" he whispers.

I nod, clutching onto his hole-ridden shirt even tighter. "Of course," I whisper back, feeling like a typical teenage girl. Raging hormones. First love butterflies. All of it is crashing around me like waves roaring onto the beach during a storm.

I welcome the feeling with open arms.

Asher shifts, and instinct has me standing on my toes.

Finally lowering his finger, he shoves his hands nervously into his dirty jeans.

"What is it?" I ask with uncertainty.

"I, um..." He swallows, and for a moment I think he might retreat. I'm worried I'll blink and suddenly watch him climb back down the trellis outside my window. "This is hard for me to say, but there's something I've been wanting to tell you for a while."

"You can tell me."

"I'm not exactly good with words." He winces.

"Is that why you always carry your notebook with you?"

"No." A crease forms in the corner of his tilted mouth. "I use that for something else."

"Oh." I frown, unsure where this conversation is going.

I'm still holding onto Asher, keeping his body pressed to mine, but he hasn't given me any hint that he wants to pull away.

"You don't have to tell me if you don't want to. I get it."

"I can try to tell you." He hesitates.

I don't answer, hanging onto every word as if it's the last I'll ever hear.

"My home life isn't exactly the best," he admits.

A knot forms in my chest with his confession. I know the basics of Asher's life but not his darkest secrets.

"My dad left years ago, and I live in a trailer on the edge of town. The pipes are always leaking, and I've carried my mom to her bed when she's been blackout drunk more times than I care to count."

"I know," I whisper, flexing my fingers, remembering the bits he's told me in the weeks since he started climbing into my bedroom in the middle of the night. "But that's why we talked about our plans, right? We both want to move to New York City and get into NYU. We will—"

His finger flies back up to my mouth and his eyes meet mine. "No, it isn't that." He looks at his feet. "That's not everything I wanted to tell you."

"Then, what is it?"

"Charleigh, you're..."

"What?" I ask him, tugging on his shirt. My heart does another jumping jack. "I'm what?"

He lifts his head, with his eyebrows pulled together. "I think I'd rather just show you. If that's okay."

A sharp gasp hits the back of my throat when Asher drags the tips of his fingers across my cheek, sending a shiver down my spine and the length of my body. No one has ever touched me like this. I've been kissed before, but this feeling with Asher is different. He's different.

His fingers move across my cheek before disappearing through my hair. He grips onto the back of my head and tilts me so I'm looking up at him. My eyes flutter, drunk on whatever feeling he's feeding me. His other hand finds my waist as he pulls me toward him. My hips land against him, and I inhale another shaky breath. My fisted hands grip onto his shirt, anchoring me to my bedroom floor.

"Asher, I..." I want to tell him how I feel, and maybe I'm a fool for trying to speak when all he wants to do is show me whatever it is he wants to tell me. I swallow my words, forcing myself to let this moment unravel.

"Charleigh." He smirks. "Just let me show you." His whispered words brush across my mouth before his lips find mine.

They press against me, stealing the breath from my lungs. I close my eyes and savor this moment, afraid if I open them, this will all go away.

Asher's mouth molds to mine. His lips are warm and soft. He parts them, allowing his tongue to dance across mine. His fingers massage the back of my head, and I press my whole body to his. My legs tingle and my heart hammers in my chest.

I tug on Asher's shirt once more, guiding him to follow me. We don't break our connection as I pull us until the back of my legs hit the edge of my bed. I lean back and scoot myself down until Asher is on top of me. He slips his knee between my legs, and his hands are on either side of my head as he lowers himself while continuing to kiss me. He keeps one hand beside my head and uses his other to cup the side of my face. He tilts my chin. Our kisses are increasingly fevered and rushed. My entire body heats, and I'm suddenly wanting him in a way I've only dreamed about. I want him to have me in a way no one else has.

"Charleigh," he says against my mouth. "Wait." It takes several attempts before he can finally bring himself to break our kiss.

"What is it?" I ask, panicked I've done something wrong. My heart sinks, and I feel the heat leave my body.

"Trust me," he says, clearly understanding the shift in my expression. "I don't want to stop. This is what I wanted to show you, and I haven't stopped thinking about it all day."

"Oh." My cheeks heat. "Can I tell you something, then?"

"Of course."

"I've wanted you to do that for three weeks now."

He laughs, dipping his head before looking back into my eyes. His hair hangs over his forehead, adding more shadows to his gaze. "I'd be lying if I said I hadn't, either."

I grin, tracing my finger along his jaw. "It's good to know I'm not alone."

His smile fades and he leans down to kiss me again, pulling back just enough to keep his lips feathering mine when he says, "You're never alone, Charleigh. Not with me."

His confession forces a lump in my throat, and I swallow around it.

"There's something else I wanted to show you tonight." Kissing me one more time, he climbs off me and sits on the edge of my bed. I sit up and adjust the spaghetti straps of my tank top, scooting along the bed to sit beside him until my thigh is touching his.

He breathes heavily, digging into his pocket and pulling out a folded envelope, the seal already opened. He hands it to me.

I look down, reading the familiar blue letters in the top corner.

"Wait." I look up at Asher, wide-eyed. "Is this...?"

He shrugs. "I applied in the spring at my old school. I didn't think I'd get an answer this soon."

"Is this what I think it is?" I whisper, struggling to contain my excitement. Blood rushes through my veins as I open the envelope. "Did you get in?" I ask him before I've even pulled the letter out.

Graduation is months away, but Asher told me he applied at the end of his junior year at his last school. Coincidentally, I did, too. It was another reason for me to tick off why I think we're meant to be.

I don't even have to open the letter to know what it says. Asher's smile is just as wide as it was when he stumbled into my room a few moments ago.

"I got in," he answers quietly. "And they're giving me a full scholarship."

"This is amazing. Congratulations, Asher." Tears well behind my eyes, but I try to hide them. It isn't that I don't want him to see me cry; it's that I don't want to make this about me. Even though I applied in the spring, too, I haven't received my acceptance letter yet, and as far as tuition goes, I'm not worried. My father agreed to pay for any school of my choice as long as I promised to finish. He happily agreed to my decision to go to NYU.

"You'll get yours soon," Asher says, as if he's reading my mind. He drags his thumb across my bottom lip. We may have only just had our first kiss and crossed a line from friends to more tonight, but this is now my favorite thing.

Asher looking at me like *that*.

Touching me like *this*.

"I hope so." I nod, feeling my mouth tug into a tiny smile.

"You will," he insists before pulling me in for another kiss.

When he eventually pulls away, I inhale an unsteady breath, wanting to keep the focus on Asher and his moment.

There's a sparkle in his eye. He's still looking at me as if he can't believe what's happened tonight.

"You're going to be incredible at NYU." I pause. "Have you told your mom?"

"No." He massages the back of his neck. "She's already terrified I'm going to leave her. I think telling her I'm going to college two hours away will break her."

I frown. "I'm sorry."

"I'll figure out the right time to tell her." He takes the acceptance letter from me and stares at it for several seconds. "I'm eighteen, so it isn't like she'd have much of an argument when I leave, but I'm foolishly hoping for something I know she's incapable of." His face remains placid. "Acceptance."

There are no words for this moment. I know Asher is right. Instead, I allow us to sit in the silence. My cotton shorts do nothing to ward off the slight chill in my bedroom, but Asher keeps me warm. I press my hands to my thighs, unsure if it's okay to grab Asher's hand. My thoughts are firing on all cylinders, scrambling to understand what we are exactly, and what this means for us.

"Do you think we'll fit in in New York City?" he asks, staring out my bedroom window. "I mean, we don't exactly fit in here, so what would make New York different?"

"I think we'll fit in perfectly. We're meant for bigger things than this, Asher. Well, at least I know you are."

I try not to let him hear the sadness in my voice. As much as I try to picture myself surrounded with flowers in the city and Asher at my side, it's difficult to imagine a life outside of the one I live now. A bubble covered in gold and luster, when it's blanketed in darkness.

"Don't do that," he argues.

"Do what?"

"Say you won't belong. You belong everywhere, Charleigh, and you'll look good on New York."

I giggle and tilt my head to the side. "I think you mean New York will look good on *me*."

"No." He threads his fingers through mine, holding my hand. "I said it right the first time. New York will look better once you're in it. It won't know what it's been missing until you're there."

I lean forward and rest my elbow on my leg and my head in my hand as I stare at Asher. I can't help smiling at him. My cheeks ache with my unrelenting happiness. "And you say you aren't good with words."

"I'm not. Usually." He chuckles and runs his thumb along the back of my hand. "But I'm falling for you, Charleigh. I've never felt this way for anyone, and I'm afraid if I tell you the depth of my feelings, you'll come to your senses."

"Can you stay for a while?" I ask, not wanting him to leave, especially after sharing our first kiss. I'm afraid I won't be able to sleep if I'm left alone with just my thoughts. "Just until I fall asleep?"

Asher pulls his cracked phone from his pocket.

It's nearly one in the morning.

"My mom is probably still passed out, so I can stay for a while." He slips the phone back into his pocket.

I slide under the covers of my bed and hold them up for Asher to slide in beside me. I don't expect to sleep with him. I'm still a virgin, and the thought of giving it to Asher tonight doesn't feel like the right time. Even though I already know it's him I would want to lose it to over anyone else in the world.

It appears Asher isn't thinking about sleeping with me, either, when he lifts his arm up to pull me to his side. After sidling up to his ribs as close as possible, I drape my leg over his and rest my hand on his chest, directly over his heart, feeling its rhythmic beat against my palm.

My eyes grow heavier by the second, and I try to fight it.

I don't want Asher to leave, but I know the moment I slip away, Asher will slide his arm out from under me and sneak back out of my window.

I worry about Asher's mother and how she'll take the news of him leaving. I think about my own parents and how my mother will never leave my father. I try to picture what they're life will look like when I'm finally gone or if I'll actually care.

Soon, though, everything fades to black, and our hushed breaths are the last sounds I hear before I finally drift off.

I wake up the next morning and crack my eyes open to the bright morning sun. Rubbing the sleep from my eyes, I sit up and look through my bedroom window. The trees are no longer swaying. It's a calm, bright, sunny morning. Every moment of last night comes flooding back to me: Asher's confession of his feelings for me, our kiss, his acceptance letter. I can't stop grinning and am anxious to get to school so I can see him again.

I spring to my feet and move toward my closet but stop dead in my tracks.

Taped to my window is a small heart cut out of paper.

Excitement courses through my veins when I hold my breath and cross my room. I peel it from the glass and ghost my finger along the front of the ink-stained paper heart.

From Asher, With Love

My cheeks grow sore from smiling, when I turn the heart over in my hand to read the message on the back.

Remember... you'll look good on New York.

My heart is still pounding as I carry Asher's paper heart across my room. My knees press into the carpet when I bend down in front of the foot of my bed and reach beneath for a shoebox my mother left under my bed after she bought me a pair of heels last summer.

I remove the lid and drop Asher's heart inside. Pinching myself, I tell myself this isn't a dream. Asher *kissed* me, and it isn't until I close the lid on his first paper heart do I realize it was his way of telling me he was falling in love with me, too.

ASHER

I spent most of my early college days just scraping by in all my classes. For the most part, it was because they were all the basic classes you're required to take before settling down and deciding on a major. I'd always had my heart and mind set on real estate. I should have mixed in a few business classes with the basic ones to keep up my interest, but against my better judgment, I didn't, mostly because I knew life can change when you least expect it. Commitment was no longer in my blood.

It wasn't until my third year of college that I finally got up off my ass and worked to earn the degree I'd always dreamed of.

Charleigh's tardiness reminds me of the first few years I spent in college, after I left her. Back when we were together, she was always the more organized one between the two of us. Everything she did was meticulously planned down to the slightest detail. At times, it was a trait I admired. Other times, it would drive me insane.

Today, she is driving me insane.

She's obviously changed over the years. Maybe Charleigh isn't the same woman she once was, just as she claims I'm not the same man I used to be, either.

Which I'm not.

I've been standing in my office, staring at the city below, waiting for her. She's nearly an hour late. I arrived at work an hour early, searching for properties within Charleigh's budget. Most of them held great potential, but there was one that stood out above the rest. It isn't too far from the part of the city I work in—only about ten blocks from my office. I want to show her that place first, knowing it's the best shot I have at convincing her to buy with me over Cyrus.

But my confidence is dwindling more with every second that passes.

I walk over to the phone resting on my desk and press the intercom button with a firm finger. "Has Ms. Keeler arrived yet?"

"No, sir," Janette replies quickly. "But, wait—"

I cut Janette off. I place my hands on my hips and turn to look back out the window. "Fuck."

"Hey, I'm sorry I'm a little late."

I whip my head toward the front of my office. Charleigh's standing in the doorway, with a coffee perched in each of her hands.

I narrow my eyes and firmly press my lips together. My teeth are already grinding. "You're nearly an hour late."

She raises her shoulders innocently, then flashes me a smile. Her dark hair is full and curled, framing her gorgeous face. She sweeps her tongue across her pale-pink-painted lips. Her chest quickly rises and falls with every breath, her breasts pushing against the buttons holding her floral blouse shut. Her black skirt hugs her full, round hips, accentuating every single fucking curve.

Shit. How can one woman be so insanely beautiful yet so nerve racking at the same time?

"I grabbed you a coffee." She crosses my office and holds her arm out, offering it to me.

I reluctantly take it and keep my narrowed eyes focused on her, ignoring the twitch of my dick.

"How did you know how I take my coffee?" The last time Charleigh and I were together, we never drank coffee. Charleigh was the only one who did since her father owned the most expensive espresso machine on the market. My mother traded hers for vodka, and for me, it was a luxury I couldn't afford.

"I didn't." She chuckles against the lid. "I ordered yours the same way I order mine."

I take a sip, wincing at how sweet it is.

"What is this?" I ask, scrunching my nose and setting it down on my desk. "Pure sugar with a dash of coffee?"

"No." She steps closer. The scent of flowers and vanilla immediately surrounds me. "It's called a vanilla latte. It's pretty standard."

I close my mouth, trying not to let her closeness affect me. We're standing almost toe to toe. I wonder if she even notices herself breaking her own boundary. Maybe it comes naturally to her without her realizing it.

I bite the inside of my cheek, tempted to lean forward and press my lips to hers. Her flowery scent draws me in. My body and mind remember exactly what she feels and tastes like, and they crave it all again. Like a drug I quit years ago, the mind remembers the high it got from knowing I'd been the only one to touch her back then. She was mine and only mine.

I clear my throat and shut off my computer before grabbing my suit jacket from the back of my chair.

"Come on." I head toward the door of my office, carrying my sickeningly-sweet coffee with me, leaving her behind.

Charleigh's heels click across the hardwood floor as she

struggles to keep up with my pace. I can't help it. It's as if my mind is telling my feet to keep a distance from her. If I'm not careful, I might allow myself to make a move I'll regret later.

Charleigh isn't a woman I can get mixed up with again. Not like the women I fucked in college or the brief moment in time when I slightly considered fucking Janette.

No. Charleigh is different, and I need to watch myself carefully.

"Asher," she says behind me. "You're walking awfully fast."

She eventually catches up to me when I reach the elevator. I toss the coffee in the bin bolted to the wall and press the call button, glancing over my shoulder. "I have to make up for lost time since you were an hour late."

"I was trying to do a nice thing and bring you coffee." From the corner of my eye, I feel her stare pinning me with daggers. "I can't help it if it took a little longer than usual. It also took me a while to hail a cab."

I turn to face her.

"You've lived here for ten years, and this is New York City. You should have expected it." My mouth is catching all the irritation in my brain and running away with it.

"Not everyone has a driver waiting for them at their every beck and call," she fires back. "Not all of us are drowning in copious amounts of money."

I grind my jaw, her words adding salt to a wound I didn't even know was open.

"You know what?" She turns her head, eyeing the door for the stairwell in the corner of the lobby. "I knew this was a bad idea. We can't work like this. I'll just work with what Cyrus sent me."

Maybe she's right. A past like ours isn't easy to forget.

She tosses her own coffee in the same trash bin before turning on her heel and briskly marching toward the stairs. I watch her leave, her ass shaking side to side against her tight skirt.

"Dammit." I run my palm down the side of my face, then jog to catch up to her before she makes it to the door. I grab her hand, pulling her to a stop.

There she is again. Drawing me in like a moth to a fucking flame.

"Wait."

She turns around. There's a sadness to her eyes, and I know it's from me. I just don't know if it's from the Asher I am now or the old one who broke her heart at eighteen.

"I'm sorry."

Charleigh laughs, ripping her hand from mine and crossing her arms. "Yeah, right, Asher. You've never been one to apologize." Avoiding my stare, she impatiently looks up at the elevator, clearly frustrated. She stamps her heel.

"What's that supposed to mean?" I ask, too stunned to focus on the slow ass elevator. Her words have, once again, burrowed their way under my skin, burning me from the inside out.

She closes her eyes and lets out a sigh, rolling her head in my direction. When she opens them again, there's still a hint of sadness, but they've brightened slightly. "It doesn't mean anything. It's been a rough morning. Let's forget it."

"Forget the comment, or forget working with me?" I ask cautiously.

Her eyes tighten as if she's trying to make up her mind on whether to trust me or not. "I guess you'll just have to wait and see." Done waiting for the snail-paced elevator, she turns on her heel, searching each corner of my office floor before she finally finds what she's looking for. I follow her gaze, and before I have a chance to stop her, she's already made it to stairwell door, pushing her entire weight into it.

She disappears down the stairwell while I stay in the doorway, holding my arm out to keep it open. "Are you crazy, Charleigh? You're really going to take the stairs instead of the elevator?"

She's already made it down the first flight before she pauses long enough on the landing to look up at me. "First of all, I'm not crazy." Then she grins. *Fuck.* "Second, you've never taken the time to use the stairs?"

"No," I tell her, rolling my eyes. I give in and follow her. "Not when my office is on the fifty-second floor. You may feel differently about using the stairs if you worked here every day."

"I don't know about that." She waits for me to catch up to her.

Our cadences match one another as our feet hit each step. I glance down, confused as to how she's able to walk down this many stairs in the heels she's wearing.

"How long have you been in New York?" she asks, trepidation in her voice. Talking about the time between when I left her and right now is like walking on eggshells.

"Since the beginning of the year."

"Oh," she mutters. "So, not long."

"Nope." I let out a heavy sigh. "It took a lot for me to agree to finally move part of my firm out here from Los Angeles."

"Do you plan on staying?"

Her question causes me to hesitate to take the next step. I nearly trip on the edge of the metal stair but quickly right myself before Charleigh notices.

She appears unfazed by her question, as if there is no ill intent or resentment laced in her words. But I can't ignore the sting to my chest.

"I planned on it," I tell her. "But I haven't completely decided. I still have business back over there and my office out in Los Angeles. I've considered switching my primary office to New York, though."

"Huh." She twists her mouth in thought, and despite us walking down the stairs, I don't pay attention to where I'm walking. From the corner of my eye, I study her face. I take note of every line and every curve. The way her bottom lip shines in the yellow lights of the stairwell to the sharp arch of her eyebrow framing her bright eye.

The corner of her mouth tilts into a playful smile when she quickly glances over at me before beginning the next set of stairs.

"I bet you'll miss the L.A. weather."

I'm thankful for the shift. Weather is good. Weather is safe.

My body lightens with our new topic of conversation, despite our never-ending descent to the first floor. I read the paint on the wall and see we're only on the forty-first level.

What the fuck?

"After living in New England my entire life, L.A. was certainly a change. I liked the warm weather, but I won't deny I missed the changing of the seasons."

"I can see that." She grins, displaying her perfect teeth. "It's like spring."

I cock an eyebrow. "The changing of the seasons is like spring?"

She laughs, shaking her head. "I meant that nature steals from itself in the winter. Flowers wilt and dry up. The trees are forced to shed their leaves. Everything becomes dark and exposed, stripped down to its barest form. But then spring comes along and gives nature a gift."

"So, what you're saying is that nature is its own worst enemy." I scoff, laughing under my breath. "Sounds like nature can be an asshole."

"Sometimes." She chuckles. "But that's the beauty in it."

"There's beauty in loss?"

She glances at me. "No, but there's beauty in its forgiveness."

I can't quite figure out what it is, but my chest is warming as we continue talking. It's as if the small pieces of the old Charleigh I chose to forget are slowly slipping back in. I remind myself to be careful to not let her in too much, though. There were reasons I pushed Charleigh away the last time I saw her, and I need to remember why before I cross a line I don't want to cross.

We travel down the next thirty flights in silence, the sound of our footsteps the only noise bouncing off the cement walls. About four flights back, I noticed Charleigh's pace starting to slow. It's now taking her nearly twice as long to travel down one flight. Her lips press tightly together as her eyes narrow. She lifts her foot as she takes a step, rolling her ankle to release the tension. I can tell she's hiding her pain from me. I bite the inside of my cheek, trying not to laugh.

"What?" She winces again, this time more noticeably. "Why do you keep looking at me like that?"

"Your feet hurt, don't they?"

"No." She gives me a side glance and tips her chin up. "I'm fine."

When we take the next step, her mouth pushes out an audible hissing sound.

I freeze. She's a step below me, but she's standing on the landing. The door to the thirteenth floor is behind her.

"You're lying." I point to her feet. "Those heels are killing you. Admit it."

"They are not. I told you, I'm fine."

"Quit being ridiculous. You can't finish out these last twelve levels. We'll take the elevator from here, and you can go home to change."

"I said I was fine, Asher. I'm not going home to change. It'll be a waste of time when we're already behind."

"Fine." I groan. "Then, I'll have my driver take us to a shoe store along the way."

"Are you kidding? I'm not wasting money on a new pair of shoes, either."

"I'll pay for them."

"No." Her eyes flash with anger and frustration. "You are not buying me shoes."

She moves to take another step but winces again. I don't hesitate; instinct taking me over.

"Come here." I step off the last step to get even with her and open my arms.

She takes a step back. "What are you doing?"

I keep my arms out, taking another step closer to her. "If you're going to be stubborn, I'll carry you the rest of the way."

"No, you won't." She begins shaking her head. "Absolutely not. I'll just take my shoes off." She reaches down, ready to remove one of her heels.

"That's disgusting, Charleigh. You'll catch tetanus or some shit like that."

She shrugs, bending down again to remove her heel. "I'll survive. Plus, if I end up catching something or hurting myself, you can carry me to the hospital."

I roll my eyes. She's nearly pulled off her shoe when I reach down and wrap my arms around her legs. She yelps as I lift her up and bend her over my shoulder. Her warmth immediately meets my chest and shoulder, radiating down the length of my body.

"Asher! What the hell?"

"Your feet hurt, and there's no way in hell I'm letting you walk barefoot."

"Put me down." She swats at my back, her arms flailing

against my muscles as she kicks her legs out, batting them back and forth. Her feet hit my ribs repeatedly.

"Nope." I begin walking down the stairs, careful as I take each step. The last thing I need is to trip and fall, dropping Charleigh along the way. I have one arm wrapped around the back of her thighs while my other hand rests on the small of her spine.

"You're such an asshole," Charleigh mutters through gritted teeth.

"I never claimed not to be." Her entire body is warm against my shoulder, and I find myself grinding my jaw once again, only this time it isn't because she's irritated me. This time it's because she's turned me on. My entire body heats with Charleigh against me.

I bite down on the tip of my tongue fighting the urge to spank her round ass next to my face for both being late and making me walk down this obscene number of stairs. My cock twitches at the thought.

I've already crossed the line, and I know it. We could have easily taken the elevator, but with each level we pass, I choose not to. It's a decision I'm aware of with every level we descend. I tell myself I'm carrying her because listening to her complain for another twelve flights would drive me insane. It's better to believe the lies than to accept the truth. She really isn't complaining that much. I should have let her walk barefoot. I should have let her go. But the old Asher I was when I was with Charleigh is starting to peek through the cracks in the walls I've built around myself. I hate to admit it, but her company is growing on me.

The silence between us swells for another few flights. As much as I'm trying to concentrate on the next step, all I can think about is my arm around Charleigh's thick thighs. My fingers pressed into the small of her back. I swallow the tension growing in my throat at the reminder of how she tastes. I squeeze her thigh, forcing myself to get my mind back on track, but the audible heavy breath sinking from Charleigh's body is too loud to ignore. My touch is doing something to her. Lighting her up inside, the same as it is me.

"So," Charleigh says, lifting her head. She grips the back of my jacket and shirt, pulling herself up far enough to look at the wall behind me. Her fists clutching the fabric of my shirt loosens it from beneath my belt. "Tell me your favorite thing you loved about L.A. Besides the food."

I laugh, wrapping my arms tighter around her thighs. I brush off the urge to slide my hand under the fabric of her skirt and sink my fingers into her just to see how wet she is. "My dad taught me how to surf. I was terrified my first time, but once I got the hang of it, I couldn't stop. Until I moved into the dorm at UCLA freshman year, it was the first thing I'd do every day."

I can tell my indulgence in sharing one of the few details about my father has stunned her. She holds her breath, her body growing heavy against mine. Her clenched fists loosen on my jacket, but she still holds on. "Oh, I, um... so, it worked out with your dad, then?"

We've reached the second floor now. Only one more flight to go until we make it to the lobby. I could easily release Charleigh and let her walk the last few steps, but I don't. I keep my arms wrapped around her, and her body pressed to mine.

I clear my throat and take the first step of the last flight. "It did."

Several seconds of silence.

"It makes me happy to know one of your parents turned out to be a good person." Her words come out low and soft.

I inhale a deep breath, unsure how to feel. Yes, my father turned out to be a decent human being, but in my mind, it was too little too late. The damage had already been done. He couldn't erase the kind of woman my mother had turned out to be, and he certainly couldn't erase what had happened to her, causing me to leave Connecticut and live with him. He also couldn't change the fact that I had left Charleigh, removing her from every aspect of my life. Moving out there on a whim in the hopes my mother's stories about him were lies was a major risk.

"Yeah." It's the single word I can think to use in response to Charleigh. Talking about my father is heavy, if only because he's a subject that reminds me of why I left her. Speaking of my father could also lead to a conversation about my mother and the fire that destroyed her and nearly destroyed Charleigh—topics I don't want to revisit. This time I shift the focus of the conversation to her.

"What about you? Was NYU everything you hoped it would be?" My thumb presses into her thigh. The feeling it gives me causes my heart to hammer in my chest.

"It was good. After my freshman year, I got a job at a floral shop down the street from campus. I spent most of my free time there, learning everything I could about running a floral business. If I wasn't in class, I was there. Otherwise, school was great."

Once I've made it to the first floor, I put Charleigh down, unraveling my arm from around her thighs. When she lands on her feet, she straightens her back and brushes her disheveled hair away from her face, smoothing it with her fingertips. She straightens her skirt and readjusts her purse on her arm, but all I can do is stare at her lips and ignore the heat in my lower belly.

"Thanks," she mutters, her eyes meeting mine.

"You're welcome."

We stand in the stairwell, and it's not until I pull my phone out of my pocket do I realize how long it has taken us to walk down the stairs. "Thirty minutes?" I say, raising my voice. "It took us thirty minutes to use the stairs instead of the elevator."

She shrugs, wincing again, the same way she did before I carried her. "Um, yeah. Sorry. I didn't think it would take that long."

"What do you mean you didn't think it would take this long?" I gesture toward the stairs. "Haven't you walked these before?"

She laughs. "Never. I was mad at you for the way you were talking to me upstairs. I didn't intend to walk the entire way, but you followed me, so I figured we could just keep going. I honestly didn't know it would take as long as it did."

I run my fingers through my hair, pushing the ends up off my forehead. "You drive me fucking insane, Charleigh. Do you know that?"

"I know I do, but you have to admit, you kind of deserved it." With her pink mouth curled into a smirk, she reaches into her purse, pulling out her phone. "Now," she says, typing out a text. "Where are we headed for the first listing you're showing me?"

"Wait," I say, hesitating. "You're still going to work with me?"

"Why not?" Charleigh's hot-and-cold attitude is beginning to give me whiplash. Though I guess the same could be said for me. We're driving each other insane, but the more I stare into Charleigh's eyes, the more I realize we're both starting to enjoy it.

I point my finger toward the top of the stairs. "Because of what you said up there. You made it sound like you might back out."

"Like I said, I was getting back at you for the way you were acting. I told you I would give you chance." She shrugs. "This is me keeping my word."

The blush on her cheeks has now faded, and her expression

is stoic. It's as if all the lighthearted conversation and energy has been sucked out of the room.

"Look, Charleigh..." My words trail off while I consider what to say. Our conversation on the fifty-two-flight descent has already been more than anything I've shared with anyone in the past decade—Charleigh being the last person I opened up to. Talking with her feels natural, much like riding a bike. For the first time in ages, it's easy, but a small part of me knows the past between Charleigh and me is anything but easy. It's complicated, messy, and tragic. "I—"

"It's okay, Asher," Charleigh says, cutting me off. "You don't need to say anything. I shouldn't have been late in the first place. This is strictly business, and I need to keep that in mind."

"Right." I nod, buttoning my suit jacket, slipping back into agent mode.

"Good," she says, the light leaving her eyes. "Now, show me the first place you have for me on your list."

ELEVEN

CHARLEIGH

I should have taken Asher up on his offer to head back to my apartment to change my shoes. Fuck, I even regret not taking him up on his offer to buy me a new pair, because now we're finally standing in front of the first location, and all I can think about is how badly my feet hurt.

"So, this is it." Asher waves his arm out to the empty office space in front of us. "What do you think of the outside?"

I don't move any closer to Asher or the building, afraid that if I do, my toes will officially go numb. In fact, that might not be a terrible idea with how much pain I'm in. I turn my head to get a better view of the surrounding area. It's in a nice part of Manhattan, only a few blocks from Asher's office. I'm thankful he didn't argue when I asked him if we could take a taxi on the way over.

"I love it. How much is this one listed at?"

"It's right at the top of your budget. There's a bit of wiggle room for negotiating."

"Oh, that's great, then." I nod, pleased to finally find a place that could be a possibility. "I'll still need to see what it looks like on the inside, though."

"Of course," he says, his mouth pressed into a thin line. His eyes narrow when he looks down at my feet. I can tell he knows I'm uncomfortable, but he's given up the fight. Instead, he walks up to the door, punching the code in to unlock it.

Once he has it open, I finally decide to move, bracing myself for the pain I know will inevitably come. Asher's back is to me, so I take the opportunity to limp to the door, putting the least amount of pressure on my toes that I can. I nearly make it to the front door, then he turns around, catching me limping.

"What are you doing?" he asks.

"Nothing," I tell him, pointing to the entrance. "I'm following you inside."

"No, you're not." He sighs, pulling the door closed. "You can't go inside when you're clearly in this much pain."

"Yes, I can." I grit my teeth, blowing hot air through my nose. Today has been one disaster after another. It was already bad enough that I woke up late and struggled to find a cab. I figured if I bought Asher a coffee it could make up for the fact that I was nearly an hour late, but I was wrong.

Asher's attitude threw me over the edge, and to get back at him, I tried to punish him by using the stairs. My plan backfired. Normally, I love wearing these shoes. They're some of the most comfortable ones I own, but they aren't exactly the best shoes to wear when deciding to walk down fifty-two flights of stairs. It wasn't all a terrible idea. Feeling Asher's arms on my body lit a fire inside me, sparking and electrifying pieces of myself that had been dead for so long. It was a familiar feeling, yet new in a way. He was stronger and more direct than he used to be. His muscles contracted beneath my fingers as I held on to him with every step he took. All I could do was focus on his large hands commanding my body, keeping me in place. I spent the entire trip down worried he'd discover how wet I'd become just from his touch, secretly wishing he would.

At first, I didn't understand why he decided to carry me the rest of the way, but I'm thankful because I don't think I would have been able to make it—especially now we're standing in front of this office that's for sale.

I wish I was carrying a spare pair of flats inside my purse right about now. Instead, I'm standing on the sidewalk, seriously contemplating the idea of walking barefoot.

"You're lying to me again, Charleigh." Asher is now standing directly in front of me.

I tip my chin up, meeting his gaze, and the longer I stare into his eyes, the more pain I'm in. "Fine." I sigh, my shoulders falling. "My feet hurt so fucking bad, I want to rip these shoes off and toss them into the nearest dumpster."

"I tried to tell you."

"I know, but I didn't want to throw another wrench in your schedule and make you more frustrated with me. I already made us late, and stopping by my place to change would have dragged this on even longer than necessary. It's almost lunchtime." I didn't realize it until know, but my chest aches with my confession. It's as if I am afraid to give Asher another reason to be annoyed with me. In reality, I shouldn't care.

I expect Asher to launch into another speech about how I'm right and this is another problem that will delay his plans. Instead, he quietly steps around me, walking back toward his car.

His driver immediately opens the back door, holding it open.

"What are you doing?" I don't follow him. My feet are on fire, nearing the brink of becoming numb.

Asher moves to stand on the opposite side from his driver, waiting for me to slip into his car. "We're going to your apartment so you can change, then we'll come back here to look inside."

Apprehensive, I glance over my shoulder. I truly wanted to look at this place. I already feel the spark inside me at the thought of its possibilities, but it'll just have to wait.

With my shoulders down and my feet on fire, I walk toward Asher's car.

"Thank you." I sigh with relief and slide along the leather. Once inside, I immediately want to cry with relief. Asher slides in, too, so he's sitting beside me. I tell Asher's driver my address, then close my eyes and rest my head back. Although I can't see him, I feel Asher's gaze on me.

"You look better already, and you haven't even changed yet."

I crack my eyes open and roll my head against the headrest. "Sometimes I wonder why I even wear these stupid things. I'm my own boss, so, technically, I can wear anything I want."

Asher hums, and the heat between my thighs expands. His hand rests on his thigh, but his pinky finger grazes my bare leg. "Why do you, then?"

"I don't know." I sigh, closing my eyes again, his touch magnifying with every second. "My mother used to make me wear them all time. At least to all the important parties and functions my father used to pull, when I needed to impress corporate cronies or politicians. I think the habit must have stuck."

"I'm surprised. You never wore them much at school. Unless you were wearing a dress."

I open my eyes again and turn toward Asher.

I smile, feeling my cheeks warm. "I didn't know you paid that much attention to what I wore."

Asher's eyes stare into mine, absorbing our conversation. He clears his throat, then adjusts himself in his seat. "Yeah, well that was a long time ago." He turns to look out his window and rests his arm on the inside of his door. The sleeve of his jacket slides back along his wrist, displaying his Cartier watch. I'm still struggling to comprehend how Asher now has the money to be able to afford a watch such as that one. Or a driver like the reflection of the one I see in the rear-view mirror. He keeps his focus on the road while I take in the car I'm sitting in.

All black leather. It smells brand new as if not a single mile has been driven in it.

When I was younger, I was surrounded by the same lifestyle Asher has now: designer clothes, fancy watches, luxury cars. My father required only the most expensive items out there, considering them essential to living an upper-class life, but I knew better. Asher's flashy lifestyle doesn't faze me.

"Are we almost there?" he asks me.

"Yeah. It's about another block."

Nerves knot together inside my stomach. The sudden realization that Asher will be standing in my apartment in a mere five minutes hits me like a barreling train to the chest.

The car pulls up to the curb, and Asher waits until his driver opens the door before he steps out. I follow him and lead him into my building. I walk slowly through up the small staircase before unlocking the front door, carrying my heels with me by the tips of my fingers. Once inside the main common area, I lead Asher up the one flight of stairs until we're standing in front of my door.

"I think my toes have officially gone numb." I laugh, although the feeling concerns me. *Is it normal for your toes to turn purple? Do I need to see a doctor?*

I glance over my shoulder as I twist the key in my lock.

When I glance at Asher, he's stifling a laugh.

"Go ahead," I tell him, my shoulders sagging with defeat. This day is an absolute dumpster fire. "Get it out. I know you want to."

"No," he says, grinning. "It's fine. I actually feel bad for you."

"No, you don't." I roll my eyes. "You're enjoying this."

His face falls, and the humor that once lingered in there is gone. "Why would I enjoy watching you suffer, Charleigh?"

I nod silently, realizing the deeper meaning behind my accusation.

When I push through the front door, I hold it open for him, but he doesn't immediately follow.

"Are you coming in?" I ask.

"Um, yeah." He blinks, slowly taking one step inside. He only goes as far enough to shut the door behind him., though, as his gaze wanders around my apartment.

My heart pounds in my chest. I've thought about Asher over the years, but I never expected to see him standing in my home. Especially not when wearing a designer suit and silky black tie.

There isn't much to it aside from the essentials: a sofa, a television, a bed, flowers. Flowers in every corner I could fit them.

"I'll be right back." I clear my throat and head to my bedroom, where I trade my dress for a blue T-shirt and my favorite pair of black jeans. I throw my long brown hair into a messy bun, then smooth on another coat of lip gloss.

When I walk back out to my living room, I find Asher standing by the mantle above my fireplace. He grabs the picture frame sitting between two bouquets of lilies.

"Is this the same flower?" he asks, studying the pressed mountain laurel beneath the glass. "How?"

The air is knocked from my lungs. I slowly step closer to him, my feet rolling with each step. "No, it isn't. You know what happened to the original one."

"The fire." Those two words fall from his mouth like an echo of a whisper. His voice hangs in the air, heavy and weighted.

"After you left for California, I picked another one, dried it, then decided to frame it." I move closer to him, taking the frame from his hands. I stare at the flower, counting the differences between this one and the one Asher gave to me the night we'd first slept together. The night everything started to fall apart.

With a shaking hand, I place the frame back on the mantle. When I turn back to look at him, he's stepped closer to me, taking in my new outfit.

"Are you ready to head back?" he whispers. He's now standing close enough to lift a hand and touch my face. He could lean forward and kiss me if he wanted.

My cheeks warm and my neck prickles at the thought of his touch, his taste. Admittedly, I want him to make a move. Mostly, I want him to touch me to be sure that what I felt for Asher all those years ago remains—or doesn't. I can't decipher my thoughts when he's standing this close to me. It's as if my mind has been clouded by a thick, dense fog. The uncertainty is both terrifying yet thrilling.

My eyes fall to his mouth, and I instinctively sweep my tongue across my bottom lip. "Yeah."

"How are your feet feeling?" He somehow steps even closer, the tips of his shoes now touching mine.

I look down at my pair of flats. "Much better." But I'm forced to look back up at Asher when he hooks two of his fingers under my chin, pulling up to meet his gaze.

"Good."

He's leaning down, his lips close enough to kiss mine. His hot breath dances across my mouth, and his eyes scan my face. I inhale, breathing him in. His scent blends with the lilies sitting on my mantle.

"Asher..." I whisper, not sure what his intentions are. It's been years since I've felt him this close, this way. It's all strange, yet familiar at the same time. I close my eyes and breathe him in, remembering the way his touch used to ignite my skin.

It still has the same power, too, and despite the anger still simmering with the way he left ten years ago, my feelings are too strong to ignore.

Your heart and your mind simply don't forget being in love.

"Asher," I start, emotion getting caught in my throat. It's been too long since I've allowed myself to truly remember what the fire took from me, and more importantly, what the fire took from Asher. "I never had the chance to tell you how sorry—"

His hand moves to the button of my jeans. He runs his thumb over the small metal circle, dipping the tips of his fingers on the inside of the waist of my jeans.

"I'm s—" I try again.

"Don't." His voice is strong, vibrating through his fingers. His eyes stay on me with a laser-like focus. He runs his thumb along my bottom lip as if he's matching what he's feeling to his memory.

I gasp. This singular touch is enough to throw me over the edge, my hums and shivers tingling their way down the length of my legs. I consider leaning forward and placing my lips against his. I'm nervous about what it would mean if I allowed him to kiss me. I shouldn't want Asher at all. He hurt me in the worst possible way. It's taken me ten years to recover from the wounds he inflicted.

Ever since that night I saw him at the bar, he's been playing the hot-and-cold game with me. There are moments, like the one where he stopped by my shop, that have me reconsidering that Asher might not hate me as much as I believe he does. Then there are moments like this morning, where I know I got under his skin. His harsh, annoyed tone and flexed jaw were enough proof that I bothered him. Despite his constant mood swings, I have an insatiable need to have him closer. I'm ready to feel him, taste him again. My thighs instinctively tighten at the thought of what it would feel like to have his cock inside me again.

His eyes roam over me, searching for answers. There's a battle raging inside him. He dips his face closer, his mouth barely brushing mine.

"Charleigh, I—"

"What?" I whisper, the word squeezing from my chest.

"I don't know," he whispers back, his fingers slipping deeper, pulling me closer. "I can't explain it."

I want to laugh, but I don't. I've heard this before. It's as if I'm living in a dream state. Déjà vu.

History repeating itself.

"You still aren't the best with words, huh?" My smile brushes his mouth, anticipation bubbling inside me. I roll onto the balls of my feet, standing on my toes. He pops the button of my jeans and slips his hand into the front of my lace thong. I hold my breath, gasping at his touch near my aching clit.

I close my eyes, ready for him to close the last remaining gap between our mouths... but disappointment washes over me when the sound of his breath forces me to open my eyes. He sighs, his eyebrows knitting as he pulls away from me. He drops his thumb from my mouth, pulls his hand out from my jeans, and steps back. He runs a quick hand down the length of his face, blowing out a heavy breath.

Cold air fills the empty space settled between us, and when I try to catch Asher's eyes, he avoids looking in my direction. He quickly moves past me, headed for the front door.

"We should go," he mutters over his shoulder, refusing to make eye contact with me.

My cheeks bloom with heat and embarrassment. I quickly rebutton my jeans and stand in front of my fireplace, confused. Two seconds ago, I could have sworn he was going to kiss me.

Every nerve in my body reacted to him, as if Asher had brought them back to life after ten years. I wring my hands, forcing the tension in my body to unfurl.

I open my mouth, ready to stop him from walking out the door, ready to demand he finish the sentence he started. Instead, I grab my phone and purse, and I follow him down the hall.

Asher and I don't speak another word to each other until we're stepping out of his car again. We're now in a different neighborhood than before, farther from the place Asher took me to before we headed to my apartment.

"I thought we were going back to the place we were at earlier?" I stand on the sidewalk, peering up at the sign above the front door.

Meme Celine's French Patisserie

"This place is better." Asher moves past me, heading straight for the front door.

I can't help but scrunch my nose. Confusion settles in. The outside is nearly falling apart, paint is peeling off the brick exterior, and the windows are covered in dust. The door is painted a faded yellow, and the sign painted across it is practically illegible.

"I think I liked the last place better," I tell him. "I'm not sure about this end of the district."

Asher glances over his shoulder as he punches in the code to unlock the door. "There's potential with this one. Trust me."

"Fine." I sigh, taking one more look at the outside before stepping in.

I follow Asher inside, stopping a few feet from the door. The space is quite a bit larger than my current shop, but every surface would need to be touched up. Other than an increase of square footage, I'm not sure this place would work. I'd probably end up putting more money into renovations than I would at the first location he showed me.

"What do you think?" He's standing near the back, in front of a set of double doors.

"I don't know." I survey the room, examining every inch, trying to imagine my business here, but my mind draws a blank, deterred by the location.

Asher turns around, but his eyes still don't meet mine. He hasn't been able to truly look at me ever since we left my apartment. He looks past my shoulder at the empty wall, absent-mindedly running his hand over the countertop.

"This space was once used as a bakery. There was a row of refrigerators over there." He points to an empty space along the wall, then points toward the back. Metal swinging doors divide the storefront from what used to be the kitchen. "There's ample space for you to work and arrange any orders or events you might have. You can easily replace the ovens with more storage or coolers."

I press my lips together, absorbing Asher's sudden change. This time it isn't solely his mood. It's in the way his body is tense, his stare cold. It's as if he's become a corporate robot, much like the version I saw the first time we ran into each other. Asher is in selling mode, completely shutting the rest of himself off from me, even the glimpses he gave me earlier today in the stairwell: carrying me over his shoulder, carrying on a conversation as easily as swimming through water, the near kiss in my apartment, his finger grazing my mouth... all of it has evaporated, and now we're back to square one.

"I'm not completely against this place. I guess I could envision it. Maybe." I frown, considering the possibilities. At this point, I'm willing to keep an open mind. "How much is it?"

"It's only four hundred thousand over your budget." Asher shrugs. He still won't look in my direction, unwilling to cross the line he's clearly drawn since leaving my apartment.

"What?" My mouth falls open as I stare at Asher, wide-eyed. I look around the space again, trying to understand how on earth this place could be priced as high as it is.

Sensing my tone, Asher finally looks at me, allowing his eyes to meet mine. "What's wrong with it?"

"Are you kidding me?"

"No." He's straight-faced, not a single hint of coyness in his expression. "This place is perfect for your expansion."

"In what way?" I ask, still shocked how he could even entertain showing me a place so far out of my budget.

"With a little updating, it's a possibility."

"You are such a hypocrite." I shake my head, crossing my arms over my chest.

"How am I a hypocrite? I promised I would show you places within reason. This one is within reason." His eyes have transformed, sparking under the dull lights of the room.

"Four hundred thousand over my budget is within reason? You called out Cyrus for only sending me listings over my budget, and here you are doing the same thing." I point at him, heat expanding across my chest. My throat suddenly feels dry, and I wish I had a glass of water. Although if I had a glass of water, it could be splashed across the front of Asher's thousand-dollar black suit instead.

"First," he starts, "I am not the same as Cyrus." His voice is strained, the veins in his neck beginning to swell. His smooth cheeks flush red, and his forehead creases with his brewing anger. "Cyrus sends listings you have no chance of negotiating on with any seller. The prices are so far apart, there is no meeting in the middle." Asher steps closer to me. He keeps his distance, but I can feel the heat radiating off his body. "Second, it's four hundred thousand dollars, Charleigh. A drop in the bucket when it comes to New York. It's not a big deal."

"It is a big deal when it's *my* money, Asher—when it's *my* business." I thumb my own chest.

"Four hundred thousand is a reasonable amount to begin negotiations," Asher counters. "Cyrus is sending you listings at least that or more over your budget. Now, if you ask me, that's more difficult to negotiate. Tell me I'm wrong."

"That's not the point." I shake my head again, frustrated. "Four hundred thousand is still a high number. Even if the seller decides to budge a little in price, that changes my monthly payments quite a bit."

"I don't understand why it's an issue."

I laugh hysterically in disbelief, resting my hands on my hips. "Now that you have all the money in the world, nearly half a million dollars may not be an issue to you, but for me, how could it not be? I told you from the start that my budget was my biggest concern. I'm taking a leap of faith with this expansion and hiring you as my realtor. I need the right place, Asher, but I also can't afford to overspend."

He shrugs, breaking his gaze away from mine as he shoves his hands into his pockets and blankly stares at the wall behind me. "You're telling me there is no room for you to consider places even slightly over your budget?"

"No," I say firmly, clenching my teeth. "I have no room." My vision turns red. The entire day comes crashing down on me, the last domino toppling over. I can tell Asher is purposely digging his way under my skin. I'm unsure if it's because of the near kiss we shared back at my apartment or if he's fishing for information. Probably both.

"What about your dad?"

My eyes narrow, and my throat burns from the inside out, shocked by his question. Blood immediately drains from my face. "What about him?"

"I don't know." Asher shrugs, his mouth turning down. "If you can't afford it, maybe he can pay the difference."

Tears well in my eyes. Anger bubbles in my chest and I

force myself not to allow Asher to see how him mentioning my father has brought out a piece of myself I choose to keep buried.

"What makes you think that, huh?" My poison-laced words drip from my tongue. "He has all the money in the world, so he must be able to help me, right?" A tear spills from my eye, sliding its way down my cheek. It lands on my chest as I stare at Asher from across the room.

His eyes meet mine again. They're vacant and empty. "Well, he did pay for your tuition at NYU, didn't he? This shouldn't be a problem for him."

Another tear spills as I clench my hands into fists at my sides. He's struck a nerve. Fury burns crimson red in my heated stare. My jaw tightens, and the muscles in my body swell.

"You know what, Asher? *Fuck you.*" I let my feet carry me out of the building, and I rush past Asher's car, ignoring his driver holding the door open for me. I don't even bother waving down a cab. I don't want to give Asher a chance to catch me outside, accusing me of using my father's money whenever it suits me.

He doesn't know anything. He doesn't deserve to know since he was the one who left.

I walk the next few blocks fighting back tears. My father never lived up to the promises he made before our lives changed. Neither did Asher. And I'm nothing but a fool for thinking otherwise.

TWELVE

ASHER

December 24, 2014

"I told you I would pick all that shit up later." My mom stumbles into the kitchen, sliding herself onto one of the kitchen chairs. Her hair is a tangled mess, and her makeup is smeared under her eyes. It looks like she got into a fight with a toaster while in the bathtub.

"It's fine. I got it." I roll my eyes and open another trash bag. I pick up an empty vodka bottle, along with a few half-empty beer bottles, and pour the stale liquid down the drain before tossing them in the bag with the other empties. They all fall to the bottom, clinking against one another.

My mom sits back in her chair, sliding her butt along the cushion until her shoulders are resting against the back. She stretches one leg out and stares at me with hooded eyes.

She lifts her cigarette to her mouth, taking a long, slow drag before she quickly blows it out. "Where are you going all dressed up?"

Her words are slurred, but I'm still able to make out what she says. I look down at my shirt, not sure what my mother means by 'dressed up'. I'm wearing one of the only three shirts I own. This one happens to be in the best condition out of all of them. I guess if you were to make a comparison to my usual clothes, my mother could be right—this is dressed up.

"It's Christmas Eve." I refuse to meet her gaze, only focusing on cleaning our small kitchen. Our trailer is one of the smallest in the park. In all honesty, it's probably considered more along the lines of a camper than anything resembling a home.

"You're going to see that slut, aren't you? What's her name again?" She grimaces. "*Charles?*"

I inhale a deep breath and close my eyes, clenching my jaw. My teeth grind against one another, and the pressure builds in my temples. "You know her name is Charleigh, Mom... and she's not a slut." I'm trying to contain my anger, knowing my mother is only saying these things because she's drunk. Charleigh has met my mother only once, on a rare occasion when she was not drunk. Only halfway there.

That was the one time my mother spoke kindly about Charleigh. Since then, she's always made snide comments about how Charleigh's family thinks they're better than the rest of us because they make ten times as much as we do. For a while, I tried to keep our friendship a secret, but once I realized I loved Charleigh more than just a friend, I didn't want to hide her anymore. I wanted my mother to know I'd found someone good and kind. I wanted her to meet the woman I was in love with.

Mom scoffs, raising her lazy hand to take another drag. "The rich and privileged are always the dirtbags. Trevor Keeler is no different." She stands, dropping her cigarette into an empty beer bottle I have yet to clean up.

My mother's comment about Trevor isn't entirely false. Charleigh's father has been having an affair with his secretary for God knows how long. Everyone knows it, even Charleigh. He doesn't try to hide it, and her mother pretends his infidelity doesn't exist. The fact that my mother lumps Charleigh in with her scumbag father makes the anger inside my chest boil.

Still carrying the trash bag, I walk over to the table and pick up the bottle. My mother's hand wraps around my wrist, stopping me. Her grip tightens, the ends of her fingers turning white. This time, I finally look at her, realizing she looks even worse up close.

"She's going to ruin you, Asher. Mark my words."

Tearing my arm from her grip, I pick up the bottle and drop it into the bag. "No, Mom. That's your job."

I turn around and head toward the front door without looking back. It's Christmas Eve, and I promised Charleigh I'd sneak into her bedroom before midnight. Snow is in the forecast, and I can already see the first few flakes coming down through our dirt-dusted window.

I sling the trash bag over my shoulder and push against the screen door. The sound of my mother's raspy voice stops me from stepping over the threshold.

"How dare you talk to me that way?" she croaks. "I'm your mother."

Steeling my chest, I turn around to find her now standing in the middle of our small living room. The strap of her tank top is loose around her shoulder, falling down her arm. It doesn't matter that it's fucking freezing outside and our trailer has no heat. Alcohol numbs the cold, apparently. But even through my frustration with my mother, it isn't until I look in her eyes that I regret the words I've spoken.

Sadness clouds her blue eyes. They're a shade darker than usual, her black makeup outlining them in dark smudges. My chest aches knowing she wasn't always this way. I'm not sure when she changed. She's been this way for so long, I can't even remember.

"I'm sorry, Mom. I shouldn't have said that."

My apology is sincere. I'm sorry for every circumstance that brought her to becoming the woman standing in front of me. I'm sorry for not being the son she wants me to be. I'm also sorry that I'll be leaving her in the next few months. I still haven't told my mother about me leaving for NYU or my full scholarship. I want to tell her, but the bigger part of me knows she won't understand how this will be better for us. If I can graduate with a business degree and start my own real estate firm, I know I'll be able to give her a better life. I simply need more time. More time for her to understand.

"Whatever. Shut the fucking door. You're letting the cold in." She waves me off, falling onto our worn, leather sofa. She picks up the remote and turns on the TV, ignoring me, keeping her eyes focused on the flashing screen. "Go on. Get on out of here and leave me. Just like your father."

"Merry Christmas, Mom." I push the screen door open and walk over to the dumpster to throw out the trash. My mother's comment isn't one I haven't heard before. Most nights she's passed out on the couch before I leave to go to Charleigh's, but on the nights she's sober enough to stay awake, she always makes a comment about my father and how he left us for someone else. All I know is he lives out in California. I may not know him well enough to form an accurate opinion, but my mother doesn't make it easy to decide who to believe. My father is a mystery, and my mother can't seem to let go of the past.

The snow glistens as it falls, coating the town in a blanket of white.

My entire face is numb, and I'm covered in snowflakes by the time I make it onto Charleigh's street. Her house is in the most upscale neighborhood in town. Large colonials run up and down each side, tall fences demarcating each yard. It's my favorite neighborhood to take note of the architecture. At least at first it was. After I'd seen Charleigh digging in her backyard that first time, *she* quickly became the reason this is my favorite place.

When I make it to Charleigh's, I sneak in the shadows up her driveway and tiptoe to the trellis below her bedroom window. I cling close to the brick wall and slide my phone out of my pocket. My screen is cracked and the top corner is blacked out. I type out a quick text to let Charleigh know I'm here, then quickly scale up the length of her house.

Charleigh meets me at her window when I make it to the top.

She immediately wraps her arms around me, burying her face in my neck.

"Oh, my God," she breathes, tensing her arms, squeezing me tighter. "You're soaking wet and freezing cold."

"It was already starting to come down when I left," I tell her. She loosens her arms around me and rises on her toes to kiss me.

I wrap my hand around the back of her head and pull her to me. She smells like she's been digging in her garden all day, and I wonder how when the ground is frozen solid and there isn't a fresh flower in sight.

When I reluctantly break our kiss, she presses both hands to my face. Her thumb grazes beneath my eye, wiping away a melted snowflake.

I grin at her gesture, but it vanishes when I see tears welling in her eyes.

"What's wrong?"

"Nothing," she whispers, shaking her head and looking down at her feet. "It's stupid."

"It's not." Hooking my fingers under her chin, I lift her gaze to mine.

She rolls her eyes and sighs. "You don't even know what it is. For all you know, it could be something ridiculous."

"If you have tears in your eyes, then I know it isn't ridiculous."

Her eyes close as she takes several slow and deep breaths. When she opens them again, the tears have subsided, but her eyes are still clouded with sadness. "My parents were fighting again. They were arguing the entire drive home from the company Christmas party. They were yelling in the foyer when I snuck up stairs. I've been hiding out here ever since."

"I'm so sorry." They're the only two words I'm able to utter, knowing nothing I can say will change anything. Charleigh needs me to escape her parents. I need her to escape my mother. I'm just hoping she gets her acceptance letter soon.

I pull her toward me, placing my lips against hers again, hoping to take away the pain. Her mouth is warm. This time, she parts her lips, allowing her tongue to slide against mine. I taste her peppermint toothpaste.

My hands slide down her neck and onto her back. She's wearing a plain T-shirt tonight, the hem hitting mid-thigh. I used to think her flowery tank top and shorts were my favorite on her, but I'm thinking I may have just changed my mind. She places her hands on my hips, gripping the fabric of my shirt. After a few minutes of kissing, I finally break my mouth away from hers. We haven't taken our relationship further than touching each other. I know Charleigh wants to sleep with me, but I haven't felt like it's the right time. I'd rather wait until I know there's zero chance of her parents finding us. As much as I want her that way, I'm not rushing it.

"I have something for you," I whisper.

"Oh, yeah?" She immediately perks. Her face lights up and she clasps her hands in front of her.

Digging inside the pocket of my coat, I find the small piece of metal and wrap my hand around it.

I grab Charleigh's hand and open it, dropping the keychain into her palm. "Merry Christmas."

Her mouth falls open in surprise, and her eyes dart up at me before landing back on her gift.

"Asher," she breathes shakily, running her finger along the flower charm, up to the golden metal heart clasp. "A flower."

"It's little, I know." My cheeks warm. I wanted to buy her the bigger size charm from the salesman working the booth at the mall, but I could only afford the smallest one.

"It's okay." Charleigh sniffs. "It's beautiful."

"You're my flower, Charleigh," I tell her, warmth spreading across my entire body. "My beautiful, little flower."

She giggles, turning over the keychain in her hand several times. When she looks up at me, tears line her eyes again. "You didn't have to get me anything for Christmas, Asher. You're all I need."

I shake my head. "It didn't cost much. My neighbor, Mr. Greer, paid me to shovel his driveway last week, so I had enough to buy it."

Her hands wrap around the keychain, and she holds it against her chest. "I love it. Thank you."

"And I love you." I wrap my hand around the back of her head again and give her another kiss.

She presses her mouth to mine, then pulls away.

"I want to show you something," she whispers. The same smile I'm used to seeing on Charleigh is back. The keychain must have taken her mind off her parents.

I follow her across her room to where she falls to her knees in front of her bed. She digs under it and pulls out a cardboard box covered in pictures of flowers, pieced and glued together like a collage. She lifts the lid, pulls out a flower, and sits back on her heels. She grabs my hand and drops it into my palm.

"What is it?" I ask, inspecting it. The petals are white with outlines of pink. My knowledge of flowers isn't as nearly extensive as Charleigh's.

"A mountain laurel. Connecticut's state flower. I picked it the first time I saw you."

"You mean the day it was raining?"

"No, that wasn't the first time." She grins. "I noticed you before then."

I smile back. "Me, too."

Keeping the flower in my hand, I slide the box closer, peering inside. The air is sucked from my lungs when I realize what's inside. I pick out one of the paper hearts.

"You kept all of these?" I ask, sifting through them. I look up to find her eyes on me.

"Of course." She shrugs, allowing her hair to fall around her face. "Sometimes, when I'm having a bad day, I'll go through them and try to find my favorite."

"Which one is your favorite?" Part of me is shocked thinking how less than an hour ago I was cleaning up after my drunk mother, and now I'm sitting on the floor with the person I love most in the world. Knowing my paper hearts have meant something to Charleigh makes my heart swell a thousand times.

She places her hand in the box, moving the hearts around. "Every day, I have a different one. It never stays the same."

"I never knew you kept them. I assumed you tossed them in the trash."

"Why would I throw them away? It's my favorite thing to wake up to in the morning." Charleigh tilts her head to the side, studying me. I can feel her eyes wandering across my chest, my arms, my face. It's as if she's lighting every single piece of my body on fire. "You say you aren't great with words, Asher. This is my proof you're wrong."

I swallow thickly. Fuck, I'm so in love with this girl, it's terrifying.

"Can I ask you something?" I look down at the box of paper hearts. I don't know why, but I'm nervous. My heart beats faster, thrumming against the walls of my ribs.

"Sure."

"What made you fall in love with me?"

She cocks her head to the side. "I don't get what you mean."

"I mean..." I sigh, pinching the bridge of my nose. "I'm not exactly the best man for you, Charleigh. I live in a trailer, and the few pieces of clothing I own all have too many holes for me to count. My phone barely works, and I have ten dollars in my wallet. I have nothing to offer you but these paper hearts." I point to the box and scoot closer to Charleigh's bed, my back pressed against the mattress.

She moves closer to me, too, pressing her body against mine. She hooks her fingers under my chin, forcing me to look at her. "I love you, Asher, and I couldn't care less whether you're poor or have all the money in the world." She sighs, swiping her tongue across her mouth. Her lips glisten in the moonlight. Leaning forward, she plants a kiss on my cheek, then places the lid back onto the box and slides it back under the bed.

Grabbing my hand, she pulls me to a stand before sitting me down on her bed, where she straddles me, pressing both her hands to my face. She leans down, tucking her hair behind her ear. I keep her close, placing both of my hands on the small of her back. "I love you for the man you are, Asher, and for the man I know you'll become."

"I love you, too." I run my fingers across her cheek. "What do you see in our future?"

"First, I see us graduating together, both of us with a business degree." Her smile reaches her eyes.

"Yeah?" I whisper.

She nods, biting down on her lip. She rocks her hips, and I fight hard not to take it any further. Although I don't want to sleep with Charleigh tonight, I won't stop myself from feeling her this way. "After college, you'll start your own real estate business and be New York's most successful real estate executive."

I smile, loving where Charleigh's imagination is taking her.

She grips my shoulders and clutches the fabric of my shirt, pulling me up toward her. My shirt makes me remember what my life is like now. It's hard to imagine there will ever be a time when I won't be scrounging for pennies just to be able to buy food. A time when I won't be living in a trailer.

"Where do you fit into this future of mine?" I ask.

With a serious expression, she brings her face to the crook of my neck. Her breath dances across my skin as she breathes me in, whispering against my flesh, "I'll be with you, silly, surrounded by flowers and paper hearts."

I grip the back of her head, threading my fingers through her hair. "I like the sound of that."

"I want you," Charleigh says against my neck.

I dig my fingers into her back, rocking her hips against me. I swell under my jeans, and it takes everything in me to hold back. I groan, moving my hands to her face, pulling it up to mine.

Her eyebrows pull together, and I see the worry in her. It's as if she's afraid I'm going to disappear.

I pull her close. My fingers dip into her floral-scented hair. "I want you, too." I swallow. "One day. But not tonight."

She inhales a shaky, unsteady breath, but softly nods. "Okay."

I place my lips to her, sending her another promise. Once she pulls her lips away from mine, we crawl under the sheets of her bed, tangling our limbs together. With her body sidled against mine, and her arms and legs draped over my body, we lay in silence, watching the snow fall outside her window and the clock turn to midnight.

"Merry Christmas, Little Flower," I whisper, with my hand over hers, holding my keychain against my chest.

"Merry Christmas, Asher."

Once Charleigh falls asleep, I stay for a few minutes. She always reminds me that this is her least favorite part of the night—when I have to leave. It's my least favorite too, for multiple reasons. Most of all, because I don't want to leave her and go home to my drunk mother, but also because of her parents. It hasn't happened yet, but I'm terrified there will come a time when her parents come to check on her and find me lying in her bed.

Charleigh has her thigh bent over my leg, pinning me beneath her. Her arm is across my chest, and her head rests on it. I press my lips to the top of her head, and her hair still smells like flowers. I breathe her in, willing myself to remember this feeling before I start my walk back home in the bitter cold. My trailer smells of stale alcohol and mold. I kiss her one more time, then carefully slide out from underneath her.

I tiptoe across the room to her desk, opening the drawer to grab the things I need. I get the scissors, cutting the piece of paper into a small heart. Taking the pen next, I press it to the paper and glance over my shoulder.

Charleigh is still sound asleep, only her hushed breathing making any noise. The moon shines on her skin, the shadows of the falling snow dance across her body, and for a moment, I imagine a life where we're both at our happiest. I can't imagine a life without her in it. I'd be a fucking idiot to lose her. An absolute fucking idiot.

Here's another heart for you to surround yourself with, Little Flower.

Flowers and paper hearts.

I flip the paper over and write the same message I always leave for her on the back.

From Asher, With Love

I fold the heart in half and tape it to the bottom of her window. I gently slide it open and get my footing on the trellis before stopping to look at Charleigh again. She's the most beautiful person I've ever known. My mother is wrong about her.

Charleigh could never ruin me.

THIRTEEN

ASHER

The wind whips against my face as soon as I step out of my helicopter. My feet drop to the landing pad, and I don't even make it to the elevator doors of my penthouse building when my phone buzzes in my pocket.

The city sky is blanketed in black with the golden lights of New York stretching out as far as the eye can see. But all I can think about is the woman I watched walk out the door a week ago. Ten years ago, I was the one who left. Although I was a coward and didn't give Charleigh the opportunity to watch me leave, instead, choosing to vanish on her like some sort of sick magic trick. Still, the ache I felt inside after watching her walk away only made me all too aware of how Charleigh must have felt the morning after I'd left her. The morning she'd found the last note I'd ever write to her taped to her window.

I'm a fucking idiot.

I ignore the growing pit of concern in my stomach and answer Janette's call.

"Janette."

"Oh, good, Mr. Egan." She lets out a sigh of relief. "You're back."

"I just landed," I tell her, nodding to my valet, Hank, who holds the door to the elevator open for me. He pushes the button for my floor and waits patiently as the lift descends.

"How was your meeting upstate?" Janette asks.

"Fine," I tell her, not caring to dive into the details of my meeting with another client who was interested in looking for properties up near Saratoga Springs. "Were you able to work on that research I asked you to do for me earlier?"

"Yes." Her voice hitches, seemingly surprised with my abrupt shift in the conversation. "I have all the information pulled up and ready to email over to you now. Do you have another meeting or closing date you'd like me to put in your calendar for Saratoga Springs?"

"No. And don't bother sending me the email. I want to know what you found. Read it to me." I give Hank another curt nod as I step out of the elevator and into my apartment. My entryway and living room are blanketed in darkness aside from the under cabinet lighting my housekeeper leaves on for me every night before she leaves.

I loosen my tie and make a beeline for the refrigerator to grab a bottle of water and sit in the large, leather chair facing the window, overlooking Midtown.

"Okay." A few clicks fill the silence while I wait for Janette. "I found a slew of articles, and it was a little difficult to sift through them, but I found one in particular that seemed to have the most accurate information. This one is dated July of 2015."

Fuck. A few months after I left Connecticut.

"Go ahead," I urge, my heart pounding in my chest.

"Trevor Keeler, former CEO of Biotech Pharmaceuticals, filed for bankruptcy this past week," she reads. "Last summer, Keeler was fired from his position at Biotech due to a history of immense gambling debt and poor investments within the company, losing tens of millions for the large pharmaceutical chain. Through further investigation, it has been discovered that Keeler has been nearing bankruptcy for the past several years, alongside scathing allegations of sexual assault and multiple affairs. Keeler finally filed for bankruptcy this week, citing poor investments and lack of sufficient funds to keep the company afloat. Bridgeport Daily News has reached out to Keeler's wife, Florence Keeler, and their legal team for further comment but have yet to hear back."

I nearly allow the water bottle to slip from my grasp and spill to the floor. It's as if all my oxygen has escaped, leaving nothing but the sickness still brewing inside my stomach. I knew Trevor was always a bastard, swindling his wife and Charleigh out of a happy life. I knew better than to assume Charleigh had it easier just because she had more money than I did. Our wounds may be two different kinds, but they run just as deep.

"Asshole." Fire burns within me at the thought of Trevor's bad dealings and how they affected Charleigh. Did that mean he didn't pay for her to go to NYU? How was she able to pay for school, then?

"Is there any articles dated after that one?" I ask Janette, swallowing the bile in my throat. "An updated one?"

"There's a small mention of him in an article eight months later, saying his company was seized by the bank and he lost all assets. A multi-million-dollar firm ultimately bought it, erasing Trevor Keeler's stamp on the company."

"Nothing about him or the family?"

"No, sir." Janette gives a resigned sigh. "Would you like me to keep looking and see if I can find anything else?"

"No." I clear my throat. "That's all. Thank you, Janette. I'll see you tomorrow."

She must be surprised by my kindness because she pauses

before giving me a warm, "You're welcome," followed by, "Um, there's something else. Your, um, your father called." She stumbles over her words, and I know she feels sympathy for me because of the state my father is in.

My throat tightens. I haven't talked to him in a few weeks. It's not that I've been avoiding him, I've simply been busy. Especially with Charleigh back in my life.

"Did he say why he called?"

"He said he's tried to reach you on your cell with no success. He's not doing well."

I rest my elbow on the arm of my chair and pinch the bridge of my nose. My head pounds and the backs of my eyes sting. The urge to drink is calling me, and while my reasons for being sober aren't because I'm an alcoholic, they're just as important all the same. Curling my fingers into a fist, I swallow down the urge and the pain inside. "I'll take care of it, Janette. Thank you."

This time, I don't wait for Janette's response. I hang up.

My thoughts swing like a pendulum. My father. Charleigh. Her father. Charleigh.

The cycle repeats as my finger hovers over her name on my phone screen.

But what could I possibly say to fix the damage I've done? What could I say that would erase the pain in her eyes I left, not only last week, but ten years ago? Especially now that I know about her father and the tsunami of torment he waged on his family in the months after I left.

I ache with a pain I haven't felt in a long time.

I haven't been able to stop thinking about how close we got last week. The scent of her hair. The heat coming from her mouth. I wanted to devour it. I wanted to devour *her*. I've started questioning every decision I've made since meeting her at the bar that first night, from visiting her floral shop and noticing those fucking paper hearts she uses as her signature on every bouquet, to the entirety of our moment of weakness last week. It was as if I would push Charleigh away only to pull her back again just to gauge her reaction to me.

Who the fuck have I become?

I think back to who I was at eighteen. The hopelessly, maniacally in love Asher. The one who would have done anything for her.

But there was a reason I left Charleigh ten years ago. It wasn't because my love for her had faded or simply disappeared. It was because I knew after the fire that everything I touched, I destroyed. I had the potential to destroy everything that was good about Charleigh.

Now the reason I left Charleigh in the first place is staring me straight in the face.

She's happy with her life, content and successful, just as I hoped she would be after I left. But that's all tainted again simply because I am back in her life . Falling for her... again.

Sheets of rain pour down across the city. Thunder rumbles in the distance, vibrating through my empty apartment. Loneliness can only be ignored for so long. Until you find it staring you straight in the face.

I'm about to close out my phone screen without calling Charleigh when I get a text from a number I don't recognize.

(646) 555-7402: I spoke with Holt earlier today. Sorry we couldn't schedule a meeting this week. He invited me to his sister Julianna's birthday party next month. I'll see you then and hopefully we can have a chat about what works best for both of us. Looking forward to it! – Weston Knight

Dammit. I'd forgotten I was supposed to set up a meeting with West this week after we were introduced at his bar opening. I type out a reply to him, then a thank you to my best friend for coming to my rescue. But just as I hit send, I get a text from Charleigh that feels like an anchor plunging into the depths of my stomach, knocking the life out of me.

> Charleigh: I was right that night at the beer garden. Working with you has been a mistake. I was a fool to put my trust in you again. I think it's best we end this before we get in too deep. Wishing you all the success in the future. Goodbye, Asher.

"Fuck!" I yell, tossing my phone onto my mahogany coffee table. The sound echoes through my apartment but is quickly drowned out by the storm brewing over the city.

Pressure builds behind my eyes, and my chest tightens. The threads of the rope that feel as though they're around my ribcage curl and tighten, squeezing the oxygen from my lungs. I lean forward and rest my head in my hands. Closing my eyes, I see Charleigh beneath the sheets of her bed... but not as the woman she is now. I see those eighteen-year-old round eyes looking up at me with every ounce of love she had. I feel her warmth under my touch as I drag my finger over her collarbone after our first time. The sound of her breath hitching as I memorize every inch, relishing in the way her heart thrashes in her delicate chest whenever I whisper in her ear.

I made her mine that night, and swore I would never let her go. But somewhere along the way, she slipped between the cracks, and I let her.

Something in Charleigh's text doesn't feel like a tepid sting. It's a sharp, burning torturous bite. It's an unexpected pain, and one I don't know what to do with. Her words are a hammer to the heart.

Fuck.

Lifting my head up, I watch the rain for precisely one second before I'm swiping my phone from the coffee table, snatching the keys to my BMW from the hook by my front door, and heading for the parking garage.

FOURTEEN

CHARLEIGH

Asher is an arrogant asshole.

I haven't spoken to him since last week. I'm still reeling from the stunt he pulled. I spent most of my week going through invoices, filling my wedding calendar for the rest of the year, and ignoring phone calls from my parents. Work has always been my escape. It's a reminder of the beauty that still exists in a world so easily clouded by tragedy.

By the time I make it home from my store, I've finally come to terms with the decision I need to make. I try not to beat myself up too much, but when I've washed my hair and begin the task of shaving my legs, I'm reminded of every reason why I knew hiring Asher was a bad idea.

My trust in him dissolved years ago, yet I was stupid enough to put my trust in him again. I run the razor up my leg, thinking back to him standing in that old restaurant space that was terribly out of my budget. The smirk that appeared on his ridiculously gorgeous face, and the way he slithered in like a snake hunting its prey. It was as if he began circling around, asking vague questions before landing on the one topic I knew he genuinely wanted to talk about.

My father.

The scars and wounds that were caused by my father are internal, settling in right alongside the ones Asher left when he disappeared. Flashes of the night my father nearly broke him come back to me. He was the one to tip the first domino of all the events to come after that night.

My breathing becomes shallower, and my hands begin to shake. I try to calm myself down, counting to ten, scared I'm going to accidently cut myself while shaving, but even when I calm my breathing long enough to finish my shower, I still haven't stopped thinking about Asher.

The thought of him persuading me to hire him, then deciding to make a complete one-eighty and show me a place he knew I couldn't afford still irritates me. Part of me wants to believe Asher was convinced four hundred thousand over my budget wasn't a deal breaker for me, but as soon as he brought up the subject of my father, he made his intentions clear. Perhaps it had to do with our almost kiss in front of the mantle. I wanted him to kiss me. I wanted to remember what it felt like to be touched by him. If I'm honest, I wanted him to fuck me right there, with the replica of the flower I'd shown him on Christmas Eve sitting in front of us. I wanted him to take me and demand I remember what it was like to be with him all those years ago. But now, I wish I'd never agreed to working with him in the first place. The pain is too great. Asher and I are a complicated web. A tangled, sticky mess we can't seem to stay away from.

After I slip into my robe, my phone rings. "Hey, Julianna."

"Hey, are you busy?" she asks.

"I just got out of the shower. I texted Asher and told him I can't work with him anymore." I breathe out, wringing out the rest of the water in my hair. "He broke my trust when I was eighteen, and he's done it again, Jules. There's too much history between us. Ten years obviously wasn't enough time for us to forget our past. We're finished."

"Shit, really?" She sighs. "I'm sorry, babes. What did he do?"

"Acted like a complete asshole." I scoff, the sting of what happened between us still prevalent. "Wait, I take that back. He *was* and *is* a complete asshole." The words spill from my mouth, but I'm not completely sold on them because, despite the person he's become, I know the man I fell in love with is still somewhere inside him.

But that doesn't change the bitterness I feel for the way he left, and how I apparently haven't been able to let it go since we've come back into each other's lives.

"Oh, no," Julianna croons. "I'm so sorry I've been out this week for the interior designer workshop. What happened?"

I resist the tears stinging the corners of my eyes, keeping them at bay. "He brought up my dad and assumed I could just ask him for money."

A sharp hiss leaves Julianna's mouth. She knows the ins and outs of my parents' tumultuous marriage and how I was always caught in the crossfire. She knows about my father's infidelity and how his failure to keep his dick in his pants bled into every aspect of our lives, forcing my father to declare bankruptcy.

"Men can be such dickheads." Julianna clicks her tongue. "I swear, I don't know why we bother."

I nod, feeling my chin wobble as I inhale an unsteady breath. "In all fairness, everything that happened with my father and him basically making our entire family broke was *after* Asher left. He didn't know."

"He still left you, Charleigh. He didn't even have the decency to tell you to your face. He left you a note taped to your window along with all the shattered pieces of your broken heart. Men tend to do that, no matter what age. *Apparently*."

"Is everything okay?" I ask, sensing there's more to her statement.

Julianna pauses. "I don't want to hear you gloat or kick your feet in excitement when I tell you."

I frown, continuing to make my way toward my kitchen, thankful we've shifted the topic away from Asher. "I wouldn't do that, Jules."

"I know. It's just... okay." She sighs, preparing herself. "I ended it with Taron."

I allow my eyes to close with relief. Now Julianna's comment makes sense. I hold my excitement at bay, as well as holding my promise.

"What happened?"

She growls in frustration, but she doesn't sound as upset or heartbroken as I thought she would be. "I showed up to the club he works at and found him in the VIP section with a waitress's mouth around his dick. You should have seen the look on his face when he saw me, Charleigh. The fucker's jaw was practically on the floor, even though he was the one who asked me to come. I thought the asshole was going to rip his dick off with how fast he pulled himself out of the skanky waitress's mouth."

"Wait..." I gape. "He asked you to meet him at the club but then proceeded to get a blow job from a waitress? While on the clock?"

"Yep."

"Wow." I blow out a heavy breath. "You deserve better, Jules."

Sadness fills me knowing my best friend deserves a man who worships her. Or at least one who isn't a complete fucking prick like Taron.

"I know, and you do, too," she adds. "Do you feel like you made the right decision with Asher?"

My eyes find the framed flower sitting on top of my mantle.

I was stupid for finding another one like it and framing it, as if it could somehow give me back a piece of my life that was ripped away. Emotion grows thick in my throat. We were almost there, with his mouth close to mine, his hands on me. But then I think about our conversation the other day, and the look in his eyes when he asked about my dad. "Yes."

I take a deep breath and look over at the counter. Anywhere else but at that flower.

"Good, because in that case, I have some news," Julianna squeaks out, soundly oddly perky. A stark shift in tone from the conversation we've been having.

"What do you mean?"

"Well... With my birthday next month, I've been planning a massive party."

"Oh, yeah?" I smile a little. Julianna goes all out for her birthday every year. Caterers, DJs, a ridiculous amount of alcohol and decorations, even a full wait staff. If anyone knows how to do an adult birthday party well, it's Julianna Capuleti, so I'm not entirely surprised when she brings it up.

"I told Holt already, but I'm going even bigger this year," she explains excitedly. "I'm inviting everyone we know."

I cock my head to the side. "Don't you always?"

"Yes. But I'm telling you, Charleigh. I'm going all out for this one and inviting more than usual. My apartment is going to be decked out. I can't wait for you to see what I have planned."

"I can't wait, either." I mean it, too.

"Maybe we can find us some hot billionaires to keep us distracted."

I roll my eyes, not knowing if Julianna realizes Asher *is* a hot billionaire. "I'm not sure that's a good idea."

"Look, I may have ended things with Taron, but that doesn't mean I've given up altogether. And neither should you." It seems my best friend still hasn't let up on the idea of setting me up with someone.

"Okay," I whisper, the corners of my mouth finally lifting.

Julianna squeals into the phone, and I smile. It feels good to hear both of us finding a bit of happiness. But I know it'll disappear as soon as I hang up. And it does.

After ending my call with Julianna, I open the silverware drawer and pick up the old, folded letter slipped underneath the stack of teaspoons. I haven't always kept it in this drawer, but the day I ran into Asher at Cyrus's office, I came home and fished through my closet to find it. It was buried in the back, pressed between the pages of an old book. I carried it out to the kitchen while reheating some leftover Chinese takeout from the night before, but I couldn't bring myself to open it. I held the crinkled paper in my shaking hands, remembering the words scribbled inside by a man who claimed to never have the right words. I held the paper between my fingers as if opening and seeing the words would hurt me all over again.

I breathe in, wishing the night that broke Asher and me had never happened. Wishing the fire never happened. Wishing my father was a different person and wishing Asher's mother could have stopped herself from becoming the person she turned into.

What would our lives have been like if Asher had gone to NYU? Would we still be together?

I look down at my hands, the letter still held between them. This note never would have existed, and I wouldn't be standing here wondering about all the what ifs. I slip the letter back under the stack of spoons and slam the drawer shut.

Frustrated with myself, I flick the switch on my kettle and drop a tea bag into my favorite mug. While I wait for the water to heat, my stomach grumbles, and I search through my pantry but find nothing. It's filled with all types of food and snacks, but it's as if my brain can't keep my thoughts straight long enough to decide what to eat.

I walk over to my couch, hoping to at least find something on the TV to calm my mind. I lay my head down on a pillow and immediately, my eyes grow heavier. I settle on a movie I've already seen, and by the time the opening credits start, I let my exhaustion take over and drag me into darkness.

FIFTEEN

CHARLEIGH

My eyes snap open at the shrill sound of the incessant beeping coming from the kitchen. I shoot straight up and gasp, wondering how long I've been asleep. I must have only been out long enough for the water in my kettle to boil since it's still beeping. Standing from the couch, I look out the sliding door to my patio. Water is pounding against my balcony. It's started raining, the clouds blanketing the sky with a deep gray. Perfect time for tea, anyway.

Once in the kitchen, I reach for the small wooden cup of honey I have sitting on the counter and swirl some of the golden liquid into my tea using the dipper.

My heart shudders, and a chill slithers down the back of my neck when I hear my doorbell ring several times in succession. The dinging sound is quickly followed by heavy knocks reverberating off my wooden door.

I drop the honey stick and stare at my front door. Waiting for what, I don't know. No one ever knocks on my door or comes over.

Then the pounding continues, its incessant knocking echoing off the walls inside my living room.

"I'm coming!" I shout, hoping it will stop whoever is at my door from knocking more.

It doesn't. The pounding continues, even up to the point of me unlocking my door and opening it.

Asher stands on the other side, his fist raised in the air. My mouth falls open at the sight of him, every inch soaking wet. His white button-down shirt is nearly translucent, clinging to his tan skin. It's wrapped around the muscles of his arms and chest, contracting with every heavy breath he draws in. Water drips from his hair, the ends mussed and resting against his forehead.

My gaze lowers to his mouth, a single drop of rain falling from his bottom lip.

"Asher." I manage to croak out his name, leaning forward and peering down the hall before looking back at him. "What are you doing here?"

"One week. One week, and you..." He breathes out but doesn't move, clenching his fists at his sides, jaw clenched tightly.

When my eyes catch his, I notice they're burning with fire.

"You," he says again. This time, he runs his hand down his face, attempting to wipe it dry, but it's impossible with how wet he is. He presses his mouth together, grinding his jaw once more. The muscles there tick, then he quickly pushes past me, stepping into my apartment without having been invited in.

Stunned, I watch him pace back and forth in the space between my living room and kitchen. He has one hand planted on his hip, while the other is gripping the back of his head as he keeps his head down. He watches his feet leaving wet footprints on my carpet.

I close the door behind me and cross my arms over my chest. "By all means..." I stand, flabbergasted. "Make yourself at home."

Asher spins around, cutting me a sharp glare.

"You don't have anything to say?" His eyebrows create a hard line above his golden eyes. My breath hitches in my throat, and I hiccup. Not because it's finally occurring to me why he's barging into my apartment after apparently racing here in this rainstorm, but because his eyes are giving me an all too familiar feeling. The one that makes my heart skip like I'm seventeen again. Like that first time he looked at me while standing in the middle of my street. The gold flecks in his eyes are just as bright like they're on fire.

I weave my arms across my chest, not wanting Asher to catch on to the way I'm suddenly willing to overlook his tantrum just because my entire body is reacting to him.

His chest continues to rise and fall, still trying to catch his breath, water dripping from the stubble on his chin.

"No," I say as evenly as possible. "I think my text said everything that needed to be said."

His nostrils flare before he closes the space between us. In what would normally take ten steps, he meets me in five. Towering over me has him invading every one of my senses. He smells like fresh rain, the heat practically steaming off his body, warming mine. I step back until I'm flush against the front door. Square shoulders and hardened muscle.

Asher presses his hands against the door, caging me in. His eyes meet mine, the flames of gold flickering in them.

"I would disagree," he growls, the heat radiating from his skin.

I narrow my eyes, defiant to my core. I shove the instinct inside the walls of my chest to stand on my toes and press my lips to his. My body aches to touch his, but I refuse to reward him when he's acting like an ass.

"Too bad," I tell him, and I duck out from under his arm and make my way back into the kitchen.

I'm humming with nerves. I need to do *something*. I spot my cup of tea still sitting on the counter. The honey dipper didn't quite make it back into the cup. A line of the sticky, amber liquid drips from the side of my mug down to the puddle of honey pooled under the dipper resting on the marble surface. I open the drawer for a spoon but quickly shut it at the first glance of Asher's note. I slam the drawer with more force than intended, smashing the ends of my pointer and middle finger.

"Ow, fuck!" I yell, jerking my hand back. I hiss, looking down at the now-red-tinted tips of my fingers. I shake my hand in air as if it will magically make the pain disappear, but Asher's hand wraps around my wrist, stopping it mid-air.

I try to pull myself away, but he resists, yanking me closer. My body slams into his still-wet chest. The shirt is clinging to his muscles like second skin. I watch in amazed silence as he holds my hand delicately in his large ones, rotating it to examine the damage I've inflicted on myself.

"I'm fine," I grunt, trying again to pull away from his grip. Being this close to him is doing something to me. Again.

Like it was last week with our almost kiss, his hand close to my clit, his touch is quick to draw a reaction to me. And I know if I were wearing panties underneath this sad excuse of a robe, they'd be soaked already.

Asher shoots me a glare. "Would you stop acting like a child?"

My mouth falls open. How dare he practically barge into my apartment, demand me to explain my text, then call me a child?

"I told you, I'm fine," I repeat, wanting him to let me go, yet at the same time, reconsidering.

Asher smirks, amusement sparking in his eyes. He keeps his gaze pinned to mine as he lifts my hand closer to his face. Achingly slowly and softly, he presses his lips to my pointer finger, giving it a gentle kiss. Then he moves to my middle finger, but this time, he parts his lips, devouring my finger. He sucks on the tip, sliding his tongue across my skin and pulling it in past the first knuckle. His cheeks hollow slightly, and his lips pop when he pulls my finger from his soft mouth. Looking at my now-crimson-tipped finger, he then flicks his gaze to mine. "Not as sweet as I remember."

I'm practically dripping between my legs. My belly hums and tightens.

Dammit.

The spell Asher just cast on me quickly fades. Anger returns to my veins, and my heart jolts with white hot bitterness.

This time, when I yank my hand away, Asher doesn't resist.

"Why are you here, Asher?"

"I want you to talk to me, Charleigh," he says, his tone more relaxed than before, but I can still sense his frustration with me. "Why did you send me that text? A week without any word. Not very professional, now, is it?"

"And coming to my apartment, soaking wet, demanding answers is?"

I hate that I want to touch him. I want to feel his mouth on me again. But this time, I don't want him on my fingers. I want more. Wanting Asher doesn't just boil down to sex, though. There's more to my feelings for him. I need to remember that. Emotion is thick in my throat, and my eyes fall to the silverware drawer.

"What is there to say?" My eyes drift back to his. "We made a deal, and you broke it."

"I didn't break our deal. We agreed for you to hire me while keeping your options with Cyrus open. I haven't been doing anything but my job, which, if you've forgotten, is to find you a new storefront."

My heart beats erratically in my chest.

Keep it together, Charleigh.

"Not that deal," I squeeze out in a tight voice. "The other one."

The hardness in Asher's expression relaxes, his eyes softening slightly.

"I trusted you, Asher, when I have every reason not to."

"Charleigh, I can't make up for what I did in the past."

"No, but it's like I've said before... you aren't the Asher I used to know. You're only using me to get ahead, or maybe you're enjoying this. Is that what that was the other day?" I point to the fireplace, then lift my hand up in front of me. "Or this? Was this a test I didn't pass?"

His eyebrows draw together in confusion.

"You don't make any sense, Asher. You push me away, then pull me back in. Then you ask about my dad as if—"

"I didn't know," he cuts in. "I didn't know about your dad."

I feel the tears coming, but I don't want them to spill. I promised myself I would never cry over my father. That would make me like my mother.

"I didn't know about what happened with your family after—"

"You left," I interrupt right back.

A stark, hardened expression washes over his face. He presses his mouth into a thin line. He takes a step closer to me, bringing his body to my shoulder until his hardened chest presses against me.

"I'm sor..." he starts but can't bring himself to finish.

Disappointment and hurt boil inside me.

"You're sorry?" I ask. "Sorry for what, exactly? Sorry for leaving me? It wasn't just you who was broken that night. I didn't even find out the details of your mom's death until I went to school the next morning and heard all the rumors floating around. You left me with nothing but a note telling me she'd died. And now, against my better judgment, I let you back into my life as if you weren't the one person who crushed me. Agreeing to work with you was a mistake. You show me this incredible place to expand my flower shop, promising it's the one." I narrow my eyes at him, still bitter that he never showed me the inside. "Then after we come back here to change my shoes, we almost kissed and... it's like you flipped some kind of switch. You completely check out and take me to a completely different location—one well out of my price range. And for what? All so you can show up at my apartment demanding answers after I fire you?" I scoff, laughing in disbelief. "Then you suck on my finger as if you're suddenly craving the taste of me?"

"What if I was?" He lifts his chin.

"What?" I ask, blinking.

"What if I was craving the taste of you?" His eyes darken.

I swallow thickly. "You're... what?"

My breathing is unstable at best when he closes the gap between us. Lifting his hand, he drags the tips of his fingers down the length of my face to my lips, then the base of my throat.

"Every fucking minute since I've seen you, I've craved you. I want you."

"You're not making any sense." I don't believe him. I can't. Not with our history. "Do you know how long after you left, I dreamed of coming back and saying these same things to me? But at some point, I was a fool because you're the one who left me, Asher. You're the one pretending our feelings for each other never mattered. You're hot one minute, cold the next. I don't know what to believe anymore or how to feel because while seeing you again has stirred up old feelings, I remember the pain that comes with it all too well. I remember it more than I wish I did." A lump swells in my throat, and my chest pricks with heat. Especially with him this close to me. Every emotion I've held the past ten years pours out of me in the form of word vomit. "You played me, and I can't for the life of me figure out why when I was dead to you already."

His eyes turn to ice. "You weren't dead to me."

"Right." I scoff. "Because severing our relationship and disappearing like a fucking ghost isn't treating me as if I were dead. We weren't perfect, but what I felt for you was real. Yet you continued on as if I meant nothing. I don't understand how you could be so okay with it."

"You aren't dead to me, Charleigh. You never were. And I haven't been okay." He swallows thickly, his neck swelling, the emotion evident on his face. "I didn't..." He sighs, focusing on his hand against the base of my throat, feeling my pulse. "I didn't intend to ever show you that place that's over your budget. I don't know. I didn't know what to do."

"What do you mean, you didn't know what to do?"

His eyes meet mine again. "I didn't know what to do with the way I'm feeling. But when I got that text earlier, I can't explain it. I felt hollow inside, and I'm sure you're thinking I've become this shallow person, and you're right. You've shown me that, Charleigh. I felt awful. Like someone had split my chest open, reached inside, and ripped my heart out. It's all so fucking confusing. You get under my skin so easily, but I can't stay away. I don't know what to do with the way I'm feeling."

"Show me," I say the words before I realize what they mean.

The darkness in his eyes deepens. With one swift move, he wraps his arm around me, lifting me to sit on the counter. My hand lands on the hard surface, shoving my cup of tea aside. The black liquid spills over the top, but it doesn't burn me. It's practically ice cold at this point. I lean back, forcing air into my lungs. Asher's stolen all of it. Heat swells and aches between my thighs. He forces them apart, settling himself between them.

"You think you're so innocent in all of this?" He leans

closer, dragging his nose up my neck and to my ear. "You think you're so fucking sweet?"

I tilt my head back and look up at the ceiling. Gasping for air, I feel lightheaded, as if I've inhaled a drug.

Asher's scent of fresh rain mingled with his deep, woodsy scent surrounds me. I lift my hand and thread my fingers through his thick, wet hair. The bottom of my robe opens, and I wrap my legs around his waist, pulling him until my hot pussy presses against his body. He's cold and still wet, causing me to hiss with the sensation it gives me.

"Do you know how badly I wanted to spank you when you made us walk down all fifty-two flights of my building?" His voice is as deep as velvet. "I wanted to punish you so fucking hard. I considered taking you right there in that stairwell."

"I don't think that would have been a good idea. Security probably has cameras all over those stairs."

"Like I would fucking care. Let them watch. You would have deserved what I was giving you."

I had no idea Asher's thoughts were this dirty, or that his thoughts had gone in that direction.

"Is that what you're doing now?" I ask, trying not to sound too turned on. "Punishing me?"

He doesn't answer as he reaches between us and tugs on the tie to my robe. The knot unravels, and with just his fingertips, he shoves each side of the fleecy fabric aside until I'm completely exposed. He hisses at the sight of me, taking his time. My nipples harden with the cold air and goosebumps spread across my skin.

Not able to hold back any longer, I pull him closer, wanting to press his lips to mine. But he stops me. I loosen my grip on the back of his head.

He gives me a disapproving tsk, clicking his tongue against the back of his teeth. He shakes his head and looks down at the honey spilled on the counter before he picks up the dipper and sticks it back into the honey jar, swirling the thick liquid. He sinks the dipper farther in and pulls it out, making sure he's gathered as much honey as possible.

He hovers the dipper over my chest, allowing the honey to swirl and drip around my breast and nipple. I arch my back as my mouth falls open, and I gasp, shivering as the gooey liquid coats my skin.

Asher watches his handiwork, every few seconds lifting his heated gaze to mine. Slowly, he drags the trail of oozing honey down my stomach and to my pussy.

The corner of his mouth lifts into a devious smirk. "The Charleigh I remember used to be sweet and kind."

"I still am," I whisper as my eyes flutter, barely able to focus on what Asher is doing to me. Stopping above my center, he brings the dipper to my pussy and slips it between my folds, quickly finding my clit.

"Shit," I hiss, pulling my bottom lip under my teeth. I bite down and close my eyes.

"Eyes on me," he orders.

I do as he says, looking down at where the dipper meets my clit. He adds pressure but doesn't move it otherwise. I roll my hips slightly, begging for him to move it.

"You think it was sweet to send me that text firing me?"

I moan, shamelessly rolling my hips again. I'm aching inside. "You think it was sweet for you to leave a note taped to my window before disappearing?"

Using his other hand, Asher's fingers slip through my hair as he grips the back of my head. He gently tugs me back, exposing my neck. With the dipper pressed against my clit, and my back arched even more, the sensation inside me builds. I might come right now if he doesn't start moving.

"I never claimed to be the sweet one." He growls, slowly and finally starting to work circles on my swollen clit. He brings his mouth to my ear. "What happened to you, Little Flower?"

A shiver breaks across my skin, and the gloves have come off. I roll my hips, the sticky wood bringing me closer to my orgasm.

"You," I moan. "You happened."

A switch is flipped.

His eyes flash with heat, carrying the weight of whatever emotions he's kept inside. He's hungry, but there's a vulnerability there. Over the past several weeks, I haven't been sure if I ever meant as much to Asher as he did to me. Memories become distorted and you start to question your own feelings. For some years, I've questioned if Asher truly existed. Did I make up my love for him? Did I love him more than he did me?

But every question is answered when he falls to his knees in front of me. "Let's see how sweet you still are, Little Flower."

Before my mind has a chance to catch up, Asher replaces the honey dipper pressed against my clit with his mouth. He's fast and rough on me, his spit mixing with the honey coating my flesh. He sucks and bites down on the swollen bud. I hiss, feeling like I'm already going to explode.

I gave my virginity to Asher years ago, but I never felt him like this.

I can't seem to get enough. My legs are draped over his shoulders, and my hands are in his hair, pressing him harder against me.

Heat builds in my belly, and my insides tighten. I want him inside me, but the sensation of Asher's tongue against me begs him not to stop.

"Asher, I'm going to come if you keep doing what you're doing."

He pulls away but keeps his head between my thighs. His

lips glisten with the honey and my wetness as he smirks. "What makes you think I'm wanting to stop this?"

His mouth finds my clit again, but this time, he follows it by plunging the honey dipper inside me. He pumps it in and out, finding the spot that ultimately brings me over the edge. I've never felt anything like it, and after the initial shock, I can't stop what's coming.

Me.

Slipping his other hand up along my chest, he grips my breast before pinching my sticky, hardened nipple between his fingers. He twists them, and a delightful pain shoots straight to where his mouth is on me.

One lap of his tongue.

Two pumps of the honey dipper.

Another flick of the nipple, and I'm coming.

My legs shake and my hips rock, riding out my orgasm. Asher continues to move his mouth on me until I've almost caught my breath. But as he was before, he's quick to move on. He stands between my still shaking legs, fire still burning in his eyes. He removes the dipper, then swipes two fingers along my wetness before bringing his fingers to his mouth. He shoves them between his lips and licks them clean. Then his hand grips my chin, pulling me up to meet his mouth.

"There," he whispers. Heated, weighted breaths feather against my lips. "Now I know how sweet you still are."

When he finally crashes his mouth against mine, he catches me on a breath. I inhale his oxygen, allowing it to fill every crevice of my lungs. I arch my back and wrap my legs around him tighter. I breathe out against his mouth, and it feels as if my body recollects every memory it's forgotten from ten years ago. His touch feels the same yet distinctive. His mouth tastes the same but different.

My body is still humming from my orgasm, but I'm already

wanting to go again. The taste of honey mixed with Asher and myself causes my heart to beat erratically.

I haven't completely understood where Asher's feelings for me stand, but when I pull my mouth away from his, I see it in his eyes. I see the love he once felt for me, the pain that ripped us apart, and fear of what this all means.

Our desire to feel one another, to *touch* one another overrides all logic.

Ten years ago, Asher and I thought we had explored every inch of one another. I'd seen his soul inside and out, but being with him now is different, and I'm feeling him in an entirely different way. He's stronger, his presence surrounding me, consuming me.

I quickly unbutton his shirt. The wet fabric peels away from his sculpted muscles and hard abdomen. I move to his belt, and with one quick move, I've unbuckled it and am shoving his pants and boxer briefs down enough to free his cock. He's hard and ready. It springs to life, and I swallow when looking at it. I don't remember it being this big. Maybe it's grown in the last ten years, or maybe this is another unreliable memory. Asher and I only slept together the one time when we were teenagers, so my memory is mostly likely fuzzy and blurred.

"Are you ready for me, Little Flower?" His voice deepens, and my body hums in anticipation.

I suck in my bottom lip, pinching it under my teeth, nodding.

Asher grabs his length and centers it in front of me before he grips my shoulder and drives himself into me.

He sinks farther, and my head falls back. His mouth finds my nipple as he pulls it in. He laps his tongue, licking up the trail of honey he left earlier. He continues to drive his cock inside me, and with each thrust he buries himself deeper. Harder.

Asher moves his hand from my shoulder to the back of my head, forcing me to look at him. "Watch us. I want you to watch what I can do to you and this sweet pussy of yours. I want you to watch me make you come."

He starts off with slower movements, eventually picking up his pace, and I watch him bury himself inside me over and over again.

"Asher." I say his name on a breath, dizzy from him everywhere. We're a sticky, wet mess, but I don't care. "Don't stop. I'm going to come again."

My insides tighten and my walls squeeze around him. I'm so wet, and when I reach my orgasm, it feels as if I'm suddenly weightless.

I'm living in this moment. For this moment. Feeling Asher for the first time in a way I've never felt.

He's different. He's older. He's more in command. And while I'm angry with the way he was last week, I can't deny the feelings he's stirred inside me. I was right when I said Asher wasn't the man I remember at eighteen. This version is stronger, bolder, commanding, and in charge.

Asher pumps himself in and out of me, faster and deeper until his eyes squeeze shut and his body quakes. His thrusts slow as his cum spills inside me. The muscles in his shoulders contract as he struggles to catch his breath. His head falls to my chest for a few seconds before I feel his lips gently press against my skin, and he leaves a trail of kisses up my chest until they land against mine.

When he pulls away, he's smiling.

"What?" I ask, laughing.

"I think my question was answered."

"What question?"

"You're still just as sweet as I remember."

SIXTEEN

CHARLEIGH

February 10, 2015

"I have to go." I smile against Asher's mouth, dreading having to break away from him.

"No." He grips the back of my head, keeping my lips pressed against his. He tastes like mint and smells like his favorite body spray.

I kiss Asher again, allowing him to slide his tongue across mine. We're standing in the middle of the street, several houses down from mine in the bitter February air, and although it's nearing midnight, I don't want to leave.

I press my palm against his chest, his heart thrashing beneath blood, bone, and muscle. I moan, feeling my thighs tense, warming as his hands slides down my back. His fingers gingerly lift the edge of my shirt, and goosebumps prickle across my skin.

"Asher," I mumble. "I really should go. I don't want my parents to find out that I snuck out. They might come looking for me."

He pulls back with a heavy sigh. His golden eyes are half closed, and he's humming with electricity. "Fine." He curls the corner of his mouth into a smirk, and it takes all my willpower to keep myself from leaning forward and kissing him again.

If I give in, I won't be able to stop.

"I'm sorry I couldn't come in and stay with you tonight," he adds.

"That's okay." I look down and drag my finger across the back of his hand, holding his in mine. "I get it."

"Yeah." He nods. "My mom went out earlier, and I just want to make sure she comes home safely. I'm surprised she went out since she doesn't get paid for another week."

Asher texted me earlier asking if I could meet him outside instead of him sneaking into my room as usual. This is one of the only times his mother has decided to walk down the street from her trailer to one of the small bars in our town. Apparently, she only has thirty dollars in her account to last her the next week until she gets paid.

Keeping up with his promise, Asher still managed to come see me tonight before going back home to make sure his mom makes it back safely to her own bed.

"I wish your mom could see what her drinking is doing to you both," I squeak out, the pain growing in my chest.

"Same." He pauses before he adds, "But I don't want to talk about her. I want to give you this." He digs inside his coat pocket and pulls out a sheet of paper folded into a heart. Not cut but folded. "An early Valentine's Day gift."

"What is it?" I ask, my cheeks hurting from how hard I'm grinning.

"Open it," he whispers, followed by a cloud of his breath. The tip of his nose is bright red, and his bottom lip quivers with the cold, his stare never breaking from the heart.

With shivering hands, I open it. The edge of the paper is frayed, as if it's been torn from a spiral notebook, but tears sting the back of my eyes when I find myself staring back at mine.

"They're yours," he whispers.

"You drew my eyes?" I ask, sniffing. "When?"

"The first time you looked at me." He chuckles. "Well, the first time you finally looked at me long enough to memorize them and draw them."

I can't stop smiling. He's talking about the day I hid behind the tree when my mother buried her wedding ring. That's what he must have written down when I watched him. I press the heart to my chest. "I love you."

"I love you, Little Flower."

"I thought I was going to have to wait until tomorrow night for my paper heart." I grin.

Asher chuckles and gives me another kiss.

"Another round of acceptance letters go out soon," I tell him, nerves getting the better of me.

"And yours will be one of them," he reassures me. I don't dive into the conversation any further both out of anxiety and helplessness. There's nothing I can do but wait, and I know we both need to get home before our parents find us gone.

After giving Asher another long kiss, we both split off in opposite directions. I walk past a few of my neighbors' houses before finally making it to my own.

My body feels heavy and tired. When I begin the climb up the trellis outside my bedroom window, I think about my father and what impact my leaving will have on his life—if any. He's always kept a safe distance from me, never growing too close, keeping me at arm's length. I was supposed to be the dutiful daughter of the highly regarded pharmaceutical CEO. I was supposed to stay within the boundaries he set since the day I was born. The fact my father agreed to my decision to go to NYU is merely a thin veil over the life I live between the four walls of this house.

My acceptance letter can't come fast enough.

I climb through the window, hoping I can be as graceful as Asher usually is when he comes to visit me every night. I lift my leg and climb over the windowsill, my feet landing softly on the carpet.

I grit my teeth and wince, sliding the window down slowly. It glides quietly, and I sigh with relief, ready to crawl under the sheets of my bed.

When I turn around, I gasp. My hand flies to cover my mouth. The lights in my room are off, but my door is swung wide open, the light from the hallway casting a large glow.

"Dad. You scared me." I press my palm flat against my chest, catching my breath.

He sits at the edge of my bed, facing the window I just crawled through. My heart plunks into my stomach when I look down and see he's holding my box of paper hearts in his lap. He doesn't speak and doesn't move a single muscle.

I clear my throat. "Where's Mom?"

"She's in bed, asleep. Where have you been?" His eyes move past me to the window. He's still clean shaven, his searing blue eyes glistening in the moonlight. A cloud of suspicion rolls through them, turning them a shade darker.

"Um..." I hold my breath and swallow. His face and body are barely covered in the shadow caused by the light in the hallway.

"It's fine," he cuts me off. He grips the box, his fingers tightening around the hard edges. "I know you were with him. You don't need to lie."

I swallow again, and this time the growing lump in my throat swells. I clasp my hands in front of me, wringing my fingers until I feel my knuckles rolling with the movements. "Dad, I don't think you understand how much I love Asher."

"That boy has been trouble for you ever since he stepped into our lives."

"How? What did he do to make you hate him this much?"

His jaw ticks as he inhales a deep breath, and his body turns rigid. "His mother has been nothing but a stain on this town, and Asher only enables her. He's sure to follow in her footsteps. The last people you need to be involved with are Asher and his mother."

"Dad." I sigh, exhausted from having to defend Asher to my father. I would never stop defending him despite my father's reluctance to listen to me. "I'm telling you Asher is nothing like his mother."

"You have no idea what kind of person his mother is, the messes she creates."

I knit my eyebrows, confused. What does he mean by the messes she creates? Maybe he's referring to her addiction to alcohol, but the way his anger is raging like a pot of boiling water, threatening to spill over, I know there's more to his statement.

"Asher is trash, Charleigh." He looks up from the box, his eyes focused sharply on me. "I raised you better than this. You won't go anywhere in life being with a boy like that. He will hold you back, dragging you down to the trailer park with him."

I bite back the tears welling behind my eyes. "He's not trash. It's not his fault his mother is the way she is. Asher's incredibly smart and ambitious. I really think if you got to know him you would see that."

I'm begging my father to understand, but I can't help feeling as if my entire life is about to get sucked out of me.

I keep my mouth shut about Asher moving away from his mother to be with me at NYU. My father is wrong. Asher isn't dragging me to the trailer park. We're barreling straight toward the richest city in the country—both of us, together. I consider if sharing that bit of information will make a difference to my father. Probably not. At this point, I don't think it matters what

Asher does. He will always be the poor boy from the trailer park, tainting the Keeler name when, in reality, it's my father who is bringing shame to our family. The remaining shred of respect I had for him has completely dissolved. There is nothing left between us now.

"What is this?" He lifts the lid of the box, sifting through the small scraps of paper.

My chest twists in pain, watching as my father's fingers graze every single one of Asher's words. He moves through them slowly, then quickly, then slowly again. The sickness in my stomach is heavy. My father was digging around my bedroom, searching for any sign that I'm still with Asher. He grabs the flower from my mother's garden and twists the stem between his fingers. The petal dances in a circle, then bends over. Before, the flower was frozen in time. Now, it looks as if what life it had left has been sucked out by my father's touch.

He drops the bloom into the box and snaps his head up. "What are these, Charleigh?" He's yelling now, the veins popping in his swollen neck.

I take a step closer, releasing my hands. My palms sweat and my fingers shake. I'm worried about what he's going to do with the box.

He stands, noticing me drawing nearer. I stop, not wanting to get any closer to him than necessary.

"I picked the flower in Mom's garden." My voice wobbles, a tear already spilling over my lashes and onto my cheek.

"I don't give a fuck about any stupid flower." He grits his teeth. "I was asking about the shreds of paper."

"Those aren't shreds of paper, Dad. They're notes from Asher."

He stands from my bed, still holding the box. He looks down, hiding his face from me, but I know exactly the thoughts going on inside his head. His body is rigid, and if I were to use a color to describe him, it would be red. A deep, dark, frightening red.

I'm still holding my breath, unsure what he's going to do with the box. My chest twists with pain again, fearing he's going to toss them in the trash.

At one time, I adored my father. I looked up to him, thinking he was the most intelligent man in the world... but all of that turned to dust when I found out about my father's infidelity. Most days, it's hard to even look at him. He has become a man I no longer admire. He became the exact opposite of the person I want to become.

When he looks up from the box, his eyes cloud over like a storm hitting the shore. I know my father will never feel any different about me than he already does. To him, reputation is more important than family. It always will be. Even if his is turning to absolute shit.

Another tear spills down my cheek as my father quickly lifts the box and turns it over. Every piece of paper falls to the floor, scattering across the carpet. Some dart straight to the floor. Others drift in the air like feathers before softly landing on the carpet. He waves his arm in front of him, ensuring every last one is emptied out of the box.

I'm still crying when my father tosses the empty box onto my bed. The dried, damaged flower I picked from the garden is now buried beneath the hundreds of hearts from Asher.

My mouth falls open, and a shuddering sob rattles my chest, breaking it into pieces. I'm unable to look away from the mess my father has created.

"You'll stop seeing that worthless boy, or you will no longer be a part of this family, and you can say goodbye to your tuition."

I'm finally able to break my gaze away to stare my father in the eye. My vision is blurred by my tears as he slowly turns around and leaves my room. I fall to my knees, crawling across the carpet in a sobbing mess. I gasp for air, releasing it from my lungs, then breathe in again. Once I've reached the pile of hearts, I start shoveling them across the floor with my hands. They're shaky and unsteady, the reality of my father's words hitting me. If I don't leave Asher, I will be left with nothing. But if I choose to leave Asher, I will still be left with nothing.

There is no winning when it comes to my father. In some ways, I think he knows what choice he is giving me. I know he is carving me and molding me to become the person he expects me to be—a hollow human being with no heart. Just like him.

I manage to grab the box off my bed and scoop the hearts back into it. Tears splash onto a few of them, spreading the ink. Asher's handwriting that makes up each letter of his messages blends, causing some of the words to become small, black ink blots on lined paper.

I swipe my fingers across my cheeks, hoping to not ruin any more of them than I already have. I finally find the flower beneath the pieces of paper and drop it back into the box on top of the hearts, the same as it was before my dad dumped them all out.

After placing the lid back on the box, I climb under the sheets of my bed, hoping they'll bring me the comfort I need in this moment. Warmth blankets my skin, and I pull the box closer to my chest, wrapping my arms around it.

It's stupid really, to be clinging to a box. The edges press into my arms, the pain a reminder of what's inside it. Asher feels trapped in that trailer with his drunk mother; I feel trapped in this house with my disillusioned parents. Secrets and whispers are woven into every surface of this house, holding their breath, waiting for the perfect moment to finally scream.

Just as I did when I was walking home from saying good night to Asher, I think of my mother and how she's managed to stay married to my father for twenty years. Every plan has been of his design, my mother a silent partner to his demands. If my father wants me to follow in his footsteps, I know I will end up like my mother—empty and alone, a hollow version of the woman she was before she met him. I don't want to end up like my her, and I sure as hell don't want to end up like my father.

As the tears begin to dry, and sleep overtakes me, I realize he gave me an ultimatum: leave Asher and go to NYU, or decide to stay with him and risk losing everything I've worked for.

The decision isn't a difficult one to make. Within seconds, I close my eyes, and my world fades to black.

SEVENTEEN

I don't regret a goddamn thing.

Lying with Charleigh pulls me back to that night. The night we gave ourselves to one another. I cling to the good parts of it, shoving aside everything that happened the moment after I trailed her collarbone for the last time. The way I thought her dad had drained every ounce of my life from me only to go home and be proven wrong.

I drag the tip of my finger across that same collarbone, noting the small flower inked into her skin. The innocence Charleigh once had is gone. Evidence neither of us are the same people we were then.

My touch stirs her awake. Her eyes remain closed, but her soft-pink lips stretch into a delicate smile.

"Mm." She hums and squirms beneath the sheets, rubbing her feet across the bed. The moonlight pours across her frame, highlighting every inch of her naked body.

I drag my finger across her collarbone once more before pulling the sheet down the rest of her body. Her nipples harden like pebbles when I trace my finger around them. The honey is completely washed away by the shower we took together a few hours ago. We were a sticky mess, but every bit of honey was worth it.

"Asher." She moans my name on a near whisper, and my dick immediately hardens, but I want to watch her. Seeing her earlier, covered in honey, with my mouth on her, did incredible things to me. I've never seen anything so fucking beautiful.

I'm craving to see it again. See her again.

I slip my hand between her thighs. "Already so wet for me." I push my fingers between her folds. They move easily until I find her clit. She arches her back, and tilts her head back, pressing into her pillow.

"I was dreaming of you," she says, rolling her head to the side.

I lean forward and press my lips to hers. "Oh, yeah?" My dick twitches at the thought of her getting this turned on by dreaming about me.

"Yes." She breathes heavily, her chest sinking on her exhale. "We were in my flower shop."

"Is that a fantasy of yours?" I'm unable to hold back my smile. "Having sex in your flower shop?"

"I didn't think it was until the dream," she whispers. I can tell she's getting close to her orgasm. Her legs constantly move as if she's restless.

"But it is now?" I circle my fingers again, pinching her clit between my fingers.

A small yelp squeezes from her mouth. "Yes."

"Huh." I tilt my head and grin. "Something to keep in mind for the future."

Charleigh's breaths become quicker and deeper with each shift of my fingers. The word 'future' lingers in the heated air between us.

We don't speak about the fact I used that word, because for us, we don't know what that even means. The last time

Charleigh and I talked about our future together, our lives were shattered and torn apart. Lives were lost.

Love comes with a price. The same could be said for the future.

Charleigh's body tenses beneath me, and seeing her come undone is my own undoing. Being here with her is a welcome distraction from the thoughts invading my mind. I stifle her scream with a kiss, pouring everything I have into her, feeling her body shudder beneath me.

Once she's finished, I pull my mouth away from hers.

"I want you inside me, Asher," she begs.

"What do you want me to do?" I ask her, heart pounding. I reach down and start rubbing myself. My cock is already hard as stone, but I need some relief while I figure out Charleigh's fantasy. "What did I do in your dream to make you wake up already willing and ready for me?"

"You had me bent over my prep table." She tries to kiss me again, but I pull back, and her face falls in disappointment.

"Not until you tell me what you want me to do." I stroke myself even faster. "What's on your prep table?"

"It's where we arrange the bouquets. Scraps of flowers and stems are usually scattered all over it. It's a mess."

"Mm," I moan. "What did I do after I bent you over your prep table?"

Her gaze hardens, zeroing in on me. "You slid your cock into me and fucked me. Hard."

I smirk. That was all I needed to fucking hear. Heat pools in my lower belly, and fire spreads down the length of my legs. The need to be inside Charleigh takes over. I'm quick to my knees.

She doesn't have the chance to react before I flip her over, move behind her, and grab her hips, pulling her ass up to face me. She presses her face into the bed and keeps her hands beside her head, bracing herself. Her ass falls back, and my hardened cock presses into her crack. She's so impatient.

I sit back on my heels and slowly run my palm over one of her round ass cheeks.

"So fucking beautiful, Little Flower." I drag my finger down the length of her ass crack before finding her wetness again. She's dripping between her supple flesh. I gather her wetness and start stroking myself to the sight of her in front of me.

Pushing up on her hands, she flips her hair and watches me over her shoulder. Her eyes bounce between my face and my hand stroking myself. Her doe eyes widen, and I can see the desire on her face.

"Trust me," I grunt, not wanting to waste any more time. "I won't finish without you." I release my hand from around my cock and center myself in front of Charleigh. I smooth my hand over her lower back before giving her ass a smack.

She yelps and arches her back before relaxing. She's facing the headboard of her bed, catching her breath.

"I've wanted to do that ever since I carried you down twelve flights of stairs with your beautiful ass practically in my face."

I can't see Charleigh's face, but I hear the delight in her voice when she says, "Well, if that's what I get as my punishment, then maybe I'll have to do it again." She likes it when I talk dirty to her.

I don't say another word before I grip Charleigh's full hips and drive my cock into her. Her whole body falls forward before she catches herself on the headboard. Her palm makes a loud smack, and her nails dig into the painted wood. I don't waste any more time before pulling out of her just enough to drive myself back inside her again. Her walls clench around me, and I feel like I'm fucking high.

Heat explodes across my skin, and there are so many things I still want to do with Charleigh. I move in and out of her but watching the way the early morning sun glistens against her chestnut hair. Listening to the little moans coming from her mouth are my undoing.

I want to savor this, and I don't want it to end, but I can't help it. She feels too fucking good. With every push, she slams herself back, meeting me thrust for thrust. Her round ass pounds into me, and white-hot adrenaline pumps through my veins with my orgasm.

Charleigh slams herself into me harder as she comes at the same time I'm spilling myself inside her. She drops her head to her pillow, but I'm quick to pull her back up. I need to kiss her. I need more even though I should be done. I slip out of her and fall beside her, then I wrap my hand around her neck and pull her to me, pressing her lips to mine. She's still working to catch her breath, and I squeeze my eyes shut, forcing myself to memorize this feeling.

Charleigh cups the side of my face and smiles against my mouth before pulling away, her forehead pressed to mine as she giggles.

"What is it?" I move my hand to tuck the stray strands of hair covering her face behind her ear.

"Nothing." She sweeps her tongue across her pink lips.

"Doesn't look or sound like it's nothing." I run my hand along her collarbone like I did earlier. "What is it?"

She closes her eyes and sighs before snapping them back open again. I notice her cheeks blooming with heat. "I never knew you were a dirty talker, Mr. Egan. You never were before." Her eyes sparkle with both exhilaration and embarrassment.

I laugh. "We only had sex one other time, Charleigh, and you were my first. How would you have known I was a dirty talker before?"

Her face transforms, and it isn't until she moves her eyes away from mine do I realize what I've said has pulled us both back down to earth. I didn't explicitly say I've slept with other women, but I've definitely insinuated it. It's not as if Charleigh should be surprised I've slept with other women in our ten years apart, though, and she isn't. But talking about our past always seems to drag up old feelings—ones we've become experts at ignoring.

"Hey, I'm not the only guilty one here." I try to pull her away from the rabbit hole I'm certain she's falling down. "You're not so innocent, I'm learning."

She giggles, and it's the most beautiful sound in the world. I hadn't realized how much I've missed her laugh. Lying with her in bed like this reminds me so much of our innocence. When life seemed simpler, but I know it wasn't.

I bring Charleigh in for another kiss, when a buzzing sounds comes from her nightstand, followed by another one, then another. Charleigh groans against me before reluctantly pulling away. She reaches for her phone and reads her text message.

Her mouth falls open on a gasp, and she shoots straight up. I sit up, worry settling in my gut.

"Fuck," Charleigh mumbles. She brings her thumb to her mouth, nervously chewing on her nail. "No, no, no, no. This can't be happening."

"What's wrong?"

She keeps her eyes on her phone, quickly typing out a response to whoever messaged her. "Selene's at the shop and said our entire refrigeration system went out overnight and the backup energy supply didn't kick in. Every single flower arrangement for a sweet sixteenth I have scheduled for pick up tomorrow is on the verge of being destroyed. It was over two hundred arrangements, Asher." Charleigh's sweet eyes fill with tears. Her chin wobbles. "Fuck, what am I going to do? I can't afford another refrigerator, and if I don't get them back in a controlled environment, we'll lose them all."

I pull her attention away from her phone, hooking two fingers under her chin. "We'll get it figured out. I'll help."

She nods as she tries to contain her panic. A tear slips from her eyes, and like a hammer to the chest, I see Charleigh's passion for her business. Flowers are her life, and I know she isn't just worried about disappointing her client. She's sad because the flowers she sacrificed never fulfilled their purpose. They died for nothing.

"I don't know how you'll be able to help, but thank you," she whispers, pulling me in for a kiss.

I kiss her back, wracking my brain with how to help. Ideas are floating through my mind when my phone rings from the pocket of my suit pants draped at the foot of the bed. I fish it out and read the name on the screen.

I look up at Charleigh. "My dad."

"It's okay." She looks down before swinging her gaze back up to mine. I have a million thoughts and questions. There's so much wedged between us. Charleigh's flower shop. Her issue of firing me. Us sleeping together. Now my dad.

It's all too much for the moment, and I can feel Charleigh sensing the weight of what it all means the same way I do.

"It's okay. Take it." She inhales a shaky breath, wiping a tear from her cheek. "I need to get to the shop before Selene has a mental breakdown."

I want to kiss or even touch her again just to tell myself this is still real, but when Charleigh's hand slips away from my cheek, I don't get the chance. She's already walking toward her closet.

Remembering my phone still ringing, I quickly answer it. "Hey, Dad."

"Asher," he says. His voice is weak, and I can tell he isn't having a good day. "You never called me back. Did Janette give you my message?"

"She did." I push my hand through my hair, glancing over my shoulder at Charleigh. The door to the closet is left wide open. She's now wearing a mini skirt and a black lace bra. "I'm sorry I didn't get back to you. Yesterday was a crazy, busy day. I was going to call you later, actually."

I can't take my eyes off Charleigh as she slips her feet into knee high boots, followed by tugging on a thin tank top. I only ever mentioned Charleigh to my father once after my mom passed and I went to live with him. After telling him I had a girlfriend I thought was better off without me, he never asked questions. Maybe it was because our relationship was new and he didn't want to push me on the details. Or maybe it was because he understood and knew I just needed time to process. For a moment, I think about telling him I'm with her now, but I decide not to change the topic of conversation to me. He's more important at the moment.

Once Charleigh is fully dressed and moves to the bathroom, I finally climb out of her bed and get dressed myself. I'd really like a shower, especially with Charleigh, but I know there's no time. She needs to leave now.

"How has the city been treating you?" My father's meek voice hits my ear again.

"It's turning out to be not so bad." I smile, watching Charleigh run a brush through her hair.

This. This is the life I envisioned with her all those years ago. I lost the dream throughout the years, and I'm not certain I have it now, but this glimpse into what it could be is pretty fucking incredible.

"Do you still plan on moving back to L.A anytime soon, or did you reconsider staying in New York after our last conversation?" He coughs into the phone, pausing a few seconds to catch his breath. A heavy wheeze follows before he speaks again. "I'm hoping the city swept you away like it did me."

I laugh, remembering my father's story about the time he lived here before he met my mother. The city meant a lot to him back then. So much that he never had the heart to sell the apartment he purchased, even after he moved out to California. It also happens to be the one I moved into at the beginning of the year.

"I don't know, Dad." I sigh, wedging the phone between my cheek and shoulder as I button my shirt. "I feel like I need to be there with you."

"No," he says, sputtering out another cough. I step into my pants and tuck in my shirt while he rides out the rest of his coughing fit. His crackling breaths meet my ear before he continues. "I told you I wanted you to branch out. I don't need you holding yourself back for me. You already have all the best doctors and nurses money can buy to take care of me. All I want is for my son to follow his dreams."

"What have the doctors been telling you?"

Silence follows my question, swallowing it whole. My father's heavy breaths drown out the sound of the shower. "They said I should be able to go home in a few days."

I straighten my back, the news of his release hitting me. "That's great. So, that means the treatment is working, then?"

He sighs. "No, son. Not exactly."

"What do you mean?" I stop buckling my belt and, with a shaky hand, I hold the phone to my ear.

"We can talk about it later, Asher. Okay?"

"You don't want me to come back when you're released?" I ask him, panic in my voice. "I feel like I should be there when you come home."

"No," he says quickly. "I know you're busy with clients and meetings. Your work is important. I just don't want you to become a stranger. I know you're an adult, but check in every once in a while, yeah?"

I smile, but there's no joy behind it. A dull ache swells in my chest and, shit, I hate it. "I will. I promise. Are you sure you're going to be all right?" A feeling of dread and uneasiness works its way into my stomach.

"We'll talk later, okay, Ash? I'll be fine."

"Okay. If you need anything, give me a call," I say, finishing up the tie around my neck. "I promise I'll be better about getting back to you."

"Sounds good." He sputters out another cough before he says goodbye, ending our phone call.

I'm digesting my father's words when Charleigh meets me where I'm standing in her bedroom near the foot of her bed. She gives me a worried smile.

"Everything okay?" Her eyes move to my phone slipped into my pocket.

I wince, unsure of how to answer her because I don't know what to make of that phone call. What did my father mean? I have half a mind to drop everything and call the airport to prepare my private jet for a flight out to L.A. But then I remember how my dad insisted I didn't.

"I'm not sure." I rake my hand through my hair, stress taking me over.

"We don't have to talk about it if you don't want." She traces her finger down the length of my face. "I should get going." She stands on her toes and gives me a quick kiss. She's half turning to leave when I grab her wrist, pulling her back to me.

"I just—" I stop, swallowing the dry air coating the roof of my mouth. Her body is pressed against mine. "I just wanted to make sure you stand firm on your decision."

Her eyebrows knit together. "You mean, did I change my mind about firing you?"

Again, a weight presses into my body. I know what thoughts are running through Charleigh's mind, but I can't help it. I attempt to give her a reassuring smile, ignoring the ridiculous pit in my stomach. "Yeah."

She gives me a teasing smile in return—one that wants me to drag her back to the bed and call out sick for the rest of the day, but I have meetings, and Charleigh needs to tend to her emergency.

She twists my tie around her hand, pulling me down to meet her. A heavy groan rumbles up my throat when my hands slide across her lower back. Her eyes sparkle in the early morning sun when she brushes her mouth above mine, not completely giving in to kissing me. "Consider me officially reconsidering."

EIGHTEEN

CHARLEIGH

I've never felt so overwhelmed in my life, and I'm not just talking about how my ten-thousand-dollar refrigerator decided to crap out on me in the middle of the night, ruining an incredibly expensive client's order. I'm talking about Asher.

Every feeling I've ever had for him has been set on fire. My body is still humming from his touch, and when I take the subway to work, I can still feel his mouth between my legs. I sit cross legged the entire way, hoping no one could sense the heat still coming off my body.

The subway is nearly at my stop when I get a text from Julianna in our group chat.

> Julianna: Bringing coffees and maybe a bit of vodka to sneak in them. I have a feeling we might need it.

> Selene: You are a saint.

> Me: You don't have to do that, Jules. I know you're busy with your own work.

Julianna: I know I don't, but I am. When my
best friends are in trouble, I'm there. And
please… I'm my own boss, so I work whenever
I feel like it. Count me in!

Selene: I love you both.

Me: Love you both, too. Hopping off the
subway now. Be there in a few!

Once the doors slide open, I push my way through the morning crowd and run up the stairs and down the two blocks to my shop. When I push through the front door, Selene is already meeting me. Her hair flies behind her, and her arms wrap around me.

"Charleigh…" She sighs, resting her chin on my shoulder. "Thank God you're here."

"Come on," I tell her. "I'll take a look at the condition of the flowers. Hopefully time is on our side. At least enough to find somewhere to keep them all."

When I reach the back room, I look through the glass doors and carefully study each arrangement and bouquet. Luckily, they don't look terrible. I have some time, but not long.

Selene nervously bites down on her thumbnail. "I haven't opened the doors because I was afraid of losing any cool air that might still be in there."

I reassure her, placing my hand on her arm. "You did the right thing."

"Okay." She huffs, planting her hands on her hips. "What do we do, then?"

"Let's start cleaning all this up, and I'll see what I can come up with."

My phone pings in my hand. Despite the internal panic, I'm

relieved to see Asher's name, so I swipe my screen and read his text.

Asher: Is this similar to the refrigerators in your shop?

Below his text is a screenshot of a Google search for flower refrigerators. The one in my shop is the first picture in the results.

Charleigh: Yeah. Why?

Asher: Give me ten.

I close my phone out, not bothering to respond or try to figure out what Asher means. I need to get these flowers organized so I can figure out what to do.

Julianna bursts through the door, tossing her cardigan on the front counter on her way to the back, a tray of coffees perched in one hand and a bottle of Vodka in the other. "I'm here with caffeine and alcohol, bitches. Let's get this shit figured out."

God, I love her.

Ten minutes must pass by, with the three of us frantically cleaning up loose flowers and vases, when my phone rings from the prep table with Asher's name flashing on the screen.

I ignore Selene and Julianna's puzzled expressions and answer.

"Hey," I breathe out. I nervously toy with a flower stem on the prep table.

"Hey." Asher pauses. "How's everything going?"

I flick my gaze up to my best friends. They haven't taken their eyes off me as they stuff flowers into vases as if they're moving in slow motion. I wave my arm at them and shake my head.

"Fine, I guess," I tell Asher on a sigh, not completely

convinced. "The flowers aren't wilted yet, but there isn't much time. I'm still trying to figure out what to do with all of them... and every other flower that couldn't fit."

"Do you know the Trinity Hotel?" Asher asks.

"Um, Trinity Hotel? I think so. The hotel is here on the Upper West side, right? On this street or the street over?"

"It's on your block, actually," he explains casually. "A few buildings down."

"Oh, it is?" I swing around just as Selene leaves the back room and makes her way to the front. Either she can hear Asher through the phone, or she already knows where he's headed with this conversation. She pushes through the door and stands on the sidewalk. I watch her as she points to her right, then looks at me. She shrugs before coming back inside.

"I know the owner of the hotel. I sold him that building a few months ago," he explains. "There's a ballroom with a complete state of the art kitchen in the back. He was about to book the ballroom for some beauty event, but the company hadn't finalized their offer on the rental fee yet. So, I put one in to outbid them. You can use their refrigerators if you need."

"What?" I place my hand to my chest, unsure whether I'm hearing him right or not.

"Yeah," he says, a few clicks coming through the phone. "You told me the refrigerator I sent you in the text was the same ones you have at your store, and I remembered seeing them at the Trinity Hotel when I showed it to my client."

"Asher." I want to cry. "You didn't have to do that. It must have cost you a fortune."

"Doesn't matter," he dismisses quickly. "If it helps you out until we find you a better shop with working coolers, then it was all worth it. When you go over there just mention my name to the front desk. They'll be expecting you."

I press my hand to my forehead. "Asher..." I croak. "I can't even begin to tell you how much this means to me."

The frayed edges surrounding the place in my heart for Asher slowly start to mend. I don't know what this means for us. For years, I held so much anger toward him for the way he left. And when he came back into my life the anger was all too real. But now, I'm realizing that while the anger was still alive, so was the love I had for him.

"You mean a lot to me, Charleigh." He reassures all my thoughts with that single sentence.

Then... silence. There's silence between us, and I know if he were here, I wouldn't be able to keep myself from kissing him.

"Listen." He exhales heavily. "I have a board meeting here in a little while, and another meeting with a client after, but once I'm all finished up I'll come down to shop to help move the flowers over or anything else you might need."

I drop my shoulders. "Thank you, Asher."

"You're welcome, Little Flower."

When I hang up, I place my phone on the table and get back to work, until I notice Julianna and Selene aren't moving. I look up to find four gorgeous, wide eyes staring at me.

"Don't." I point a stiff finger at them before wagging it around the room. "We're not talking about this right now. We have work to do."

But when I look down and shove another flower in the vase, I can't help but smile.

AN HOUR LATER, the girls and I have finished arranging the last bouquet and gathered a few of them to take over to the Trinity Hotel for our first run. A few minutes after ending my call with

Asher, I walked the three buildings down the hotel and told the front desk clerk who I was. She showed me all the refrigerators in the kitchen before taking me to the staff entrance at the back, which would make it easier to use. The refrigerators were more than enough for the sweet sixteen order and all the flowers I hadn't been able to fit, regardless. I decided to close the shop for the day, considering I knew this would probably eat up most of my day.

I've just completed my second run over to the hotel when my phone rings in my pocket. I'm hoping it's Asher, but my chest deflates when I see Cyrus Temper's name instead.

"Hello?" I answer.

"Hi, Charleigh Keeler? This is Amanda at Cyrus Temper's office. I'm connecting you with Mr. Temper now."

I pull the phone away from my ear, confused with her introduction. "Oh, um, okay."

Barely a second passes before I hear Cyrus on the other end. "Ms. Keeler," he practically sings. "How are you?"

The tone in his voice is odd. In the times I've spoken with him, Cyrus is a fairly stiff man. In a way, he reminds me of my father. He is always in business mode, but today, he has a bit of personality. "I'm doing okay. Better now than earlier, actually. How are you?"

"You never emailed me back with your thoughts on the listings I sent you. Unfortunately, a few of them are off the market now."

I blink rapidly. Apparently, we're skipping the artificial pleasantries.

"I'm sorry I never got back to you." I press my hand to my forehead. "I've been incredibly busy."

He huffs, then clicks his tongue. "Well, that's precisely why we were looking for a bigger shop for you, isn't it?"

"Well, yes." I swallow. "But I—"

"It looks like I have a few other listings I can send your way," he interrupts. "The market is tightening, so we'll want to jump on these as soon as possible."

I open my mouth to tell Cyrus I'm reconsidering working with Asher. In our first meeting, I briefly told him I was working with another agent, and when he pressed me on who, I caved and told him it was Asher. He hasn't brought him up since, but I didn't miss the way his jaw clenched at the mention of his name.

My confession sits at the edge of my tongue until Julianna bursts through the door with the biggest fucking grin I've ever seen on her.

She whizzes past me, scoops up two more bouquets, looks directly at me, and winks. "Asher Egan must love more than just you riding his trouser snake for him to book this hotel for you. Wow."

Panic climbs up my neck, and my jaw drops. My hand flies to cover the bottom of my phone, but I know I'm already too late. There's no way Cyrus didn't hear Julianna's big mouth just now.

"*Oh, my God,*" I mouth to her.

She shrugs and silently giggles. "Oops."

I gape at her while she leaves me standing in the middle of my shop, dumbfounded. I hadn't even told her about me sleeping with Asher. I refused to tell Julianna and Selene earlier, sticking to what I meant when I said we had work to do. They dropped the subject, but they must have gathered something happened between us for Asher to go to these lengths to help me out. At least Julianna has figured it out. Selene's been hard at work, carrying armfuls of flowers over to the hotel, barely taking the time to look up from her feet, talking only long enough to tell us she was able to convince her sister London to come to Julianna's birthday party.

My cheeks are flaming, and the obvious silence on the other

end becomes loud. "Mr. Temper? Are you still there? I'm so sorry."

"I'll email over those listings now, Ms. Keeler," he clips. "Let me know when you find one that interests you. Have a great day."

My mouth falls open again when Cyrus abruptly ends our call.

I stand frozen in my shop until the heat leaves my face and chest. I want to be angry with my best friend for embarrassing me, but she may have done me a favor. There's no way I can work with Cyrus now. Not when I'll be wondering if he's thinking about me with Asher.

Despite my desire to hopefully never see Cyrus Temper again to save us both the embarrassment, I hope Julianna is right. I hope this means Asher does care for me in ways that mean more than just sleeping with him, because if not, I'm not sure my heart will survive getting burned again.

This time, mine will be going up in flames.

NINETEEN

ASHER

February 11, 2015

I'm waiting for Charleigh in front of the school. There are a few cars already parked in the lot, but it's still too early for most of my classmates to be here.

Charleigh messaged me to meet her out front earlier than usual, telling me it was important. Of course, I didn't hesitate.

I haven't seen her or spoken to her since last night in the street, when my mom spent her night out drinking at the dive bar down from our trailer park. Luckily, she made it home safely, but she fell asleep with a cigarette in her mouth and a beer bottle dangling from her poorly manicured fingers. I woke up this morning to clean up her trash before heading out for school.

Nerves swirl inside me. I can't wait to see Charleigh. She is the one constant in my life, reminding me there is more out there than stale cigarettes and empty beer bottles.

When her car pulls into her usual spot, I immediately cross the lot and sit in the passenger seat. Her long hair shields her face from me. My eyes move down, taking in the box of paper hearts sitting in her lap, along with an envelope sitting on top, the familiar blue NYU letters stamped in the corner.

"Oh, shit, you finally got it." My mouth quickly pulls into a grin. "Congratulations. I knew you'd get in, Little Flower. I fucking knew it." I can't contain my excitement. I'm fucking bursting at the seams.

I reach forward and wrap both my hands around her head, turning her to face me. I plant a giant kiss on her pink lips and pull her back. There are tears in her eyes, but they aren't ones of joy and celebration. They're tears of fear and sadness. All the happiness I felt at seeing her acceptance letter is sucked out of me and the car. The air turns cold, and a deep dread fills my gut.

"Wait..." I pull my eyebrows together. "You didn't get in?"

She sniffs and shakes her head. "No, I did. My mother handed me the letter this morning." Her eyebrows dip, and her bottom lip trembles. She won't look at me.

"Then, what is it?" I ask, uncertainty still lingering. Does she not want us to go together anymore? Terrible thoughts begin to edge into my mind. I run my hand down her cheek, trying to console her and beg her to tell me. "What's wrong?"

Charleigh sniffs and her chin quivers. Tears spill down her cheeks. "My dad found it."

"What, the letter?"

She answers with a shake of her head and places her hand over the box of my paper hearts. Then it hits me.

I reach out and place my hand over hers. One of Charleigh's tears drops onto the back of my hand. She looks up at me, her eyes transforming into two glass orbs, tears lining her black lashes.

"I need you to take it." Her voice wavers.

I know Charleigh is protective of the messages I've written for her, but I can't understand why it's made her this upset. She looks broken, as if a piece of herself has been fractured.

Her father must have done more than find the box.

"Charleigh." I tuck a loose strand of hair behind her ear. "Are you sure you want me to take them?"

"Yes." Her words are more forceful this time, her hand stiffening beneath mine. "I can't leave them there. He'd found the box when I went back to my room last night. He was waiting for me and threw all the hearts all over the floor. He was angry, Asher. He's angry that I'm still with you, in love with you." She inhales a shaky breath, sliding her hand across the top of the box. "He..."

"He, what?" I adjust myself in my seat, leaning closer to her. I wish we weren't sitting in her car right now. I wish I were closer to her.

"He—" She breathes in, tipping her head back against the headrest. Her long, brown waves press against the fabric behind her as she rolls her head to the side. There's a battle being waged inside her heart. "He told me he won't pay for me to go to NYU anymore unless I break up with you."

"Oh, Charleigh." I cup the side of her face, threading my fingers through those long, dark waves. Tears spill down her cheeks. I can see the consequences of her father's words weighing on her. She's exhausted, and I can tell she hasn't been sleeping well. Dark circles line her tearful eyes. She was crying even before I got into her car.

"I'm not going to leave you, Asher." She rushes her words, hardening her gaze.

"Charleigh, no." I shake my head, soothing my thumb across her cheek. "You can't give up on NYU."

"He's only doing this to hurt me. He doesn't care about me. He only cares about himself. Why should I sacrifice my happiness for him? I can find another way to pay for school."

"I know it's hard for you to deal with your dad, but I also know how hard it is when you don't know how you will pay for things: school, food, shelter. Your dad may be an asshole, but he's also giving you the best chance at being successful by paying for college."

I hate that I'm defending Trevor Keeler, but despite my hatred for him, I can't let Charleigh give up her chance to go to NYU because of me.

"I can apply for scholarships," she suggests. "Grants, financial aid—I don't know. I'll figure something out."

"Scholarships, maybe. Grants, possibly," I tell her. "Your parents can still claim you on their taxes, so you probably won't qualify for financial aid, but it doesn't matter. That's going down a road of uncertainty—unnecessary uncertainty."

More tears spill from her eyes, and my chest twists at seeing her so upset. She wasn't expecting me to give her all the reasons why she should agree to her father's ultimatum.

It tears me apart thinking about a life without Charleigh, but she deserves more than this life she's been living. She deserves to live out her dream... even if it's one without me.

"You want us to break up?" Her eyebrows dip, tears welling along her eyelashes.

I pull her toward me, pressing my forehead against hers. "I want you to live the best life possible, even if that means it's a life without me."

She pulls back. "That's not the life I want."

I look out the front windshield, watching our fellow classmates pour into the building. "We can't always get what we want, Charleigh." I'm trying not to get frustrated with her, but I can't help feeling hopeless. I always knew Charleigh's relationship with me was a risk—a risk bound to break one if not both of us.

I'd fight like hell to keep her, but even I know there is a limit. Is this it?

I turn back to face her. This time I don't bring my hand to

her cheek. She reaches across the center console, pressing her palm flat against my chest.

"I'm not leaving you, Asher. I just need some time to figure this out. Maybe my father will change his mind."

She doesn't even believe her own words. I highly doubt her father will suddenly change his mind about me.

The pain in her eyes is unbearable, though, so I lean forward, pulling her against me. She takes it one step further, climbing over the center console and sitting on my lap. She straddles me, her knees resting against the sides of my thighs.

I wrap both of my hands around her face. They're slick and wet from her tears, mingling with the warmth in her cheeks. I search her eyes, hoping I'll gather the strength to do the right thing, but my love for Charleigh is too strong, and I'm weak.

"I'll keep the box."

"Thank you." Charleigh sighs against me. Her body relaxes as if she's releasing the large breath she was holding. "I love you."

"I love you, too."

I tuck her hair behind her ear, then press my mouth against hers. Her lips are a mixture of salty and sweet—sweet from her lip gloss, salty from her tears. She pulls away from me and runs her hand through my hair, pushing it off my forehead.

I grin, allowing her love for me to smooth over all the doubt. I wipe her tears away from her cheeks. "Let's go in. We have that big math test today, and I can't be distracted."

She giggles, and it's the most beautiful sound.

"Okay."

"We'll be okay," I reassure her, not completely sure myself.

"We will," she agrees.

Charleigh and I head into the building together, with me carrying her box of paper hearts.

TWENTY

ASHER

I don't breathe a sigh of relief until the last stroke of Allen's pen meets the contract sitting between us. It's been a long road of convincing him to stick with me as his realtor, but we've finally sealed the deal. After clearing up the swirl of rumors floating around the city about me, Allen agreed to stay on as my client. In the end, he told me his decision was based on his previous experience working with me, and while the offer Cyrus presented to him was enticing, it wasn't enough for him to ditch me.

Allen stands from the end of the conference table and shakes my hand, promising to get in touch when he's in the market for another apartment building. I wait until he and a few of other employees gather up the scattered paperwork before heading back to my office. I can't wait to get to Charleigh's shop to help her get the rest of the flowers over to the hotel. It's been nearly six hours since we last spoke and it's driving me crazy.

I haven't been able to stop thinking about her, working when all I can think about is the spark in her eyes when she looks at me. We haven't talked about what yesterday means for us, but for the first time in years, I feel hope.

I didn't realize how empty I'd become until Charleigh came back into my life. She filled me with her sarcasm and defiance. She pushed me to open myself back up to the possibility of feeling again. And now I've had a taste, I can't stop. I don't want to stop.

Once I'm in my office, I'm double checking my inbox when Janette's voice comes through on my intercom.

"Mr. Egan? Cyrus Temper is here to see you."

I stare at my phone, wide-eyed. Why the fuck would Cyrus Temper want to speak to me?

"I'm about to leave, Janette. Have him schedule a meeting with me for another time."

"I tried, sir. He says it won't take long and it's important."

Reluctantly, I groan and check the time on my phone before answering Janette. "Send him in."

Before Cyrus steps into my office, I stand from my chair and close out my computer. I don't plan on staying long. This isn't the first time I've had a meeting with Cyrus face to face. I met him last year at a fundraising gala in Los Angeles. He wasn't there for long, claiming he had a slew of clients to return to in New York. Everyone rolled their eyes at his comment, especially me. The sleaziest real estate brokers are usually the ones who stroke their own egos. Cyrus Temper is no exception.

Janette knocks on the door before opening it, allowing Cyrus to follow her into my office. She closes the door, giving us privacy.

Cyrus is one of those men who makes his presence known when he's walking into a room. What he lacks in integrity and personality, he makes up for in appearance. His suit is perfectly tailored like mine, but he's always worn an ostentatious color underneath it—baby pink or pale yellow, sometimes with a dark blue tie wrapped around his neck. His brown loafers are very outdated but probably cost more than the bright gold watch resting on his wrist.

He holds his hand out to me. "Asher. Good to see you again." He flashes me a grin, his stark white teeth nearly blinding me.

"You, too, Cyrus." I nod, putting on a saccharine smile. "I don't have long. I was on my way out the door, actually."

"Oh, your gorgeous secretary out there made me aware." There's a sinister spark in his eye that leaves me unsettled. "I wanted to congratulate you."

"On?" I pinch my eyebrows, tilting my head in confusion.

He laughs as if I should know exactly what he's talking about. His belly bounces, and I cringe on the inside. "Your firm landed in *Fortune*'s top 100 fastest-growing companies, correct? Number two, if I'm not mistaken."

"Oh." I nod once, sitting on the edge of my desk. I cross my feet at the ankles, tucking my hands into my pockets. "Yes, it did. Thank you."

"How old are you again?" He moves around my office, pretending to study the pictures I have on the walls.

"I'll be turning thirty at the end of the year."

Cyrus clicks his tongue as he paces my office. "Wow. *Fortune* 100 before you hit thirty. Quite an accomplishment."

I shrug, not sure what he's getting at with this conversation or even why he's here. "Well, becoming a real estate broker has always been a dream of mine. I worked hard to build this business and basically haven't stopped chasing this dream since I was a kid."

"Not without a bit of help from your father, no doubt." He stops, holding his hand out. The pleasantry in his voice is now gone replaced with bitterness with a hint of disdain.

I remain silent, unsure of where this conversation is headed.

"He helped some," I finally offer. "My love for real estate

began long before I lived with him, but he certainly taught me a few things. He worked out of a firm down on Wall Street before deciding to move out to California. I didn't realize you two had met."

"Years ago, when he was a big name here in the city. It's been a while since we've talked or seen one another." He grins, the corners of his thin lips curling. "Give him my regards."

I clear my throat. "I will."

I watch as he walks over to the small bar built into the far wall of my office. He fills a glass with some of the water from the pitcher, dropping a lemon wedge into it before he holds his glass up to me, turning the corners of his mouth down and wrinkling his forehead, then points to the bar.

He's silently asking me if I'd like a glass of my own water. *Fucking asshole.*

"No, thanks." I shake my head and move toward the door, holding my arm out for him to follow. "I apologize, but I was just on my way out, remember?"

"One more thing," he croaks. He takes a sip of water then walks over to where I am, standing in front of me. He's at least an entire head shorter than me, and he smells like cigarettes. I want to vomit. The scent makes me feel as if I've suddenly grown seasick. My stomach wobbles, remembering the way my mother used to smoke over a pack a day, the scent embedded in the only three shirts I owned at the time.

"I thought you were here to offer your congratulations," I quip, my nerves unsettling. This fucker needs to get out of my office. Now.

He smacks his lips and runs his hand over his mouth. Two beady eyes stare up at me as the gold chain around his neck glints in the light of my office. "I came down here to deliver a warning."

I narrow my eyes, pinning him with daggers. "A warning?"

"I'm onto you, Mr. Egan."

"You're *on* to me?"

"Yes," he says, matter of fact. "Allen Simon is a good man, and I was disappointed to hear he'd back out of my deal before crawling back to you. But alas, in this business, I guess you win some and you lose some. It's the name of the game, and as you know, I like a good match every now and then."

I don't answer him, instead clenching my jaw so tightly I'm convinced my teeth will crack. Everything about Cyrus Temper makes me sick.

"But just when I thought our game with Allen Simon had played out, the opportunity with Charleigh's Florals appeared."

My stomach does another turn, causing tidal waves inside me. I clench my jaw, feeling every muscle in my body tense. I try not to allow Cyrus to see my reaction at his mention of Charleigh's flower shop, but it's too late. His eyebrows slant and his eyes narrow as if I've already confirmed his suspicions, whatever those suspicions may be.

"You know," he continues, amused with where he's taking this conversation. "It wasn't interesting or surprising to me when she mentioned you at our first meeting weeks ago. After all, Allen Simon had been deciding between the two of us. It didn't occur to me even when she told me she was a graduate of NYU or that she was originally from Connecticut. Then I decided to do a little digging."

I clench my hands inside my pockets, making fists. My nails dig into my palms. Hearing Cyrus talk about Charleigh is bringing out a side to me I rarely ever share. A side that would do practically anything for those I care about. Especially Charleigh.

"You're from Connecticut as well, aren't you?"

"How would you know that?" My blood boils.

"Oh, please." He sneers. "It's a matter of a simple internet search, Asher. Not that difficult. You can learn quite a bit about someone: where they're from, where they went to school, what their family is like. I know the history between you and Charleigh. And I know about your mother."

"What exactly do you want from me then, Cyrus? Yes, I knew Charleigh when we were younger. So what?" I bite my tongue, resisting the urge to drive my fist right into his smug grin.

"I don't want anything from you," he spits. His face turns a deep shade of red, and the veins in his head bulge. "I just want you to know that I'm on to you. Just like your father, you're a scammer and a cheat."

"You knew my father?"

"Christopher Egan was a lying, cheating prick. It was no surprise when he ran out of this city, dragging his tail between his legs. And just like him, you'll fuck anybody to close a deal."

I straighten my back and tighten my fists. I'm not entirely sure if he's making an accusation about me fucking my clients, or if he's talking about my father as well. I didn't even fucking know he knew my father. My nails cut into my palms even harder, but I don't give a shit. They can bleed for all I care. "What exactly are you accusing me of?"

"I think you know exactly what I'm accusing you of, you little shit. Like father like son." He snarls, sniffing before he wipes his hand across his big, red nose. "You and your reputation are on the line here, so I think it'd be wise to think twice before pulling out that tiny dick of yours. Just watch yourself, because I won't hesitate to expose all your secrets." He points a stocky finger at my chest. "All of them."

I'm not a fan of threats.

I step closer to Cyrus. He lifts his chin just to keep his eyes on mine. I look down on him, forcing myself to remain calm. I don't know exactly what he's insinuating. Does he know

Charleigh and I share a past? I don't know how much of mine and her personal life she's shared with him, but I doubt she has. Charleigh isn't the type of person to share the pieces of her personal life with strangers. I can't imagine a world where she's told Cyrus about our past. Still the thought of him threatening me in my own office pushes me to the edge.

"Get the fuck out of my office," I grind out.

With an evil smirk, he scoffs and lifts his glass of water to his mouth. With narrowed eyes, he swirls the water in his mouth before turning his head to the side and spitting. A gush of water sprays from his mouth and onto my desk. Spit and water droplets coat the surface of my mahogany desk. *What the actual fuck?*

I move an inch closer, clenching my fists at my sides.

He wipes the back of his hand across his dripping mouth. Slamming the glass down on my desk, he turns to me with a smile. "You'll want to clean that up before it ruins the wood. Would hate to see such an expensive piece of furniture go to waste." He pats my chest a few times.

Goddammit, I want to punch him in the fucking face. But I also know if I do, the asshole will call the police and press charges. I'd play into his hand perfectly. I'd give him the satisfaction.

He gives me one last smile that makes me reconsider. Consequences be damned.

"It was good to see you, Mr. Egan. We'll be in touch."

CHARLEIGH

After wrapping my mouth around the opening of the large, clear bottle, I tip my head back and down a large swig before passing it to Selene with a sour expression. The liquid burns my tongue, leaving a blazing trail down my throat before splashing warmly into my stomach.

"See?" Julianna beams, taking the bottle from Selene. "I knew we would need this." She tilts her head back, taking another swig, her long, chestnut hair catching the afternoon sun pouring through the windows to the front of my store. Selene and Julianna sit on one of the display tables, their long legs dangling over the edge, their feet hovering just above the floor.

I'm sitting cross legged on the checkout desk beside the single-wrapped flowers with paper heart tags, and the single serve bags of floral tea in brown bags with my store logo on the front.

Selene is still wincing from her shot when Julianna offers her the bottle of vodka for another swig. She silently shakes her head, shimmying her shoulders in disgust. Julianna then sticks her arm out toward me, but I shake my head, too. One shot is enough. I take a sip of my tea sitting beside me, hoping it will mask the taste of vodka coating my mouth.

Three hours of walking up and down the block carrying thousands of flowers is exhausting, but I feel so relieved knowing a sweet sixteen party won't be ruined. And I have Asher to thank for that. Still, the thought of needing a better, larger storefront weighs heavily on my mind.

"So..." Julianna leans back and gives me wink. Somehow, she still looks perfect despite us rushing around all day. "Are you going to tell us why your super-hot, billionaire ex went out of his way to save the day *after* you supposedly fired him yesterday?"

"Oh, my God." Selene groans, grinning widely. "I've been dying to hear all day." She looks at Julianna before looking at me. She grips the edge of the table and leans forward, eager to hear my juicy gossip.

I hold back my smile, biting on the inside of my cheek. "I *did* fire him."

"Ok*ay*." Julianna waves her hand. "And...?"

I roll my eyes, no longer able to hide my feelings. It's not that discussing relationships with my two best friends is embarrassing, but there's something about my love for Asher that I've always kept to myself. Part of it is probably due to the fact our relationship when we were younger was mostly kept secret. Especially from my parents. There's always been part of me that's been tied to the idea that speaking about it out loud will make it unreal.

I take another sip of my tea and play with one of the single-wrapped flowers. I rub my thumb over its velvety petal. "After I sent him that text, I'd resigned myself to never seeing him again. Sort of how I felt when he left before. But then he showed up at my door."

"Showed up?" Selene asks, intrigued.

I look up to them both. They've stopped moving their legs, hanging on my every word.

"Yeah." I blow out a heavy breath. "He was at my door, soaking wet. He was angry I'd fired him via text."

"Well..." Julianna scoffs. "He doesn't exactly have a right to be upset when he left you a note breaking up with you."

"I know." I nod, trying not to think about that. Julianna has a point, but I can't hold the note over Asher's head forever. We were kids, and that night wrecked us both. We won't be able to move forward if I can't let go of the past. "But he told me he hasn't stopped thinking about me since we ran into each other that first night. He said he'd never felt a pain like the one when he'd read my text. He felt hollow, as if I'd ripped his heart out. And that's saying a lot because he's been through more pain than anyone I've ever known."

Silence befalls both my best friends. Julianna's face no longer holds judgement.

"Wow." Selene sighs, her shoulders falling.

Julianna sits up and tilts her head. "You really love him, don't you?"

My chin quivers. "It's been ten years. I used to think love died with loss. I thought love died with pain."

"There's no expiration date on love, babe," Selene says softly.

I look at her as a tear slips from my eye, and I shake my head and sniff. I can't believe I'm crying, but honestly, I haven't felt this vulnerable in a long time.

"Selene's right," Julianna agrees, wrapping her arm around Selene. Selene rests her head on Julianna's shoulder and places her hand on her knee. They both look at me with reassuring smiles. "It's okay to love again," Julianna says. "I know I said men are scum, and for the most part they are."

Selene and I both giggle.

Julianna laughs but inhales a heavy breath. "But not all of them are dicks."

"Right," Selene agrees with a sharp nod.

"I thought we'd have love figured out by now," I confess. "Others we know around our age are married and with kids." The vodka seems to have been my own personal truth serum.

"Everyone goes at their own pace, I think," Selene says, gazing longingly through the front window of the shop. "I want to focus on my career and what I truly want from it before looking for someone to share my life with. Growing up the way I did makes you hesitant to rely on anyone other than yourself."

I don't press her on her meaning. I know Selene doesn't want to work for me forever. She's a writer, and words are her life, but the thought of coming to the shop every day and not seeing her bright blue eyes, blonde hair, and thousand-watt smile is depressing. I don't even want to venture down that road right now.

"As you should." Julianna places her hand over Selene's.

"Agreed." I smile, finishing off the rest of my tea before it gets cold.

"It sounds like you have it figured out, though, Charleigh," Julianna says, eyeing me across the gap between our respective seats. "I think?"

A shiver makes its way down my neck at the memory of Asher tracing my collarbone this morning. "Maybe. I hope."

Julianna quirks a brow as the corner of her mouth curls. "Now, the real question is, was I right earlier?"

"Right about what?"

"About you riding his dick."

"Oh, my God." I groan, tossing the single flower I've been holding back into the bucket with the others. I roll my eyes but square them back on my best friends. My heart races and my cheeks heat. "But the answer is yes."

"I knew it, you slut." Julianna points at me, and the three of us erupt into laughter.

The sun hasn't quite set all the way. The orange glow pours into my shop, highlighting my flowers in the best possible light. It warms my soul. I check my phone. Still no message from Asher.

"Oh, shit." Selene pops up from Julianna's shoulder and quickly checks her phone before bouncing off the table.

"What is it?" I ask, surprised at her sudden change of mood.

"I forgot I promised my grandmother I'd visit her before visiting hours were over at the hospital." She turns to me, her shoulders dropping. "I'm so sorry. Do you need anything else here?"

"No." I wave her off, hoping off the checkout desk. I point to the backroom where there are remnants of dissected flowers everywhere. "Of course, you go right ahead. I'll clean the rest of this up."

"I'll go with you, Selene," Julianna says, grabbing her cardigan from where she tossed it earlier. "I have an appointment with a caterer at my place in an hour, anyway. He's bringing over a shit ton of samples for my party."

I give each of my best friend's a hug and thank them immensely for their help today. Once they're gone, I send an email over to my client, letting him know all the flowers for his daughter's sweet sixteen were saved. I breathe a sigh of relief, thankful to salvage my reputation in this city. I hardly ever dare look at the reviews on *Google,* but it's a necessary evil. The last thing I'd want is someone saying I allowed all their flowers to die, ruining their event.

Because as much as humans don't realize, in moments of celebrations and mourning, the little things mean the most.

I linger in the back room, ready to start my massive clean-up operation, when two arms wrap around my waist. I fall back against a hard wall of muscle and immediately feel him tower over me. His mouth hits my ear and, fuck, my stomach is doing that fluttering thing again.

"Don't clean up just yet, Little Flower."

"Asher." His name falls from my mouth, soft and hushed. All I've wanted to do is tell him how grateful I am for what he did with the hotel, but he stops me.

"I know." His mouth touches the hollow of my ear, and his voice vibrates down the length of my body.

I'm already wet for him again.

I turn around in his arms, pressing my hands to his hard chest. Tilting my chin up, I stare into his eyes. "No. I need to tell you. Thank you doesn't begin to cover how grateful I am for what you did today. You truly saved me from losing this client."

He tucks my hair behind my ear. "Seriously, Charleigh. I'm just sorry I wasn't here sooner to help you. I got stuck in a few meetings, but I tried." Sadness flickers in his expression, though it's gone before I'm even certain I've seen it.

I laugh and tilt my head back. "Will you just accept my offer of gratitude?"

His face falls, and he studies mine as if he can't believe I'm standing in front of him.

I think back to my conversation with Selene and Julianna.

Love doesn't have an expiration date.

Is what I'm feeling for Asher still love, or is it something new? It feels a lot like the love I had for him back then, but there's an undercurrent of grief and pain in there, too. There are layers to what we once had now. It's complicated in a new way that's both exhilarating and terrifying.

"Charleigh." He sighs, then inhales a nervous breath. "What I did today doesn't even make up for the pain and heartache I've caused you, and I'm not just talking about ten years ago."

"Asher." I rise up on my toes and wrap both hands around his, holding them between us.

"I was an asshole and I'm not afraid to admit it." He hooks two fingers under my chin.

"You know..." I smile. "I never thought I'd hear you admit to being an asshole out loud."

"Well." He slinks his arms around me and down my backside. Slipping his hands under the back of my short leather skirt, he grips onto both of my cheeks and lifts me back onto the prep table. "I'm a changed man, remember?"

After opening my legs, he stands between them. I slip his suit jacket off his broad shoulders and wrap his tie around my hand like I did this morning to pull his face down to mine. "Why don't you remind me again?"

Asher crashes his mouth against mine and rolls his hips forward. His erection is clear, straining against the zipper of his black slacks. He presses his length to my wetness. I know I'm soaking and ruining what is probably thousands of dollars' worth of designer pants, but Asher doesn't seem to care. He parts my lips with his tongue, sliding it against mine. He tastes me and sucks on my bottom lip as if he can't get enough. I whimper against him, my heart expanding with every kiss and touch.

I move to undo his belt and tug his zipper down. His cock springs free, and I immediately wrap my hands around it and rub my thumb over the tip.

Hissing, Asher tilts his head back and closes his eyes. "Fuck, that feels good," he says between clenched teeth.

I tug him closer, rubbing the end of his cock along my wet pussy. "Do you feel that? Do you feel how wet I get for you at even the slightest touch?" My thighs are shaking, and my pulse quickens.

"Yes." He hisses, rolling his head back and looking down at

me. He traces his finger down my face before letting it fall to my sweater. I lift my arms as he removes it, then reaches behind and unsnaps my bra. The cool air hits my skin, and my nipples harden. I'm left in nothing except my knee-high boots, with my leather skirt bunched around my waist. "How about we make your fantasy a reality?" He looks at the mess of flowers and stems surrounding me. "This is the prep table you were talking about, correct?"

"It is." I'm forcing myself to even out my breathing. I lift my left hip and start to roll to the side, bending my leg. I hold my knee against Asher's sculpted abs, twisted at the waist. Leaning back on the table, I prop myself up with my arm and with my other hand, run my palm against my exposed bare ass. I didn't wear any panties today, and I can tell Asher's pleased. "But you had a different view of me."

His eyes darken, and his hand smooths over my ass.

"No." He growls. "I want to watch you as my cock fills you. I want to watch you come." He brings his other hand to my mouth and pushes his thumb to my bottom lip, prying my mouth open. "I want to watch your pretty mouth gasping for air when you orgasm."

A yelp climbs up my throat, and I jump when he smacks my ass. A jolt of electricity shoots down my leg before his hand moves to my knee, parting my legs for him, once again. I lie flat on my back and press both of my knees to his frame.

My gaze rises to his face, and I see the change in him. He's looking at me differently. He's looking at me as if I'm his lifeline. He's looking at me as though if I weren't here, he wouldn't be breathing.

The gold flecks in his eyes intensify, and my mouth falls open as soon as he slips himself inside me. He fills me up, pushing in as far as he can. His body meets mine, and I arch my back off the table, not caring how many flowers are beneath me.

We're surrounded by them, and the scent fills every one of my senses. I breathe it in as I gasp for air. The table rocks and shifts with every thrust, but I welcome it.

It's true, I had a dream about being with Asher in my flower shop, and now I wonder how many dreams we can make a reality. The future is terrifying when it's let you down in the past.

Asher grips onto my breast, flicking my nipple with his fingers. He keeps his eyes on me as he moves above me – inside me. There's nothing but the sounds of our heavy breathing, the creaking wooden of the table, and the setting sun pouring through the tiny window.

We don't speak. There's no dirty talk, despite earlier, or Asher wanting to fulfill my dream. We've transitioned into something else. He's fierce and commanding, but there's also vulnerability in his movements. He's quick yet measured. Hard yet soft. He grips my shoulder, holding me in place. Heat pools in my belly, and my thighs shake, nearing my release. I chase it, not wanting to drag it out. I want to feel every bit of what I'm feeling with Asher. I want to jump off the cliff without hesitation. And I do. My body quakes as my body hums with my orgasm. My mouth falls open as I gasp for air, my eyes pinned on Asher.

And he's watching me, just as he said he wanted to. Four more thrusts, and he's falling apart too, and I feel myself tighten around his cock. He stiffens, holding onto me as he vibrates with his orgasm. His cum spills into me, and I inhale a breath at the sensation.

He falls to my chest, pressing his face to my flesh, turning until his ear presses against my beating heart. I bring my hand to the back of his head, threading my fingers through his brown strands. I hold my breath, and I can't explain it, but tears build behind my eyes. Not from being with Asher now. Not from being heartbroken. Tears threaten to spill realizing we aren't who we were before. Our feelings for each other may have stemmed from who we were then, but the flower has bloomed into something else.

Then the reality hits when he lifts his hand and traces his invisible line across my collarbone. I hold my breath until my lungs burn.

Because despite how beautiful this feels with Asher now, the ugliness of the past will always remain.

TWENTY-TWO

ASHER

February 12, 2015

Three dollars and thirty-six cents.

I finish counting the change the clerk handed me after buying my mother a pack of cigarettes and stuff the money into my pocket. I haven't been to Charleigh's since she handed me her box of paper hearts and told me about her father's ultimatum. I stuffed the box into my closet, hoping it's safer there than at Charleigh's.

But I can't stop staring at her most recent text, begging me to come over tonight after her parents go to sleep. Part of me is afraid of the risks, but the other part of me wants to see her. By the time I make it to my street and my trailer comes into view, I decide the benefits far outweigh the risks. They always do when it comes to Charleigh.

I slowly open the metal screen door, unsure whether my mom is still awake or if she's passed out somewhere in our trailer.

I walk through the living room carefully. After turning down the hallway, I peek through the bathroom door. My mother isn't in there, either. There's no sign of her anywhere.

Perhaps she left while I was out. At least that's what I think until I make it to my bedroom door, which is swung wide open. A deep, intense smell of cigarette smoke hits me.

My mother is standing in the middle of my room, a cigarette hanging from her dry lips. Smoke circles in front of her face. Her hair is tangled and teased. It looks like she hasn't brushed it in days.

"Mom." I instinctively search my room, wondering why she is in here. She's never in my room. Most of her days are spent either on the couch or sitting at our small kitchen table. The only rational reasoning I can think of is that she was looking for money. "What are you doing in my room?"

"What the fuck is this?" Her words come out muffled as her lips try to work around her cigarette. Ash falls to the carpet, dissolving into the gray fabric. A wrinkled, white paper envelope is crumpled in the firm grip of her clenched fingers.

It's my NYU acceptance letter.

I pinch the bridge of my nose and try to remain calm, hoping to say the right thing not to send her over the edge. "Mom, it's not what you think."

When I look at my mother, her eyes are spread wide open. Black makeup is smudged around her bloodshot eyes.

"What the fuck is this?" she screams, repeating her same question. My breath catches in my throat, and I lean back when she charges toward me, slamming her fists against my chest. Her breath reeks of alcohol.

I scrunch my nose and press my lips together. The stench is enough to make me want to vomit. I'm shocked she's reacting this way. My mother may be an alcoholic, but she's never laid a hand on me.

"Mom," I grunt, her fists pounding against my chest. She's pushing me backward down the hall. The floor is littered with empty beer bottles, clothes, and trash. I try not to trip as she forces me out of my room. I grip her wrists when she continues to push me until we're in the middle of the kitchen. "What are you doing?"

"You ungrateful son of a bitch." She's screaming in my face. Her cigarette has fallen out her mouth, and now she's spitting all over my face. Beer-scented saliva flies from her mouth as she continues to yell. I'm finally able to push her off me, and she stumbles backward, clearly drunk.

It takes her a second before she's able to correct her footing. She grips the edge of the kitchen table, her body swaying as she straightens her back. My acceptance letter is still clenched in the palm of her other hand. The tips of her fingers are white with how much pressure she's applying.

"Was this your plan all along? To leave me?" She stands up, rolling her head back. Her chin is tipped up, her top lip curling in anger. She charges toward me again, grabbing a half-empty bottle of vodka from the kitchen counter. She wraps her free hand around the neck of the bottle, using all her strength to throw it in my direction. The bottle flies from her hand, rocketing straight at me. I quickly duck, the bottle narrowly missing me before it crashes behind me and shatters against the old wooden cabinets, causing the liquor to splash to the floor. A puddle of clear liquid pools around us, with shards of glass scattered across the linoleum.

"What the fuck, Mom? Are you crazy?" Blood rushes from my body as I stand, looking at a version of my mother I've never seen before. I knew she had issues, but I've never seen her like this. "You don't understand. I'm doing this for us."

Maybe we're past the point of reason, but I don't want to give up trying to reach the better part of her if it is still inside her, buried beneath all the hurt and pain she's feeling.

She laughs hysterically, grabbing another open bottle of liquor from the counter. This time, she doesn't throw it at me.

She lifts it to her mouth, taking a giant gulp. She keeps her eyes pinned on me, a flurry of anger building inside her. The mouth of the bottle suctions to her lips, making a loud pop before she drops it at her feet. The glass doesn't break, but the liquid pours out of the bottle slowly, flowing like a river. The entire kitchen floor is covered, and the heavy scent of alcohol fills our trailer.

She wipes her mouth with the back of her hand. "Right. For us." The corner of her mouth draws up into a slant, and she continues to laugh sarcastically. "That's what your father said. And Trevor."

"Trevor?" I jerk my head back, shocked. My jaw drops.

"Trevor fucking Keeler." She sneers.

"You mean Charleigh's dad?"

She laughs again, revealing more of her yellow-stained teeth. "They're all the fucking same. It's always the ones who have all the money. They treat you like trash, ready to toss you out like a whore whenever it suits them. They treat you like you're nothing." She steps closer to me, her feet tripping along the way, and points a lazy finger, leaning slightly forward. "*Nothing.*"

I place both of my hands against my head, tugging on the ends of my hair as I digest my mother's confession. The need to vomit rises in my throat.

Did my mom have an affair with Trevor Keeler?

"What does this have to do with Trevor?" I stare at my mom, scared of her answer. I'm not sure I can handle her admitting to me she's had an affair with Charleigh's dad.

"Trevor Keeler is nothing but a liar. Your father lied to me, too. When I told him I was pregnant with you, he said he wasn't cut out to be a father. Said it wasn't what he wanted for himself." Her red eyes line with tears as her chin quivers over her clenched teeth. "He took everything from me. The apartment down by Wall Street, the money—everything he promised me, he took."

My eyes follow my mother's theatrical hands. She's waving them around as if she's reliving the time she was with him. Each movement she makes is dramatic, and what she's saying isn't making sense. I have no idea the kind of man my father is. She's never given me the chance to know him, and as far as I knew, he didn't desire to know me. This is the most she's ever spoken of him.

"My dad worked and lived on Wall Street?" I ask. My throat burns at the thought of my mother keeping this a secret from me. How could I have a father who worked on Wall Street, yet my mother and I live in a trailer that is nearly falling apart?

"Doesn't matter, anyway," she seethes. "You're leaving me, and you'll end up just like him—cold and heartless, with nothing to show for it but a fucking packed wallet. You'll be alone, Asher." She lifts the letter, holding it between us. "I mean, shit, you've already started."

"Mom, I told you, I'm doing this for us. I can give us a better life." The burning sensation in my throat grows, working its way into the pit of my stomach.

Tears stream down her face. Trails of black makeup are drawn along her skin. "You aren't doing this for me. You're doing this because of that fucking Keeler girl. I warned you about her, Asher. She's going to ruin you. This is proof enough." She lifts the letter again. All I want to do is rip it from her grasp, but I'm afraid of what she might do if she catches me trying to take it from her.

"Mom," I beg. "You aren't listening to me. If I go, I can create my own business. I can take us out of here."

"You know what I should do with this?" She holds the paper up, shaking it in my face. "I should fucking burn it. That's what dreams are, anyway, Asher: nothing but piles of ash."

"You're losing it, Mom." I swallow, unsure of her next move. Does she really intend to burn the letter to prove a point? "You need help."

"I want you to get out," she says, closing her hands into fists. The paper crumples in her fingers. "Leave."

"We can just—"

"Get the fuck out, Asher!" she screams, squeezing her eyes shut. Three lines crease the corners of her eyes as a tear slips from under her lashes. Her small frame shakes with anger. Her eyes are narrowed, fuming with hatred for me.

I've always known my mother is troubled, deep down. There are issues lying under the surface of her alcoholism, driving her to keep going back to bottle after bottle.

"Fine," I tell her. I've already had enough. I need to leave this trailer before my head explodes, and I hope by the time I come back, she'll be passed out on the couch again. Maybe by tomorrow she will have forgotten finding the letter and arguing with me.

"That's right!" she yells after me. "You keep going back to her. You'll burn for this, Asher."

I keep my pace steady, ready to leave my mother behind. There is only so much I can take from her. I don't need to stay and beg her for reason. There is no reason left inside her. Hasn't been for a long time.

I walk until I reach Charleigh's house. I stay focused on my feet hitting the pavement. Every step is a step farther away from my mother and another closer to Charleigh. I don't bother checking Charleigh's house as I usually do before climbing the trellis. I don't even warn her that I'm coming up. But she meets me as soon as I make it to the top and tap on her glass.

"Asher," she whispers, pulling me tightly against her.

I wrap my hands around her face, pulling her to me. "I love

you," I muse against her mouth, immediately feeling relieved. It's like I've taken a big breath, and Charleigh's my oxygen.

"I love you, too," she whispers back.

"We're still going to NYU, right? Me and you?"

Her eyes dance between mine, concern etched into every line of her gorgeous face. "Of course. Me and you. Promise."

"Okay, Little Flower." I nod, relief settling in my bones. I pull her in for a kiss and walk us toward her bed.

Charleigh takes the hint and grips onto my coat as she walks backward. When her legs hit the edge of the bed, she unzips and slips it down my arms. My hands are quick to her face again. I pull her in, pressing my lips to hers as if it's a matter of life and death.

She sits on the bed and crawls back on her elbows until her head meets her pillow. I crawl to her on my hands and knees, slipping one between her legs. I rest both hands beside her head and look down at her.

"I want you," she says to me, looking me in the eye.

"Are you sure?" The moonlight streams across her face, and I want to bottle up this moment and stay here forever.

"Yes." She grins before it fades. She lifts her hand and traces my bottom lip. "I don't think I've been more certain of anything in my entire life."

"Even more than your love for flowers?" I muse, leaning down until my mouth is hovering above hers.

She tilts her chin to meet me. "Infinitely more."

A jolt of electricity shoots to my heart. Knowing she loves me more than her flowers speaks volumes, and I know I love her too. I grind my erection against her thigh, unable to hold myself back.

Charleigh giggles before having me move aside for us both to climb under the sheets. I've never been with anyone else, and neither has Charleigh. We don't know what we're doing, but there's something beautiful in knowing we're each other's first and equally inexperienced. I feel better knowing she won't judge me for not knowing exactly what to do.

I pull out the condom I've kept in my wallet for the past few weeks and hold it between us. Charleigh's doe eyes stare at it before swinging to mine.

"I don't really know what I'm doing," she confesses.

"It's okay," I tell her, giving her a kiss. "We can go slow."

She nods and bites down on her bottom lip. Nervously, we both get undressed under the covers without talking. Once we're both naked, I slip on the condom and climb over Charleigh.

"Are you ready?" I ask her on a shaky breath.

She nervously inhales and keeps her hands to her chest. I lean down to kiss her, hoping to wipe away any nerves.

"I'm ready," she assures me when I pull away.

"Okay." I center myself in front of her. "Tell me if it hurts too much, and I'll stop."

"You could never hurt me, Asher," she says and fuck, I fall in love with her even more.

When I push myself inside Charleigh, I've never felt anything like it. I keep my focus on her, and for a few moments, she squeezes her eyes shut. But the more I move, the more she starts to relax, and it isn't long before I can tell she's enjoying it as much as I am.

After a few more movements, her body tenses around me, and I quickly cover her mouth with my hand to muffle her moans.

When the heat reaches my belly and I reach my orgasm, I stare into Charleigh's eyes. They soften with an emotion I've never seen on her before. It's as if she's never felt anything like this in her life. Neither have I.

How is it possible to fall even further in love with someone?

When we're both finished, I remove my hand and quickly replace it with my mouth.

"Are you okay?" I'm nervous. Why am I nervous? "I didn't hurt you, did I?"

"No." She sweeps her tongue across her lips and shakes her head. "Not at all. In the beginning, it hurt a little, but it didn't last long. I liked it." She bites down on her lip again. "Was it good for you?"

I giggle. "Is that even a real question? Of course, it was."

I give Charleigh one more kiss before I crawl off her and sneak into her bathroom to wrap the condom up with toilet paper before tossing it into the bin. I get dressed, then crawl back under the sheets of Charleigh's bed. She's still lying in just her bra.

We lie together in silence, and I trace her collarbone, my finger ghosting her skin, hypnotized by this feeling. A giggle erupts from her, but it abruptly stops when the light in her room turns on. The sound of the switch flicking causes my stomach to flip. I barely have a chance to look over my shoulder before I'm ripped from Charleigh's bed.

Large hands grip my shoulders, and a sharp pain shoots down the length of my spine when I'm knocked to the floor. I've barely opened my eyes to see what the fuck is happening when I see Trevor Keeler hovering above me. One fist is clutching onto my hole-ridden shirt while the other fist is reared back. A sickening face fueled by rage stares at me, wide-eyed, filled with a fury I've never seen before.

"No, Dad!" Charleigh shouts. "Stop it!"

When his fist connects with my face, my ears fill with a piercing ring. Bones crunch, and I can't figure out which part of my face he's broken. My nose? My jaw? Radiating pain echoes everywhere. I don't have the energy to fight back, too caught up in trying to understand what is happening. Blood must be spilling down my nose because my upper lip is warm and wet, and a metallic taste fills my mouth.

I turn my head on Charleigh's carpet and crack open my eyes long enough to see Charleigh kneeled at the edge of her bed. She's clutching onto the sheets, screaming and begging her dad to stop. Tears stream down her face, and all I can think about is how I want to wipe them away.

"Please, Dad!" she cries. "Get off him!"

I roll my head back to face Trevor above me. "You fucking piece of trash. How dare you touch my daughter."

The sounds of Charleigh's shrill scream and Trevor's rage mix into his fist driving into my face again. Another round of pain radiates across my body, and when I don't fight back, I'm surprised to realize Trevor suddenly stops.

"Trevor!" I turn my head to my right, seeing Charleigh's mom standing in the doorway. She runs toward him, throwing him off me.

He falls back, his breathing savage and ragged. His rage and anger toward me hasn't faded. I roll to my side, covering my face with my hand to try and figure out where the bleeding is coming from. I feel lightheaded and sick, but I manage to sit up. I consider speaking up, fighting back, but I know anything I say will only make the situation worse. I don't care that Trevor has beaten me; my concern lies with Charleigh. After I leave, I don't know what will happen to her, and I don't want to add more fuel to the fire. As much as it fucking pains me and I know I'm going to regret it, I don't fight back.

"Get the fuck out of my house," Trevor barks. The veins in his neck pop, and his muscles tense. He isn't paying attention to his daughter or his wife. He stands and stalks over to me, and I wince when he grabs another fistful of my now-bloodstained shirt, ready for another blow. Instead, he points an angry finger in my direction.

"You'll never see my daughter again. Do you understand, you worthless piece of shit? If I ever see you or hear from you again, I'll call the police and tell them you raped her."

"Dad," Charleigh sobs. She's still on the edge of the bed, her shoulders racking uncontrollably. "I love him. Don't do this."

He ignores her, and my heart breaks. Fear creeps in, and I know there's no turning this around. Charleigh's future is lost with me in it.

"Get out *now!*" he screams in my face. Spit lands on my bloodied face, but I don't say a word when I pull myself to a stand. Charleigh's mom is kneeling on the floor behind Trevor, her hands covering her mouth. Charleigh's leaning forward, and I can see it in her body, the way she wants to leap forward and follow me. But I just look at her with a blank stare, silently begging her not to.

"No, Asher," she whispers, tears streaming down her beautiful face, pleading. "Please."

Holding my hand to my jaw, I silently turn around and walk out of Charleigh's room. It's the first time I've ever left her bedroom through the door, and it takes me a moment to find the stairs. My heart shatters with every step, and I don't breathe until I can no longer hear Charleigh's cries coming from her bedroom.

I hold my hand against my face the whole walk home, wondering how many bones are left broken. But the closer I get to my trailer park, the deeper a chill sets in my bones. At first, I think I'm losing it. Maybe it's the blood loss. Maybe it's my broken heart. But a bright orange and red glow comes from the top of the fifth trailer into the park, and I know it isn't either of those things. Clouds of dark gray smoke pour out, flames flickering toward the front.

I immediately sprint home, running as fast as my injured body will allow. My feet slide and kick along the dirt when I reach my driveway. I don't regain my footing until I land on the first of three steps leading to the door.

"Mom!" I scream.

Blood drains from my body, prickles making their way down my spine. I'm standing in front of the door, trying to turn the lock, but it doesn't budge. Heat surrounds me when it shouldn't. It's fucking winter.

"Mom!" I shout again, pounding on the door.

She doesn't answer. The flames have grown. The door is warm, not quite hot to the touch. I step back, then use every ounce of strength I have, slamming against it with my shoulder. It flies open, and I stumble forward.

Smoke slams in to my face, clouding my vision. My eyes sting, and a sharp pain hits the same shoulder I used to open the door. I struggle to get back to my feet, the pain reverberating down the top of my arm. I look down to see some of the fire has caught on the sleeve of my shirt. The acrid scent of burnt fabric and singed skin fills my nostrils. I slap my hand against my arm, trying to put it out. Luckily, the flames are relatively small. It doesn't get past my shoulder.

I hold my hand against my arm, pinning it as close to my side as possible. It feels like pins and needles shooting up my arm with any attempt to move it.

"Mom!" I roar.

Smoke shoots to the back of my throat. I start coughing, covering my face with the back of my arm. It's nearly impossible to see through the smoke, but I continue making my way back toward the kitchen.

My mother isn't on the couch. The only other place she could be is in the kitchen. A brief sense of relief washes over me when my feet finally land on the linoleum floor. I'm headed in the right direction. There are flames lining parts of the floor, snaking their way up the curtains. It quickly eats away at the fabric, drawing closer to the ceiling. I rub my eyes, clearing the smoke a little. When I open them, I finally find my mother passed out. She's lying in the middle of the floor. There's blood pouring out from the side of her forehead, mixing with the pool of liquor around her. It shines, reflecting the flames surrounding her. Her eyes are closed and she's lying on her side, her arms relaxed beside her. The flames are inching closer to her feet, the flickering edges dancing closer to her toes.

I frantically search for a way to break through the fire. The flames are circling her, creating a barrier between us.

"Mom! Wake up!" I cough again; the back of my throat engulfed in searing pain. I squint, trying to find a clear path that will lead to her. There's none. "Mom!" I lunge forward, hoping to grab her. There's a large group of flames blocking me from getting to her, but I don't care. I need to grab her and pull her out.

"Get him out of here."

Firm arms wrap around my waist, stopping me from getting to my mother.

"Stop it!" I yell, fighting against him. "I need to help her."

He pulls me, ignoring my plea. "Don't worry. We've got her." His heavy, deep voice rumbles against my back, and he ushers me out, passing me off to the next firefighter. "Get him out of here. Make sure he gets checked by a medic," he tells the other man.

After he hands me off, the man wraps his arm around my waist. The doorway is cleared more than when I entered my trailer. He helps me walk down the stairs and takes me straight to one of the ambulances. They ease me onto a stretcher, laying me back. I'm struggling to sit up, wondering if they've pulled my mom out yet. The paramedic pushes against me, holding me back.

"Stay still. We need to examine you," the paramedic says, but I don't care about me.

"Is my mom...?" I ask, choking on the words, forcing them out. I'm going to vomit all over this fucking stretcher.

"Their pulling her out now," the paramedic says, examining the injuries to my face and head. They aren't even from the fire. His eyes meet mine. "I'm sorry, but we don't think she made it."

With heavy-lidded eyes, I stare up at the raging flames quickly covering every surface of my trailer. My arm burns, and my skin stings, the pain spreading into my chest. My head pounds, and I know it isn't from the fire. It's from when Trevor's fist connected with my face. It feels as if I'm getting stabbed by a million pins and needles. The pain expands across my skin, but I ignore it. I'm more worried about my mother, hoping to hell the paramedic is wrong.

I think about our last conversation. She blamed Charleigh for the reason I was leaving her. My mother was trapped, helpless, and unconscious in our burning trailer. I didn't believe her when she said it, but my mother threatened to burn my acceptance letter. I wonder if she followed through on her threat and that was the cause of the fire. Guilt consumes me.

If it's true—true that my mother spiraled after I left—I'm not sure how I'll be able to handle it.

Being with Charleigh has come with repercussions. We've been fighting an uphill battle, defending our relationship to anyone who stands against it—my mother, her father—but at what cost?

I roll my head to the side, looking at my trailer engulfed in flames. A tall, billowing cloud of smoke continues to rise from the top of the frail roof and windows. The only life I've ever known is burning to the ground and I will forever spend the rest of it knowing it was my fault.

The death of my love for Charleigh... and now my mother.

ASHER

I helped Charleigh clean up the prep table and organize her new inventory from the back that didn't require refrigeration. As I carried handfuls of black tins, she filled me in on how she's experimenting with selling products other than flowers, working on tying them into the full floral aesthetic she has going on in the store. Along with the white ship lapped walls and buckets of floral arrangements in every corner, I think it fits from a business perspective. After stacking the tins of candles on a small table near the front of the store, Charleigh locks up the shop, and I offer to take her back to my place for dinner.

I'm nervous when I shouldn't be, but that's how Charleigh's always made me feel. She's incredibly out of my league. Always has been. My stomach grumbles, and I silently pray she agrees.

Her stomach growls, too, and she laughs, hiding her embarrassment by covering her face with her hands. "Oh, my God." She groans into her hands before lowering them. "I didn't realize I haven't taken a minute to eat all day. I'm surprised the one shot of vodka I had with the girls earlier didn't knock me on my ass considering my tolerance for alcohol is basically non-existent. Especially when it comes to an empty stomach."

I lift my eyebrows. "So, that's a yes, then?"

"Absolutely." She beams, and I feel like I'm a fucking teenager again passing a note over Charleigh's shoulder.

On the drive over, I call my personal chef and ask him if he doesn't mind whipping up something for us to eat before he heads out for the day. After ending the call, I slide closer to Charleigh in the back seat and don't take my hands off her until I'm forced to when my driver pulls up in front of my building.

Charleigh dips her head down, eyeing the building from inside the car, looking past me. She leans forward and presses her hands to my thighs, trying to get a better view of the skyscraper in front of us. I can't keep my eyes off her. She steals my breath, and her mouth falls open.

"What is it?" I ask.

"In the ten years I've lived in New York, I've never ventured to this part of the city."

"Really?"

She turns to look at me. "Well, yeah, this is the more glamorous side, where the richest investors and mega brokers of Wall Street live. At least that's what I've heard. A far cry from the likes of an almost-thirty-something flower shop owner."

I give Charleigh a nervous smile, hoping she isn't judging me for my lifestyle now. In a way, it's as if we've swapped places. Not that Charleigh is as broke as my mother and I were growing up. Charleigh's apartment is incredible, located in a great part of the city, where every building is made of one hundred-year-old brick, and there are wrought iron railings adorning the front steps.

My driver opens my door, and I step out, holding my hand out from Charleigh's. She takes it and doesn't let go. With our fingers entwined, she follows me inside the building, pushing through the bronze revolving door.

The front lobby is massive, with marble floors stretching all the way to the back. Walking beside me, Charleigh gazes at the lobby, wide-eyed.

I give Chuck, the doorman, a quick wave in greeting, and lead us to the elevator.

When the doors slide open, I pull Charleigh inside and press the button to my apartment at the top floor. I'm quick to push her against the wall. I can't help it.

"Asher," she whispers when my nose meets her neck. She bends it, allowing me more access. I breathe in, burying my face deeper into her neck. My lips meet the hollow of her ear, and my body is pulsing, the sensation making my cock spring to life.

"I've always loved the way you smell," I hum against her skin. "Like you've been digging in the garden all day."

"Have I always smelled like this?" She giggles, grabbing my hand and placing it between her hot, wanting thighs. She presses my fingers against her already swollen clit, and I want to pinch myself that this is really happening.

"Yes," I growl, thinking back to her apartment and her shop. Even to the little flowers she kept pressed between the pages of her history textbook. "Like a million fucking flowers."

"Hmm," she moans, pressing my fingers harder against her clit. I love how eager she is. "I'm glad my scent is so memorable."

I kiss her behind her ear, and she shivers beneath me. I've barely moved my fingers, but I can already tell she's about to come. With my fingers pressed to her clit, I wrap my other hand around her neck. Her body shudders underneath mine, and she grips my shoulder. She's gasping for air when she stiffens, coming all over my fingers. Fuck, I wish we had more time in this elevator. I don't even care if Frank the security guard is watching the security cameras and sees what we're doing. But I'm fucking starving, and I want to spend more time with Charleigh. I want to enjoy this before she somehow disappears and slips through my fingers.

I haven't told her about Cyrus coming to see me this afternoon, or the threat he made to expose me, whatever the fuck that meant. I'm still trying to wrap my head around it and, honestly, I'm convincing myself he isn't serious. Cyrus wouldn't risk playing with me when I've proven myself to be true competition in this city.

For now, I want to focus on the woman who has always turned my world upside down.

"Oh, Little Flower," I whisper against her hot skin. "What are you doing to me?"

"Nothing." She breathes out. "I'm simply doing what I've always done."

"No." I shake my head as I move my hand from the pulse in her neck to her chin. "You're doing something to me." I grip onto it and steal her breath with my mouth.

She moans, and her body melts into mine. She wraps her hands around the back of my head, keeping my mouth pressed to hers. My cock twitches, but I tell it to calm down, at least until I get some food in my stomach.

When the elevator dings and the doors open, I wrap my hand around Charleigh's again, leading her into my home.

"Come on." I drop her hand and remove my suit jacket, tossing it onto the sofa lining the front entrance. "I'm starving."

Charleigh stops and doesn't walk any farther inside, instead looking around my place with intrigue.

The floors are covered in a deep brown hardwood. Thick wooden beams stretch across the ceiling.

She gazes at my place, tentatively taking one step, then another. There's a large kitchen opening up to the living space. Set on the dining room table are two plates filled with steak, asparagus, and some kind of roasted potatoes. Two glasses of red wine are also set out. I look around, wondering if my private chef is still here, but the blue kitchen towel is folded on the counter next to the stove—a clear indication he's gone for the night.

The apartment is dark, with only the bit of light coming from the undercabinet lighting in the kitchen and a few lamps scattered around the main living area. I stand by the dining room table, studying our plates, expecting Charleigh to want to sit down and eat, but she doesn't. She's too wrapped up with the size and look of my place.

I cross my arms and watch her, unable to wipe the smile off my face.

When she spots the tall floor-to-ceiling glass windows lining the entire floor, she walks across the room until she's only inches from them.

I join her and stand beside her.

"Your place is..." She pauses, taking a breath as she presses her whole hand to her chest. "Your place is incredible. I've never seen the city from this view."

"It's my father's place, actually."

"Really?" She snaps her head in my direction.

"Yes." I nod, pressing my hand to the glass and gazing down at the city.

"Your father used to live here?" she asks. "He wasn't always in California?"

I'm assuming she's guessing based on the last note I ever left her, given that I never talked about my dad before I moved to live with him, and the time I carried her down the stairs after I'd shared a slice of my life back in California.

"No, he's a New Yorker, actually," I tell her, feeling myself open up to her in a way I never do with anyone else. "I didn't know this until I left to live with him, but he used to work in the city... as a real estate executive for one of the brokers on Wall Street."

"What?" She turns to face me and crosses her arms over her chest. "He was in real estate, too?"

"The night of the fire, my mother told me something." I scratch at the stubble lining my chin. I hate talking about my mother sometimes. A wave of guilt always follows the memories. Especially the ones where she'd look at me with empty, bloodshot eyes. "It didn't make sense at the time, but later, after I moved to California, my father told me the story of how they met."

Charleigh's delicate neck bobs as she swallows. This is the first time I feel myself opening up to her completely.

Fire spreads across my chest, and instinct tells me not to continue, but then I look into Charleigh's eyes and fall for her all over again. She's the only person on this earth who has ever truly seen me.

"Before I came to your house that night..." I stop, emotion swelling inside me. "The night your dad found us, before I snuck into your bedroom, I had an argument with my mother. She was nearly black out drunk or high on some kind of drug. I doubt she was clearheaded about anything she was saying, but she mentioned my father living here on Wall Street, in this apartment." I look around, taking it all in. Pieces of my dad still linger. Large pieces of art hang on every wall. Each surface is appointed with care and precision, just how his home is back in California.

"So, how did they meet?" Charleigh asks.

"I didn't know until I went to live with him, but he and my mother met when she worked at one of the restaurants down the street. Every day, he would go in for coffee, buying enough to supply each of his coworkers. At that time, he was an intern for one of the firms. After a couple weeks, he gathered the nerve to ask her out on a date, and it wasn't long before their relationship grew. He fell for her fast and found himself stuck between building his career and building a life with her. He wanted both, but the more time he spent climbing the corporate ladder, the more my mother grew paranoid. Eventually, her paranoia got the better of her, and no matter what my father did, she wouldn't change her mind." I rake my fingers through my hair, shoving it off my forehead.

I sit on the bench of the grand piano set in the middle of the room. "My mother told me my father lied to her; said he wanted nothing to do with her when she told him she was pregnant with me. But that wasn't true, Charleigh."

Her eyes well with tears as she slowly walks toward me. I part my legs, and she settles between my thighs, standing in front of me as she cradles my face with her small hands and pulls me up to gaze at her. I place both of my hands on the small of her back, slipping them under her sweater to feel her skin.

"What *was* the truth?" she asks softly.

"After I moved to California, my father never went out of his way to tell me the truth. In his eyes, he wanted to build our relationship organically and not dwell on the past. But after a while, I remembered what my mom had told me, and I was dying to know. One day, after one of our surfing sessions, he finally broke down and told me. My mother didn't tell my father she was pregnant with me until he had decided to leave the city after they split. He didn't find out about me until I was two years old. She wrote him a letter, explaining that she had a child and needed his support money. He showed me the letter. He stepped up, offering to help in any way he could. She only ever wanted the money, never intending on letting me see him. You know, my father said he tried to reach out to me every week. He'd call, but my mother always ignored him, or when she did answer, she'd tell him I didn't want to speak to him. He sent child support, but she never used it on me. That's how she was always able to afford to pay for her drugs and her drinking habit.

Unless she'd run out, then she would go snooping through my shit for money. He asked time and time again for me to fly out to visit him for the summer, but my mother never allowed it."

"He never took her to court over it?" Her eyebrows pull together.

"No." I frown. "I never asked him why he didn't, but I think he assumed I was living a good life. Maybe he didn't want to rip me away from the only home I'd ever known."

She runs her thumb under my eye.

"I don't hold it against him, though," I say, softly. "He was good to me when I did move with him, and I think if I had left her before, she would have died sooner."

"Do you still have a good relationship with him? He called you this morning."

"I do." I smile weakly, though sadness consumes me. I try not to think of my father's illness often, although I care deeply. It's tough to continue business when all I can think about is him. "He's, um..." I can't get the words out easily, never having spoken of it out loud to anyone other than my father. "He's dying of cancer. I've told him I want to be there for him, but he insists I continue to work. He says that's all he wants for me, so that's why I'm not there."

"Oh, Asher." She kisses me, then wraps her arms around my body, pulling me to her. I press my head to her chest, listening to her heartbeat while trying not to cry. I hold my tears in as she runs her hands through my hair. "I'm so sorry."

She loosens her grip around me and places her hands on my shoulders, but I immediately catch the sadness in her eyes. They cloud over like a storm in the horizon.

Inhaling an unsteady breath, Charleigh's chin wobbles, and the city lights catch the tears lining her lashes.

I run the back of my hand down the length of her face. "What is it?"

"I'm just..." She gulps. "I'm just thankful your dad turned out to be a good person, and I hate knowing that he's suffering. I spent years wondering if you were okay, so it makes me happy knowing he turned out to be great. It's as if sickness always consumes and steals away the best people. My trust in father figures isn't exactly stellar."

She looks away, and I draw her attention back when I wrap my arms around her again, pulling her to me.

"I read what happened to your dad and his business." I clear my throat. "I'm so sorry, Charleigh."

She nods and sniffs. "After you left, I was crushed."

Her broken-hearted stare rips me apart. The pain is still clear in her expression. The echoes of our past are still alive, its beating heart thrumming between us.

I make a conscious effort to hold myself together, focusing on my breathing as Charleigh continues.

"All my plans were destroyed that night I watched you walk out my door." A tear spills over and slides down her cheek. "I just stared at the empty doorway, willing you to come back. I couldn't look at my father or how your blood dripped from his fist. He turned to me with fury and threatened me to not disappoint him again before storming out of my bedroom. Our relationship changed that night. I kept my head down for the remainder of my time at home, mostly because I didn't have the strength to look up. I was a withered soul, broken and lost. You were the one person I felt who saw me, and when you left, there was no one." Charleigh shrugs, emotion building inside her. "My mother never spoke of that night again. She went about her life as if we lived in some alternate universe, like a *Stepford Wife*. Like she did every day when she found out about my father's affairs and lies, even if it hurt her. The deal was sealed on me holding out hope I could turn to her for anything. I knew I couldn't."

I wipe her tear away, wishing I could erase the pain. Regret settles in my bones.

"What happened when you went to NYU?" I ask.

"When the news broke of his bankruptcy, my hope of going to NYU dissolved. My father came home and told me he wasn't paying for me to go to school anymore. All our money was gone." Her voice fades, nearing a whisper. She shakes her head, blinking away the tears. "

"I left for the city as soon as I could," she continues. "I realized my mother was never going to change. She would pick my father over and over again. So, when I left, I left them both and my life behind. I wish I could say it was an easy decision, but it doesn't matter how much hatred you hold for someone, letting them go can still be difficult. It's more like I've resigned myself to disappointment and regret. Disappointment wishing it could have been something different. Regret it had to come to this, where we live in a world as complete strangers. My mother messages me all the time, hoping one day I'll change my mind." She laughs and rolls her eyes. "Ironic, considering she'll never change her mind about my dad."

She inhales a deep, cleansing breath, her eyes brightening slightly. "Anyway, as soon as I could, I packed everything I owned into two overnight bags and took the train to Grand Central. Found a job working for a florist near NYU and stayed in the apartment above the shop. My father never paid a dime for my tuition, and I scrambled to apply for student loans. I pressed on despite my family's reputation. Didn't matter, anyway. In a city of eight million, I wasn't anyone of significance. Between classes and work, it wasn't easy to balance, and most days I wasn't sure I'd make it past sophomore year." She shrugs. "But here I am."

After sliding my hands down her body and to the back of her legs, I pull her up for her to my lap. She straddles me on the piano bench, pressing herself as close as she can get. I hold her against me, wrapping my arms around her, not wanting to let her go.

"You are the strongest, most resilient person I've ever known," I tell her, meaning every word. My chest expands, and it's as if I've been holding my breath for the last ten years. The barbed wire I've kept wrapped around my heart unravels.

Charleigh shakes her head slowly. "I was only trying to survive."

"No. You were living, Little Flower. You continued to breathe and live and turn your dream into your reality."

Her eyes search my face. "And you did the same."

She smiles, pulling me closer. When she brings her mouth to mine, I smile against it.

"I have a confession," I mutter.

"What is that?"

"I'm falling for you all over again, Little Flower."

She chuckles and teases my mouth. "I must warn you, Mr. Egan, I'm falling for you, too."

I flatline. My heart stops beating, and it isn't until she kisses me does it start again. Her soft mouth warms my soul. Charleigh has brought me back from the dead. She's painted my world with her flowers, brightly-colored clothes, and goodness. She's moral and pure. I don't deserve her when all I've brought to her world is pain and chaos.

But for the first time, no one is standing in our way. Not my mother. Not her father.

It's just us.

She rolls her hips and rubs her center over me. I already know she's bare under her skirt and, fuck me, it drives me wild. My cock swells and my stomach tightens. Chills slither down my legs, and my stomach still grumbles.

"We haven't even touched our food," Charleigh teases.

"You're right." I raise her arms above her head and remove her sweater, then unclasp her bra. Arching her back, she looks up to the ceiling. I pinch her nipple, flicking my thumb over the hardened pebble before bringing it to my mouth. She moans, and I've never felt closer to her than I do now.

I pull her nipple into my mouth and suck on it before snapping it back. "I'm fucking starving."

TWENTY-FOUR

CHARLEIGH

"Now, how am I supposed to get through the night with you dressed like that?"

I sit on the plush velvety bench in Asher's walk-in closet and finish clasping my silver, sparkled stiletto around my ankle.

I say walk-in closet, but it's more like a bedroom. Asher's closet is the size of a fucking bedroom.

I giggle as he looks at me through his reflection in the full-size mirror he's standing in front of. He's finishing tying his black tie around his neck. My heart swells seeing him wear it over a dark, cobalt-blue shirt, deviating from his usual stark white business attire.

"It's just a gown, Mr. Egan," I tease, walking over to stand behind him but off to the side. Even in heels, his tall frame still eclipses mine. I breathe in his deep, woody scent. The gold flecks in his eyes sparkle, but they narrow when he twists to pull me in front of him in the mirror.

I fall back against his chest as he runs his hand up the length of my thigh, then through the center of my chest. My black dress is covered in silver, turquoise, and yellow sequins in the shape of flowers. He slips his fingers under the tiny spaghetti strap over my shoulder that wraps down to the small of my back. Heat pools between my thighs.

His eyes dance across my reflection as if he's trying to decide which part of me he wants to devour first. "This isn't just a gown, Little Flower."

I quirk a brow. "Do you like it?"

He clicks his tongue against the roof of his mouth. His hands slide all over me, landing on my hips. He jerks me back, and my ass hits his erection behind his black slacks.

Bringing his mouth to the hollow of my ear, he breathes into it, "What do you think?"

I moan, biting down on my bright red-painted lip. Thankfully, my hair is tied back in a row of low-pinned braids, exposing my neck. My skin prickles with goosebumps, and I shiver.

"We need to get going or Julianna will kill us for being late to her birthday party."

"No kidding." He smiles against my skin. "Holt's been texting me endlessly, begging me to get there before he kills her himself."

I laugh and cover my mouth to stifle it.

Asher's eyes fall to my feet in the mirror. "Are you going to be able to make it all night in those heels?" They dart up to mine. "I'm not going to have to carry you all the way back home, am I?"

I love when Asher talks to me like this. There's something primal in his voice, as if I'm his and no one else's. I love feeling like he can't get enough of me, and the fact that he's talking about his apartment as if it were *our* home, not just his.

I roll my hips back. "If you do, are you going to punish me for it?"

The corner of his mouth curls, and I fight to keep my

composure. Julianna seriously will kill me and Asher if we're late.

Asher brings his mouth back up to mine, his voice hits my core, and I'm convinced I'm going to come on the spot from it. "You can count on it, Little Flower."

I exhale and leave him in front of the mirror before I get myself into too much trouble. With Julianna, at least.

ASHER KEEPS his hand on the small of my back when we step out onto the rooftop. Golden string lights hang from one end of the building to the other like a thousand tiny stars against the black sky. The city sits below us, continuing on for miles. Music pumps through the speakers, vibrating the concrete at the balls of my feet. Hundreds of people mingle and move about. I don't recognize a single one of them. Julianna really does know a shit ton of people. I guess that's what it's like when your last name is Capuleti.

I focus on Asher's hand resting on the small of my back as we make our way into the party. It's been nearly two months since he showed up soaking wet at my apartment. And the night he took me to his apartment, telling me about his dad, has brought us even closer.

We haven't talked about the future, and I think, right now, we don't need to. Other than him helping me find a bigger storefront. The first place Asher showed me went quickly off the market, but we're still looking. I haven't responded to any of Cyrus's continued emails, even after I sent him one after the last phone call I had with him, declining to work with him. Thankfully, his emails stopped two days ago. But Asher and I are taking our renewed relationship day by day.

I feel a bit of peace knowing the only ones standing in our

way this time is us. Though Asher's hand on my back tells me he wouldn't want me anywhere else than with him here at my best friend's thirtieth birthday party.

"About fucking time!" Julianna shouts over the music. She lifts her arm in the air from the other side of the roof and waves us over.

"Yeah." Asher leans down, speaking into my ear so I can hear him over the music. "She definitely would have tracked us down and turned us into a crime scene for being late."

I giggle and elbow him playfully in the side. The smile that blooms on his face is enough to melt my panties... if I were wearing any.

When we reach Julianna, she's standing with Selene, her sister London, and a man I've never seen before.

"Happy Birthday." I smile, wrapping her up in a hug. I hold her out at arm's length, taking in her silver-sequined mini dress and the diamonds scattered in her hair. She looks like a disco ball. "You're stunning."

She flips her pin-straight brown hair over her shoulder, eyeing me up and down. "As are you, babe."

She turns her eyes to Asher and points to me. "You better keep your hands off my girl until you get home. She's mine while you're both here."

Asher scoffs, laughing. "Now, that's an unfair request. You're setting me up for failure."

Julianna narrows her eyes, then smiles. "Let's see if you pass the test, then, Mr. Egan."

"No guarantees," Asher offers up with the smile that makes my heart jolt.

Selene laughs, passing Julianna to give me a hug. "Don't scare Asher away just yet, Julianna. They just got here and haven't even had a drink by the looks of it."

Selene wraps her arms around me. "You look beautiful," she

says into my ear. "I love this dress. It's very you." She loosens her hold on me. Her blonde locks are pulled into a low, side mermaid braid. It drapes over her bare shoulder—a sharp contrast to her black, off-the-shoulder mini dress.

"Thank you," I tell her. "So do you, as always."

Selene steps back and holds her arm out to London. "Remember my sister, London?"

"I do." I grin, pulling her in for a hug.

London's pink lips spread into a soft smile. She returns my hug and tucks her long, raven hair behind her ear. Her and her sister are truly night and day. The thin gold rings on each of her fingers glint in the lights.

"It's good to see you, Charleigh." She tilts her head to the side. "I'm sorry we've only met the once."

Selene links arms with London. "Hopefully, you'll be able to see her more often. Still trying to convince her to move here."

London rolls her gray eyes, her glittery eyeshadow sparkling as much as her rings. "She won't let up. But I'm still not sure."

"I run a large corporation in Boston," the man beside London chimes in. I'd almost forgot he was standing in our group. He curls his lip. "Makes it difficult to move."

"Oh," London says, placing her hand to her forehead before placing it on the man's shoulder. "This is my husband, Heath."

"Nice to meet you." I smile, taking in his sharp, clean appearance. He's taller than Asher, and his brown eyes darken.

"You, too." His mouth twitches with barely a smile in return.

"What corporation do you run?" Asher asks, and I release a breath. I look at London, and she gives me a small smile before tucking herself under Heath's arm.

"My family owns and runs RealLine."

Asher's eyebrows shoot up. "The pharmaceutical company?"

"Yes." He nods, scratching at his freshly-shaven jawline with a blank expression. "That's the one."

"It's my birthday," Julianna chimes in, rolling her eyes. "This conversation is boring, and we're here to celebrate." She looks at Asher and me. "You both need a drink."

"I agree," Asher says, pulling me closer, resting his hand on my hip.

"Should we go over to the bar?" I ask.

"You can," Julianna says, glancing over her shoulder. "But there are servers walking around with trays of champagne and cocktails, so whichever you reach first."

Asher looks over our group, searching the crowd. "Is Holt here?"

Julianna waves her hand flippantly. "I think he's over by the bar talking with some of his coworkers from the magazine."

"Oh," Selene says, looking at Julianna. "Didn't you say Lottie Anderson was here?" She eyes the group. "She's one of the top columnists at Holt's magazine. I love reading her articles."

"I think so," Julianna says.

"I'll see if I can flag her down later," Selene mutters.

The music grows louder and switches to a more upbeat tune. A server happens to pass by us, and Julianna swipes two glasses before she hands one to me, then Selene. London grabs one too, slinging it back before the three of us get the chance.

"That's the spirit, London," Julianna cheers, raising her glass in the air. She hoots and hollers, clearly enjoying how her massive birthday party is playing out.

"Didn't realize this is where everyone was gathered." Holt suddenly appears beside Asher. He shakes his hand, then Selene introduces London and Heath.

Holt takes a sip of the brown cocktail perched in his hand.

"Selene was just telling us about one of your columnists, Lottie Anderson," Julianna blurts out.

Selene shoots Julianna a glare. Her cheeks flame red as she lifts her glass to her mouth and downs the fizzy drink in one gulp.

Holt eyes Selene, then grins deviously. "Oh yeah?"

"I like her articles," Selene mutters, not meeting Holt's eye.

"Huh." Holt clicks his tongue. "You're not a bad writer yourself. At least that's what I've heard. I've never read your work."

"I've been working on a novel, so I don't have much to show right now."

Holt winks at Selene. "I doubt that."

I'm stifling my laugh when Asher leans down and brings his mouth to my ear. "I see West by the bar, so I'm going to go grab a drink. I'll be back later."

I lean into him, feeling his breath feathering my neck. "Okay." I remember him saying he's meant to meet with West tonight to discuss the expansion of his bar chain.

Asher gives me a soft kiss on the forehead before leaving the group.

Another waiter stops by, offering more champagne. I still haven't finished the glass in my hand, but I grab another one anyway. I quickly finish my first and place it back down on the silver tray.

"Hell, yeah," Julianna says. "Let's go dance."

Julianna grabs my and Selene's arms, already pulling us away. "London, let's go."

London finishes her new glass of champagne and follows us, leaving her husband standing with Holt. The four of us move out onto the dance floor set in the middle of the rooftop. It glows brightly beneath us, the tiles changing from bright blue to red to green with the music. We dance in a circle, and I lift my hands in the air, feeling free and content. I'm swaying my hips when Selene leans in, shouting over the music.

"You look happy."

"I am happy!" I shout back. "It's Jules's birthday."

"No." She grins, nodding in the direction of the bar, where Asher disappeared to. "With him."

Warmth radiates my body, and I know it isn't just from the two glasses of champagne. "I am happy."

"It's about freaking time!" Julianna yells, holding onto London's hand as they both sway to the music. London's caught up in the beat, closing her eyes, swaying her head back and forth.

I'm losing myself to the beat, too, allowing the alcohol to hit my blood stream while keeping my attention on where Asher is standing at the bar. He's leaning against the wooden counter, his eye on me. We're at least a hundred feet apart, but there's an invisible thread tying me to him.

"You've got to be fucking kidding me." Julianna's jaw practically drops to the floor. Her cheeks flame red, and fire burns in her eyes.

"What?" I ask, looking over my shoulder.

"Rome Montgomery." She spits his name out with disgust, curling her lip and scrunching her nose.

"Who's Rome?" Selene asks, her eyebrows pulling together.

"Only the biggest, and I mean the *biggest* asshole in the entire world."

"Why?" London asks her. "What did he do?"

Julianna gives a mock laugh, tilting her head back. "He's only terrorized me since we were kids. When we were ten, he put gum in my hair and walked around our private school telling everyone to call me Bubblehead. Our family and his have been at odds since before we were even born. He's been taught to hate us his entire life and continues to make horrible statements about us publicly. One year, he accused Holt of publishing an article he claims to have published in his own magazine. Of course, it was all a lie."

"Wait," Selene cuts in. She closes her eyes and shakes her head before opening them again. "He owns a magazine, too?"

"Among other things," she mutters.

"Which one is he?" London asks, standing on her toes, attempting to look over the bobbing heads of the dancers surrounding us.

Julianna crosses her arms defiantly. Her boobs push out and her cleavage deepens above the cut of her disco ball dress. "The arrogant asshole headed our way."

I search the crowd for anyone headed in our direction and quickly catch sight of who Julianna is talking about. Tall, dark hair, and a sharp jaw. His dark hair is slicked back perfectly, and he runs a hand over the top as he zig zags his way through the crowd.

"Oh, my God." Selene gapes. "He's gorgeous, like dangerously gorgeous."

"No, he isn't." Julianna huffs. "Trust me, if you knew his personality and who he is deep down, you wouldn't be saying that."

Selene quirks her eyebrow. "I don't know about that."

"He's just another corporate billionaire prick living off his family's wealth and fucking any woman who even bothers to glance in his direction," Julianna mutters, then scoffs. "I need another drink."

I keep my comments to myself about her being a billionaire who inherited her family's wealth, too. Instead, I keep things light.

"Didn't you say you hoped we'd meet a few hot billionaires at your party?" I ask, stifling myself from laughing too loud. I point to Rome. "Well, there's one right there."

She groans and rolls her eyes. My best friend isn't amused. She delivers me a glare, then she leaves the three of us on the dance floor, meeting Rome before he has the chance to meet us.

"Julianna!" I shout. "What are you going to say to him?"

She yells over her shoulder. "I'm going to find out who invited him here, then kick his ass out!"

"Shit," Selene hisses, and the three of us rush to follow but keep a decent space behind.

Despite her anger, Julianna gently pushes her way through her party guests, careful not to take it out on them, stopping every now and then to smile, promising to catch up later. But her face falls the second she's standing toe to toe with Rome. Her usual full lips press tightly together, and her nostrils flare.

Selene, London, and I watch the exchange between them as if we're flies on the wall when, in reality, we have front row seats.

Rome's mouth lifts in to a grin, and there's a look of satisfaction in his eye. He simply stares at Julianna as he shoves his hand into his pocket and pulls out a small black box tied with red ribbon. Julianna doesn't even move to acknowledge it, keeping her daggers pinned on the man in front of her.

"Happy Birthday, Lark." He narrows his gaze as Selene jerks her head in my direction.

"*Lark?*" she mouths, and I simply shrug. I have no clue.

"What are you doing here, Montgomery?" Julianna asks, crossing her arms over her chest. Her entire body is stiff and rigid. She's full of rage, and I can only guess her vision has turned red at this point. As red as the blood-red tie Rome is wearing.

"It's your birthday," Rome flatly says. "How old are you turning today? Forty, is it?"

Julianna grinds her teeth, her muscles in her jaw tightening. "Thirty, asshole."

"Oh, right." Rome looks down at the box before stuffing it back into his black pants. He taps his finger on his forehead and fake winces. "Sorry."

"You can save your fake apology," Julianna grinds out, not backing off. "Why are you here?"

"You know, you sure are acting like a brat for someone who's turning thirty." His eyes darken.

"Why are you here?" she repeats.

"I was invited."

"By who?"

With his hands in his pockets, he bends slightly, bringing his eyes in line with Julianna's. "Who do you think invited me, brat? I'll give you one guess."

"I'm not playing your game, Rome."

"Oh, come on, Lark," he teases, scrunching his nose. "Games are fun. Just like birthday parties. They make things interesting."

Julianna's gorgeous eyes thin into two slits laced with poison, directed squarely at Rome. "Have I ever told you how much I hate you?"

"Only about a million times since we first learned to speak."

"Right." She huffs, pointing at the elevators. "Well, I still hate you, and it's my party, so I want you to leave."

"Not just a brat, then." He scoffs. "Still a firecracker, as always, I see."

Julianna stands her ground and stays silent, crossing her arms over her chest.

"I'm not leaving." Rome straightens his back. "It would be rude of me, considering your brother invited me. Don't you think?"

"Holt would never invite you," Julianna barks back. "He doesn't hate you nearly as much as I do, because a level of hatred that high would be impossible to compete with, but his venom for you is still there."

"Obviously not enough to keep me away from celebrating the day you graced this earth with your glorious presence, though, now, is it?"

"*Leave.*"

Rome ignores her, searching the crowd with a look of pleasure on his face. I can tell he's enjoying this game. "Is your boyfriend here? What's his name again?" He looks down at Julianna. "Honestly, you go through so many, I can't keep up."

"I want you to leave." Her chest has stilled, and her body has hardened.

Rome opens his mouth, but is stopped when Holt moves in between them. He doesn't have a chance to speak, either, before Julianna aims her piercing stare on her brother, ready to throw more daggers.

"You invited him to my party?" She points an angry finger at Rome.

Holt trades innocent glances between them before his shoulders drop in defeat. "Hear me out."

"No." Julianna's eyes line with tears, and suddenly, it's as if her anger has dissolved into hurt. "I don't need to hear you out when it comes to the Montgomerys."

"You told me you wanted to invite everyone." Holt tries to defend himself.

Julianna scoffs in disbelief. "Not Rome!" she yells. "I didn't mean for you to invite Rome Montgomery. He's our family's enemy and all they do is ruin everything they touch."

"Rome is..." Holt starts.

Julianna immediately shuts him down. "I don't care what he is. I don't want him here."

She turns to Rome, her anger fueling her once again. "I

want you to leave. Now." She turns to her brother. "Both of you."

Julianna leaves Rome and Holt where they are, disappearing into the crowd gathered around them. Holt holds up his hand, calling after her, but he gives up quickly, knowing it's no use. When you've made Julianna upset, it's best to give her space.

"I'll go after her and make sure she's okay," Selene says to London and me.

"I'll go with you," London offers.

I search the crowd. This party is massive. I never thought the rooftop of a building could hold so many people. "I'm going to find Asher and see if he can talk to Holt and let him know what's going on," I tell the sisters. "I'll find you after."

"Okay." Selene gives me a kiss on the cheek before walking away.

Rome and Holt are still standing where Julianna left them. I don't pay too much attention to them before searching for Asher. Holt is deep in conversation with Rome, so I don't bother asking him if he knows where Asher is, either.

I push through the crowd, wanting to find him as quickly as possible so I can get back to my best friend. I decide to start with the last place I saw him, at the bar.

TWENTY-FIVE

WEST

I hate people. Well, maybe not all of them.

It's a laughable philosophy to live by for someone who owns a chain of bars and craft breweries. My business *is* people.

But I've never had more conviction in that belief than I do now.

Staring out at the sea of wealthy fuckers willing to suck this person's cock to squeeze every last dime out of their filthy rich assholes makes me reconsider my career path.

Ironically, I'm one of these wealthy fuckers now, but I didn't grow up like them. I'm not a trust-fund baby, and I don't strive to stand beneath the spotlight. I don't want to be known for my name, and I don't want to be known for my money.

In truth, I don't think I want to be known—a constant battle when I want to continue to grow in my business and build a life for myself.

"West?"

I break my attention away from the sea of wealthy fuckers to see Asher Egan walking toward me.

He's wealthy, but not a fucker. I like him.

"Hey, man." I give his hand a shake.

He runs his fingers over the top of his hair. "I'm so sorry I've missed you these past few weeks. I hope you don't hold it against me."

I laugh and shake my head. "Not at all. I've been busy, too, so I get it."

Asher points to the bar set up beside us. "Would you like to grab a drink, and maybe we can talk about your plans?"

After I order a beer and Asher orders a seltzer and lime, we sit on the barstools lining the glass barrier running along the edge of the roof.

"Are you having a good time so far?" I ask Asher, nodding to the party goers.

He glances over his shoulder before turning back to me. "Yeah, I'm here with my girl, Charleigh. She owns a flower shop on the Upper West Side. She also happens to be best friends with Julianna."

"Oh." I nod, swallowing my beer. "She was at my opening for the garden, right?"

"She was." He nods, too, a small smile blooming. "We weren't exactly on good terms then, but we're working on it."

"She seems nice. Congrats, man."

"Thanks." He rests his elbow on the edge of the glass. "So, Holt told me you were interested in expanding your breweries. How many do you have right now?"

Oh, yeah, Holt. Again, wealthy but not a fucker. I like him, too.

See, I don't hate *all* people.

"Just the four," I answer.

Saying the number out loud seems small and insignificant. Much like the way I've felt most of my life.

"I know it isn't many." I wince, feeling intimidated all of a sudden. I did a little research into Asher Egan. Son of a wealthy New York real estate executive, he's just the same. But a little deeper dive showed me Asher didn't always come from this world. Much like me.

Not the same world, but not far from it.

"That doesn't matter." He waves me off, stirring his seltzer with a small, black cocktail straw. "You've built quite an empire already from what Holt has told me. Adding more properties will only build on that success."

I give him a closed-mouth grin before taking a drink.

"So, are you originally from New York?" he asks. "A part of you gives off the New York vibe, but something tells me you haven't always lived here."

"Could be the beard." I point to my chin, then laugh it off. "But no. No, I'm not."

Charleigh, Asher's girl, walks up to us. "Sorry to interrupt," she sheepishly says, turning in on herself. She quickly places her hand on Asher's shoulder and whispers in his ear.

I flick my gaze to the ground, thinking about Asher's question and what I'm going to say. My first instinct is to lie or graze over the ugly parts, fishing for only the brightest parts. My past is dark and ugly—one I've spent years running away from.

When my gaze lifts back to Asher, a flicker of black catches my attention, tearing me away from the couple in front of me. The wind is knocked from my chest, and I'm left gasping for oxygen. Sometimes, no matter how hard and how fast you run from your past, it has a way of finding you.

Silence replaces the noise, and all I can focus on is the raven-haired girl on the other side of the party. There's a break in the crowds, giving me an unobstructed view of her. At first, I think I'm mistaken. It can't be her. It's simply impossible. But when she lifts her hand to tuck her long, black hair behind her ear, each delicate golden ring wrapped on every single finger glinting in the light, I know the impossible is possible.

A small, red, heart-shaped birthmark stamped between her thumb and forefinger.

My heart stops.

I swallow the blazing heat in my throat, and just when I think I'm already starving of air, I lose more when I recognize the man she wraps her arms around.

"West?"

I dart my eyes to Asher, looking down at him still seated in the barstool.

I'm no longer sitting across from him. I'm standing. The pipes in my airway squeeze and strain to fill with oxygen. My lungs burn.

"I, um..." I swallow, nearly choking as I step backward. "I need to go." I continue backing away. To where, I have no fucking idea.

"Wait..." he says.

I'm suffocating. My chest is hard as a rock, and I can't fucking breathe. I can *feel* the blood draining from my face. I take another step back but trip on something metal. It clangs to the concrete, rattling and grabbing the attention of the wealthy fuckers surrounding me. I catch myself on the arm of a chair before busting my face.

"Are you okay, man?" Asher asks. He's standing from his stool now, and Charleigh's hand is covering her mouth.

"Yeah," I breathe out, bending to pick up the small, metal end table. All eyes are on me. Their stares are burning a hole in my back. "I just... I need to go." My gaze quickly slides over the crowd, panic setting in.

Without another word or glance, I turn and walk as fast as I can to the elevator, leaving her and every single one of the wealthy fuckers behind.

TWENTY-SIX

ASHER

Turns out, I did end up having to carry Charleigh home. I carried her from Julianna's party to the car, then again from the car to the elevator.

She's still conscious, her three glasses of champagne not completely knocking her out. I wouldn't exactly call her drunk but definitely teetering on the line. While unsteady on her feet, though, I decided to carry her the rest of the way. It just gave me another excuse to hold her, anyway.

"You didn't have to carry me *all* the way home," Charleigh mutters against my chest. "I could have walked from the car to the elevator. I'm not drunk." With her legs over my right arm, and her back resting against my left, I maneuver my arm to reach inside my front pocket to tug my keycard free.

I remind myself to grab the spare keycard I keep in my office next time I'm there to give to Charleigh. Holding her in my arms makes me want to never let her go. I want her in my life. I want her in my space. I want her home.

The light on the black box turns from red to green, automatically taking us up to my level.

"I know I didn't have to carry you," I grunt, adjusting her in my arms. I look down as she looks up at me with her gorgeous, hooded eyes and whisper, "I wanted to."

Her cheeks blush red. Or it could be the alcohol swimming in her bloodstream keeping her warm.

"Did you enjoy Julianna's party?" I ask.

"I did." She grins.

"I hope she had a good time. I know she was probably looking forward to tonight since her last birthday."

Charleigh laughs, tilting her head back. "She was, and I think she did." Her laughter wanes. "But I think the encounter with Rome threw her for a loop."

"I wish I had been there." I can't help chuckling. "I'm sure Holt regrets his decision to invite him."

"You've never met Rome?"

"No." I shake my head, sighing. "Holt's mentioned him a few times but never in a good way. I'm just as surprised he invited him."

"I wonder why he would do that when he knows the history with Rome's family and his own. Not to mention Julianna's."

"I don't know." I press a kiss to Charleigh's forehead.

A slow, wide grin spreads across her face.

"What?" I ask her.

She lifts her chin and looks up at me, never allowing her smile to falter. "I'm kind of disappointed."

I chuckle. "For someone who is disappointed, you certainly don't look it."

She lays her head on my chest, the numbers above climbing with every level. We're almost to my apartment. My scent mingles with hers while she wears my suit jacket. The sleeves are entirely too big on her, and it's practically swallowing her whole, but she looks sexy as hell wearing what's mine.

"I'm disappointed because I didn't make you."

"Make me?" I look at her quizzically.

"Carry me." She shrugs her shoulder, looking back up. "If I *made* you carry me, I thought that meant you would punish me for it. But you're doing this out of the kindness of your own heart."

I bite back my grin. Electricity shoots across my chest.

Fuck, this woman has me. All of me.

"Who said I still wasn't going to punish you?"

Wrapping her arms around my neck, she lifts herself up a little closer to bring her face to mine. Her lips brush my mouth.

"That's more like it, Mr. Egan."

"I'm glad we have an understanding, then, Little Flower."

The elevator stops on my level, and the doors slide open. I don't let Charleigh go when I carry her through the threshold. She keeps her hands around my neck and lifts herself to bring her mouth to mine again. This time, we don't stop kissing. I part her lips with my tongue and breath her in. She's flowers and champagne and beauty.

I carry her through the entryway and am about to lower her out of my arms when I stop, hearing a crunching sound beneath my feet.

Looking down, I quickly lift Charleigh back up before her bare feet touch the shattered shards of glass sprinkled across my floor. They glitter in the darkness. A chill slithers down the length of my spine as I back up toward the elevator before finally putting Charleigh down. I hand her silver heels back to her. On a panicked breath, she slips them back on as I take a step back toward the glass, taking in my apartment. Someone has been here.

"Asher..." Charleigh hisses in the dark.

I push my arm behind me, urging her to stay back, and press my finger to my mouth before holding it out to her. "Wait here," I whisper.

Her eyebrows knit together, and she presses her hand to her chest. She shakes her head but stays where she is.

I pull my phone from my pocket and dial 911 but keep my finger hovered over the green call button.

I search my apartment in the dark. Every light is off, the only illumination coming from the city. Every single frame mounted on the wall in the entryway is busted. My father's art pieces and photographs are all destroyed. Glass is scattered across my floor. The cushions of my furniture is upturned, the fabric sliced and torn. The material inside is spilling out, lying in mounds all over my floor. It looks like a fucking animal went rabid in here.

When I get closer to my living room, I realize the damage done to the furniture wasn't chewed apart, though, it was done by a knife. Clean cuts stretch from one end of the cushions to the other.

I glance back at Charleigh to make sure she's okay and still standing close to the elevator. With her hand held up to her mouth, she nervously bites down on her nail.

I turn back around to search the living room, getting closer to the piano. The bench is smashed in, practically snapped in half. All the keys are broken, some missing, popping completely off and sitting at my feet.

I start racking my brain as to how this happened. Charleigh and I were only at Julianna's party for a few hours, and no one can access my floor without a keycard, and I'm the only one with one.

I call my security guard quickly. "Lincoln, I need you to check the security cameras for the last three hours and pull the data from my key box in the elevator to see when it was last used. Email over the footage and data as soon as possible."

I hang up and call the police.

After giving them the initial info, I check to make sure the rest of the apartment is clear. Afterward, Charleigh joins me in the living room, and the dispatcher assures me they're sending an officer out, but she stays on the line and asks, "Do you have an idea who would have broken into your apartment, sir?"

Charleigh is staring at the piano with tears streaming down her face. My gaze falls on the sticky note taped to the top of the broken pile of wood.

I tear the note off, reading the four words scribbled on it.

LIKE FATHER, LIKE SON

"Yeah," I sigh, the air leaving my lungs. "I have a pretty good idea who."

TWENTY-SEVEN

CHARLEIGH

February 12, 2015

"Mom?"

"I thought you fell asleep," she says softly, stepping into my room. "At least, I was hoping you did."

I roll over, turning my back on her. I can't look at her. My heart is too broken, too lost. The bed sinks behind me with her weight, and I close my eyes, feeling another tear slip from under my lashes and down my cheek. All I've been doing is crying.

"Talk to me, sweetheart."

"I don't want to talk," I whisper, staring at my bedroom window. It's a silly notion, but I'm secretly willing Asher to come back. Vivid images of him climbing through my window come to me every few minutes, but then they're gone the second I blink, and my heart breaks all over again.

The wounds are fresh and raw, tearing me apart.

"Please, Charleigh." She places her gentle hand on my shoulder. "I'm here."

I stare at the window with nothing but pain.

"Why do you stay?" My voice is gravelly, and my throat is sore.

"What do you mean?" Her voice is so soft. So gentle.

I half turn in my bed and face her, keeping my arms tucked under my head. "Why do you stay with him? He's a monster."

Her shoulders fall as she tilts her head. She's looking at me with sympathy as if I wouldn't understand if she tried to explain. She's looking at me as if I wouldn't understand what it's like to love someone.

"You wouldn't—"

"Understand," I cut her off, hardening my expression. I roll back over. "Save your excuses and reasons for Dad. He falls for them more than I do."

My words sting the tip of my tongue. I know I've just hurt her with my brutal honesty, but the flood gates have opened, and all my reservations have disappeared. It's hard to feel empathy for someone who never stands up for you against those who hurt you. It's even worse when that someone is your mother.

"I know you don't agree, but it's true." She sighs, and I feel her straighten behind me. I don't move. "But you wouldn't understand."

"Understand why you choose to stay with someone who consistently hurts you?" I ask her. "No, Mom. No, I don't understand it."

She doesn't answer. All I hear is her soft breaths.

I close my eyes, feeling like I might burst. I swallow the lump in my throat, reciting a silent mantra in my mind to not fall apart. I'm on the brink, my toe slipping on the edge of the cliff.

"I don't understand why when I'm in love with a good and decent human being—one who would do absolutely anything to protect me and love me—he is stripped from my life," I continue. "Dad took away the only person I've ever truly loved. He took the only person to ever truly see me," I tell her, the words spilling out of me. "Your daughter's heart is broken, and you did nothing to stop it. You did nothing to stop *him*. Again, you chose him over me."

"All I ever do is choose you." Her voice quivers. "But you have to understand, Charleigh. I love him, too. These things aren't always black and white."

A silent sob escapes my chest with a shudder. I roll forward and press my mouth to my pillow. I don't want my mother to hear my cries. The scent of flowers mingles with my tears, and I know the smell is coming from her as well as me. She always smells like flowers, and it makes the pain all the worse.

I inhale a deep breath before pulling away from the pillow and keep my focus on the window, hoping Asher won't follow through on my father's threat. I'm hoping I haven't lost him completely and this will all be solved in the morning when I see him at school.

"Just leave me alone, Mom," I manage to choke out. "*Please.*"

She doesn't speak another word, and neither do I. She pats my shoulder before she rises from my bed. I feel her absence behind me, and the hollow ache in my chest grows.

My world has turned black.

"Try to get some rest," she says, her voice farther away. "I love you, sweetheart."

I close my eyes and hope my new black world swallows me whole.

I WAKE up in the morning to a world of white, feeling no more rested than before I fell asleep last night. Light pours into my room, and I'm facing my closed bedroom door. Then the memories of yesterday come barreling into me at full force.

I scramble out from under the sheets, sitting up as I snatch my phone from my nightstand. My screen lights up, the picture of Asher kissing me in the snow coming to life. My heart thrashes inside my chest, certain I'm going to find a message, but when I see there's nothing, my heart is ripped open all over again. Asher's silence is a dagger piercing my flesh and bone. With every passing second, it digs in a little deeper, twisting its way into me.

I wipe the tears from under my eyes and turn my head to look at my window. I stared at it so long last night, willing Asher to appear, and I still am, even in the blanket of snow outside. The sun is shining, and the sky is a bright blue, not a cloud in it. Opposite of how I'm feeling on the inside. The sun reflecting off the snow is blinding, but I'm bounding off my bed the second I see a square piece of paper taped to the outside of my window. I open it and reach my arm under, tugging it off the glass, careful not to drop it. Shivering, I close the window and stare at the paper.

My hands shake, and I struggle to take in a breath. It's the first sign of Asher since yesterday. A letter. A bad feeling washes over me, knowing if it were good news he wouldn't have left this for me. He would have texted me or called.

I stumble backward until the backs of my legs meet the edge of my bed. I slowly sit down, not taking my eyes off the letter pinched between my fingers. Shakily, I start to open it.

Fresh tears spring to my eyes, seeing no *From Asher, with Love*. The words blur the second I read my name in Asher's handwriting.

Charleigh,
I know it isn't right to leave you a letter like this,

but as I sit here at the hospital, writing these words, I don't see any other way.

After I left last night, I walked home to my trailer engulfed in flames. My mom was inside, passed out. I tried to get to her, but it was too late. According to the paramedics, she had already inhaled too much smoke, and there was no reviving her.

The police said it was an accident. They concluded she'd gotten drunk, spilled alcohol all over the trailer, then fell asleep with a cigarette in her mouth. All it took was one ember to fall, setting our world on fire. Everything is lost, turned to nothing but ash. And now I'm facing an ugly truth.

My mom is dead, and I have nowhere to go. At least I didn't until about an hour ago.

Somehow, the police got in touch with my dad. I guess they interviewed our neighbors and one of them told them they'd heard my mother talk about my dad before and handed over what information they had about him. Since I'm eighteen, they said I didn't have to go with him. I'm a legal adult, and he has no authority over me. But honestly, I don't know where else to go if not to him. I have nothing but a few dollars in my pocket. I don't even have a phone.

Anyway, my dad bought me a plane ticket as soon as he heard of my situation. My flight leaves in a couple hours, and I'm heading out to California as soon as I sign some paperwork and the nurse finishes placing a splint on my nose.

But as I sit here in this sterile, white room, with

the nurse about to walk back in, I can't help but let the guilt eat at me. I know my mother had her issues, but all I can think about is the last words she said to me before I left. I'll be living with this guilt for the rest of my life. I can't take what I said to her back, but I believe I can fix what will be.

I know you love me, Charleigh. And I know we had our plans to go to NYU together. But I also know that for me, it was all a pipe dream, no matter how badly I wanted it. Because for people like me, dreams don't come true. When I first met you, I knew you were too good for me. You have the life I've always dreamed of and every possibility in the entire world to do whatever your heart wants. You see, Charleigh? Whereas you have the world in the palm of your hand, I have nothing in mine.

I couldn't save my mom. And I couldn't save us. But I can save you from me.

I dragged you into this mess I call a life—my life. You don't deserve it, and I can't ignore the signs any longer.

As much as it pains me to say, your father is right.

I'm sorry for what happened with him tonight, but it would be foolish of me to continue believing there could ever be a future for us. So, go live your future.

Go to NYU. Get out of this town, and get out of Connecticut. Surround yourself with hearts and flowers. Whatever it is, do what makes you happy. Live your life the best way possible. A life without me—one that affords you every opportunity.

I don't know what the future holds for me, and I

can only hope the decision to live with my dad and to leave you isn't one I'll regret. Even so, I'll at least be at peace knowing I did what was best in this moment. I hope, if not now, then eventually, you will find peace, as well.

Thank you for your love, Charleigh. I'm sorry I couldn't save your box of paper hearts in the fire, and I'm sorry I couldn't give you all of me. The best of me.

But when someone asks me in the future if I've ever been in love, I will confidently say yes, that I loved someone with every fiber of my being.

I'm just sorry our love wasn't enough to save us.

Goodbye, Charleigh.

- Asher

I USED to believe four words could change everything, but as another tear spills onto Asher's name written on his letter, I realize the number of words doesn't matter. Two is enough to drive the final nail into the coffin before burying it in the ground, never to see daylight again.

TWENTY-EIGHT

CHARLEIGH

My apartment is cold when I step inside, wrapping my arms around myself, attempting to create some sort of warmth. I'm still wearing Asher's suit jacket, and I could have sworn it was keeping me warm earlier. Although that could have been the champagne from Julianna's party. But the buzz I felt has worn off, and now I'm cold. Freezing cold.

I step into my apartment and can't shake this eerie, violating feeling even though it wasn't my apartment that was broken into. It was Asher's.

But with the security Asher has, and the people surrounding him, I'm surprised a place like his could be vandalized.

An icy chill is still stinging the back of my neck when Asher moves from behind me to face me.

"Little Flower," he whispers, hooking his fingers under my chin. I lift my gaze from his feet to find his golden-flecked eyes. They're as bright as flickering flames.

"I'm okay." I clear my throat and dart my gaze away from his. A knot forms in my chest, and I feel sick. I think back to the police sitting in Asher's apartment, taking our statements. I wanted to vomit when I heard Asher telling them he thinks Cyrus Temper was behind the break in. I wanted to vomit because I knew it was my fault. All of it. If I hadn't considered working with Cyrus to find me a bigger shop, then drop him to work with Asher, this wouldn't have happened.

"Why do I get the feeling you aren't?" he asks, pulling my gaze back up.

I look away from the floor and wrap both of my hands around his cradling my face. "I am. I'm just cold."

"Okay." He pulls me forward and presses his lips to my forehead. I breathe him in, finding comfort in his deep, woodsy scent. His mouth is warm and surrounds me like a security blanket, and suddenly, I feel safe again.

"Why don't I make us some tea?" he asks.

I simply close my eyes and nod in response.

"We're safe here," he reassures me, speaking against my forehead.

My eyes are still closed when his mouth leaves my skin. I feel his absence immediately and open my eyes.

He leaves me standing in the entryway and moves to the kitchen, where he finds my electric kettle on the counter, fills it with water, and sets it back on its base before flipping the switch.

"Do you think they've arrested Cyrus by now?" I ask, worrying my lip.

"Hopefully." He sighs, running a hand through his hair. He shoves it off his forehead, the muscles in his arms flexing below his rolled sleeves. "He was caught on camera using my keycard in the elevator, so it should be an open and shut case. He doesn't have much of a defense."

"But he'd have the money to pay for his bail if they set one, right?"

Asher hangs his head low as he grips onto the edge of the counter. "Probably."

When he lifts his head, his brow is furrowed, but his eyes are soft. We don't speak another word, letting the truth sink between us. Cyrus clearly has it out for Asher, and my gut twists, telling me this isn't the worst of his retribution. While being questioned by the police, Asher filled them in on the day Cyrus had shown up at his office, threatening to ruin his reputation. He'd said the same four words to him that he'd left on the note. That's how Asher suspected him almost right away.

I wanted to ask Asher why he didn't tell me about his encounter with Cyrus the day it happened, but I was in no place to judge. I didn't tell him about the day he overheard Julianna say something about me sleeping with Asher when I was on the phone with him. I was embarrassed for what Julianna said, and I didn't think Cyrus would care. All these seemingly insignificant moments have turned into ones that clearly pushed Cyrus over the edge.

Asher pushes off the counter and turns around, searching for the supplies for tea.

Watching him move effortlessly in my apartment breaks the chill over my body. Seeing him here feels right. And despite the fear Cyrus has put in us tonight, I feel safe and at peace with Asher here, in my home. Suddenly, I'm blanketed in warmth.

I spent a decade holding anger and resentment toward him for leaving the way he did, but knowing now what he went through that night, I imagine myself in his shoes. A domino effect he couldn't stop from happening. The fight with his mother that led to my father beating him that then led to him going home and finding his house engulfed in flames – his mother passed out inside it.

Asher's trauma came all at once, crashing down on him in a

few short hours, and he felt helpless. The only thing he could do was wave the white flag and leave. While I wonder the situation would have turned out if he had said goodbye that morning instead of leaving me a note, I know I would have convinced him to stay, and I know he wouldn't have left.

Sometimes life forces you to make decisions. Even ugly ones.

I meet Asher in the kitchen and stand at the end of the island, watching as he removes two mugs from the cabinet. He sets them on the counter and pauses, staring down at them before swinging his gaze up to mine. He sighs. "I'm sorry I didn't tell you about Cyrus."

"Don't." I blink back the emotion. "You don't have to be sorry. Maybe I wasn't clear in letting him down and telling him I was working with you instead. Do you think he knows we're about to go under contract with a new space? Maybe that's why he's upset."

"Maybe." Asher shrugs. "You did nothing wrong, Charleigh."

Asher's reassurance does little to calm my nerves. I know he's right, but clearly the truth doesn't matter when it comes to Cyrus. Three weeks ago, Asher found the perfect location for my second flower shop, well under my budget. I was thankful he'd found a gem after losing out on the first he'd shown me, and he was thankful I'd placed my trust in him again. We're set to close in a couple weeks.

I give him a small smile, convincing myself to believe Asher's words. The kettle beeps as the water inside boils. Asher blinks and returns to his task of making tea. He opens the silver-ware drawer and reaches for the spoons, but his hand stops, hovering over them. My heart drops into my stomach, remembering what sits inside.

I press my hand to my chest and take a tentative step closer, standing on the other side of the drawer. I look down with watery eyes, a tear splashing on the handle of one of the spoons.

When I look up at Asher, he's still staring into the drawer as he slides his note out from under the spoons.

"Asher, I..." I start, but the words get caught. I swallow, and I don't know why I'm nervous.

I don't take another breath until he finally swings his gaze up to me. "You kept this?"

My heart beats against flesh and bone, and I count the beats. "Yes," I whisper. "It was the last and only proof I had left of us."

"Why is it in your silverware drawer?" he asks, his brow furrowed, but I see the heartache in his eyes.

"I dug it out of my closet after I ran into you at Cyrus's office. I don't know why I pulled it out. I was going to read it but couldn't bring myself to do it."

"So, you haven't read it since putting it in here?" His eyes fall to the drawer before lifting again.

The golden flecks sparkle, and I've never felt more vulnerable than I do now. Asher is aware of the words inked into the paper. He was the one who wrote them. But there's something sacred about it. Like once he'd given me the words, they were only meant to be mine. Now I feel cut open and exposed, my darkest thoughts and feelings dug up from the grave where they've been buried for years.

"No," I confess. "I haven't read it since the first time. I remember how it felt to read it then, and I wasn't sure if I'd feel the same way. It's been ten years, but I don't think time matters when it comes to us."

He clears his throat. "It doesn't." A light smile plays on his mouth. "You know... it's funny." He toys with the open end of the note as if he's deciding whether to open it all the way or not.

I look at him quizzically. "What's funny?"

"When I was writing this, I was thinking you were probably going to read it, wondering how someone who claimed to never have the words suddenly had so much to say."

I laugh, but the echo of heartbreak is intertwined with the humor. "I wasn't thinking that at the time, but you're right; it was a lot of words for you."

He steps closer to me and cradles my face in his large palm. I lean into his touch and peer up at him.

"I never had the words until I gave my heart to you, Little Flower." He leans down and kisses me.

I wrap my arms around his neck and rise onto my toes, pressing into him. I'm still kissing him when I lower my hand and grab the note, pressing it to his chest, over his heart. I hold it between us and pull my mouth away from his.

He keeps his forehead pressed to mine.

"I don't know if I'll ever be able to read it again," I whisper, pulling away. "Afterward, I tucked it into the back of my closet and didn't pull it out again until after graduation. I buried it in a box with just that flower. I didn't know it then, but I'd also buried my heart in that box, too." I nod toward the mantle.

Asher doesn't speak. He simply nods and places the letter back on the counter. The water in the kettle is no longer at a rolling boil. It simply sits, steaming.

Asher lifts his hand and wraps it around the back of my neck, urging me to look up at him. A tear slips from my eye. "And now?" he asks. "Is your heart still buried?"

I give him a small smile. "No." I move to unbuckle his belt, untucking his shirt from his black slacks, too. My hands slowly work to undo each button. "And it feels pretty fucking amazing to feel the sun again."

The echoes of pain I felt reading his letter dull, replaced by

Asher's renewed promise. The gold in his eyes spreads as he slips his hands around my back. He grabs onto the zipper, undoing my dress. His hand glides across my skin, and I feel lit from within.

"It does feel amazing, doesn't it, Little Flower?"

TWENTY-NINE

ASHER

The scent of burning flesh isn't easily forgotten. Neither is the taste of blood. It stays with you, sinking into your every memory. Over the years, I've found myself dreaming of that night. Flashes of Trevor Keeler's venomous face hovering above mine, his red eyes piercing me. The metallic taste of my own blood on my tongue, filling my mouth. Then I'm standing in front of my trailer, emblazoned and burning. I stay where I am, grounded to the dirt, my feet unwilling to move. My mother is trapped inside, screaming my name to come and save her, but all I do is stand there, frozen against the glow of fire, breathing in the smoke.

Smoke fills my lungs, and I cough, unable to inhale a clean breath. I'm starving for oxygen, and it paralyzes me.

"Asher!" My mother screams from behind the thin, metal storm door.

My chest squeezes, and I try to lift my arm to reach out to her but can't.

Suddenly, my eyes snap open.

Wide eyed, I find myself in Charleigh's bed. She's turned her back to me, and my arm is draped over her naked body.

I breathe in, but I choke. For a moment, I wonder if I'm still trapped in my dream but I'm not. Smoke floats over Charleigh's body in the moonlight, and I cough again. I shoot up from the bed, shaking Charleigh in the process.

"Charleigh," I choke. I cover my mouth with my arm and dart my eyes to the bedroom door.

A bright orange glow flickers at the end of the hall, toward the front of Charleigh's apartment.

"Charleigh." I shake her. "Get up."

She stirs, and when she coughs, she shoots straight up. She twists in the bed to face me, waving her hand. "What is happening?"

"I think your apartment is on fire," I say, a chill prickling down my spine. "Come on."

The both of us hop out of bed, and Charleigh quickly slips into a pair of shorts and grabs my shirt off the floor, slipping her arms into it, only fastening the first two buttons. I hastily step back into my boxer briefs, not caring that I'm practically naked.

I'm stuck in this nightmare again. Panic sets in, and my chest feels hollow, slowly filling with smoke.

I swipe my phone from the nightstand and grab Charleigh's hand, pulling her out into the hallway, only to stop when I see my mother lying in the hallway. She's on her back, her eyes closed, caked in dried mascara. An empty bottle of whiskey rests in her hand, a puddle of brown liquid pooled underneath her. The flames coming from the front of Charleigh's apartment dance across her lifeless body.

"Asher!" Charleigh yells beside me. I snap my head to the left. She's using the collar of my shirt to cover her mouth.

I blink and quickly glance back down the hallway, the blood draining down to my feet. My mother is gone. I swallow my nerves, hoping the fire isn't out of control. I swing my attention back to Charleigh.

"What do we do?" she asks, panicked.

I cover my mouth with my arm, ignoring the scars on my bicep from the last fire I survived.

"We need to see if we can get out the front door," I tell her.

Smoke slithers down the hallway, clouding my view of Charleigh even though she's standing in front of me.

"If not, there's a fire escape outside the living room window!" Charleigh yells back, coughing after every other word.

"Okay, come on." I squeeze her hand. The smoke stings my eyes, and I try to blink it away.

Charleigh follows my lead as I turn the corner, the living room coming into view. Flames cover the sofa situated in front of the window, blocking the fire escape. Every piece of furniture is engulfed in fire, even the plants Charleigh has placed in nearly every corner of the apartment. Angry red and orange flames threaten to catch onto the curtains lining the front windows. Shards of glass stick out from one of the panes of the wide-open window. The blazing flames rage, building faster than my mind has a chance to catch up to what's happening.

I yell over my shoulder. "The fire escape is blocked by the fire!" Dialing 911, I raise my phone to my ear.

"911, what is your emergency?" The man on the other end asks.

I open my mouth to answer but stop when an eerie feeling washes over me.

"Cyrus." I feel Charleigh stiffen as her hand grips onto mine, her nails digging into my skin.

I look at her eyes before turning back around, following her what has her attention.

When I turn around, I find Cyrus standing by the front door. With narrowed eyes peeking through his swollen, round face, he glares at Charleigh and me with an expression full of hatred and darkness.

The glint of the silver lighter in his hand flashes in the bright glow of the fire. He flicks the lighter with his fingers, constantly popping the top up, the metal clinking over the sound of the fire. A cloud of smoke shields him from complete view, but his expression is unmistakable.

"Hello?" The man on the phone says. "This is 911. What is your emergency?"

"I think you'll find it in your best interest to hang up right now," Cyrus bellows, lifting his chin.

I tighten my grip, fear settling into my bones. "Hello?" the man repeats in my ear.

Cyrus's jaw tightens, and his brow furrows.

Swallowing thickly, I lower my phone with a shaky hand. It slips from my fingers and falls to the floor beside my feet.

"Good boy." Cyrus sneers.

Goddamn motherfucker.

I curl my fingers into a fist at my sides.

My heart thumps in my chest, raging against my ribs, and my mind dances, figuring out how I'm going to get us out of here safely.

I swing my attention to the flames now crawling up Charleigh's green, velvet curtains.

"There's no one to pull you out of the fire this time," Cyrus yells over the flames.

My stomach flips.

The room is quickly filling with smoke, and Charleigh hasn't stopped coughing since we stepped out into the hallway.

I squeeze her hand and talk to her over my shoulder. "Keep your shirt sleeve over your mouth."

She nods and lifts her wrist to her mouth, placing the white ends of my sleeves to cover her nose and in a makeshift mask.

"What do you want from me?" I ask Cyrus, shooting him a glare and pinning him with daggers.

"I want your fucking attention," he barks.

"Is that why you broke into my apartment?" I ask, coughing and stepping farther into the living room. "To get my attention?"

I stick close to the kitchen island, keeping one eye on Cyrus and the other on the fire raging on the other side of the living room. It's getting dangerously close to where we are. Charleigh's hand slips from mine, but she remains close, stepping into the kitchen.

"That means you got my little note, then, didn't you?" Cyrus curls his lip.

"What did you mean?" I ask, lifting my chin. "Like father, like son?"

"Your father fucked his clients." He quirks a brow, scoffing. "The women, at least. I was skeptical of some of his male clients, but who honestly knows what lengths your father was willing to go for money and power?"

I swallow, wondering why my father never mentioned his past with Cyrus, knowing I was coming here for work. Perhaps he thought Cyrus wasn't a legitimate business threat any longer since it's been over twenty years since they worked in the same city. Perhaps he didn't even know about this feud. Although I haven't known my father my whole life, I don't believe Cyrus. My father isn't the kind of man to fuck everyone over. His years of sending money, despite my mother's mismanagement of it, is proof he has integrity.

"You're a liar," I boldly tell him, steeling my chest. "And I don't fuck my clients." I shouldn't press him when he has the power, but I can't help it. His lies about my father, and me, are getting under my skin.

Cyrus laughs manically; his attention now focused on Charleigh. "What about this little slut, then, huh? Explain her."

Charleigh freezes, and her eyes widen, her eyebrows pulling together. She's terrified, and every instinct in my body is yelling at me to save her, to protect her. I don't want her to end up with the same fate as my mother, trapped inside with no way out. Me being at fault.

Watching her now, I know I wouldn't survive without her. A life without Charleigh isn't a life at all. I've done it once before, and I was nothing but a hollow human being. I'd die right along with her.

Charleigh slinks closer to the end of the island, to the side Cyrus can see, her eyes constantly bouncing between us and the counter. I follow her attention, catching sight of my letter on the countertop where we left it earlier. She glances at Cyrus quickly before swiping it up in her free hand.

"Explain, motherfucker!" Cyrus bellows.

Charleigh shudders, jumping and lowering her hand holding my letter to her side.

The fire has spread, growing dangerously close. Heat pricks my skin, and I step closer to the kitchen. I grind my jaw, my impatience growing thin. We don't have time for this.

"I don't have to explain shit to you," I bark back. "Move out of the way, and we won't turn you in."

Cyrus laughs, rolling his head back, then wiping his chin with his round fingers. "You think I don't already know the police are on their way? They tracked you the minute you didn't respond to that call." His eyes darken. "We aren't going anywhere."

My stomach sinks, and I'm sick.

"What do you want from me, then?" I ask, giving in, playing along.

"I want you to admit the truth." He growls. "I want you to have a backbone where your father didn't."

I swallow, my breaths shallow, nervous with what Cyrus wants me to say.

A spine-tingling chill slinks down my back.

"I caught your father fucking one of his clients when I followed him one day. It's how I knew he would cheat to win and how I knew you would, too. I've lost out on millions of dollars because of you Egans." Cyrus spits. "Then when this whore stopped returning my calls, I remembered her mentioning you before, and I knew. I overheard her friend mention you on the phone, then I followed you to her shop and caught you fucking her in the back room." His gaze darts to Charleigh before he turns his daggered eyes on me. "But that wasn't the first time, was it? You already knew what her dirty little cunt tasted like."

I grind my jaw, certain I've cracked a few teeth. Fucking, creeper.

"Fuck you, Cyrus." My vision turns red, and I lunge forward, tackling him.

Charleigh's screams filter over the sound of crackling flames. The smoke swells, and I'm weakened by it. The second I land on top of Cyrus it takes a moment for me to catch my breath. I cough, wanting to inhale a clean air, but I can't. My throat tightens and my lungs burn.

Keeping Cyrus pinned to the floor, I glance over my shoulder long enough to shout to Charleigh. "Get out of here, Charleigh! Now!"

I'm unsure whether she's heard me between Cyrus's grunting and my tight throat.

Then Charleigh's sprinting down the hallway. She picks up my phone from the floor and runs back toward me.

"Asher!" she yells, her eyes darting over my shoulder. I look back down at Cyrus beneath me but am knocked off balance. His fist connects with my jaw so hard, I fall back. My spine slams into the floor, and flames rage beside my head. I turn and look, scrambling to back away. The heat is intense, almost too much for me to bear. Memories of my mother flash through my mind, and panic takes over.

I turn my head to look back up at Cyrus. Smoke billows between us, but his venomous eyes are unmistakable.

He wraps his hand around my neck and lowers himself, bringing his face as close to mine as he can. My throat burns, and my vision blurs, black dots appearing at the sides. All I see is Cyrus's beady eyes above me.

"This is the last time you'll take money from me, fucker." He hisses. "This is the last time an Egan takes everything from me."

He keeps one hand wrapped around my neck, squeezing. He uses the other to keep it pinned on my windpipe, straightening his arms. Sitting up, his face turns beat red, and the veins pop in his round neck. He's using as much pressure and strength as he can to kill me.

I lift my arms and bat at his. I'm growing weaker, and my eyes start to grow heavy. I don't have the strength to keep them open. I try to fight back, but all I see is Charleigh sitting under the tree in her parent's backyard. Round patches of wet dirt stained into the knees of her jeans. Her long, brown hair curtaining her beautiful face. Me hastily drawing her round eyes in my sketchbook, just in case I never had the gift of seeing them again.

My hands start to fall away from Cyrus's arms, and my mind drifts. It floats away, and the smoke and heat overwhelm me.

I've almost completely surrendered when Charleigh growls above me. My eyes snap open with as much energy as I can summon, watching the end of a large flowerpot smash against the side of Cyrus's head.

The ceramic cracks against his skull, and his usually beady eyes spread wide. I squint, a chunk of the pot and clumps of dirt falling all over me.

Cyrus's hands let up, and he topples to the side. I'm still straining to breathe. I inhale sharply, gasping for air. I roll to my side, coughing. My jaw is wide open, but despite his hands being off me, there's still no relief. I look up at the flames, inches from my face, and I scramble to sit up and back away.

"Asher." Charleigh kneels beside me. She grips onto my arm, urging me to stand. "We need to get out of here."

I quickly wrap my hand around hers and stand, ready to head for the door, but I stop when I see a barrier of flames blocking the front door.

"Shit," I blow out.

"Come on," Charleigh says, pulling me back down the hall. "There's a ladder outside my bedroom window."

I nod and lead her down the hall. We stick close to the wall, avoiding the flames crawling across the floor, setting her carpet on fire.

When we make it to her bedroom, I slide the window open and help Charleigh climb out first. She grabs onto the thin, metal ladder and starts her descent. I'm quick to follow.

I don't inhale a clean breath until my bare feet land on solid ground. With my hands on my knees, I try to clean out the smoke from my chest, worried I've inhaled too much. Charleigh's hand is on my back, but my own worries subside, focusing on her.

Wrapping my arms around her, I pull her to me. She snuggles into me, resting her face on my chest. I press my cheek to the top of her head and breathe an uncomfortable sigh of relief.

I kiss the top of her head, then wrap my hands around her face, pulling her to look up at me. "Are you okay?"

Tears streak her cheeks, and worry is etched in her round eyes. She nods and sniffs, her eyes falling to my neck. "Are you?"

I swallow thickly, looking up at her burning apartment. Each window glows a bright red and orange, and I think of Cyrus inside, lying there unconscious, surrounded by fire.

Flashes of blue and red lights surround us, covering the brick building of Charleigh's apartment. I turn and look around at all the fire trucks and police cars. A crowd of onlookers has gathered around us and on the other side of the street.

I look back down at Charleigh, running my thumbs under her eyes, wiping up her tears. I inhale an unsteady breath and notice that this time it's a little easier to take in. I look into her eyes, thankful for the gift of seeing them again.

"Yeah, I'm okay." I press my lips to her forehead and breathe her in. "You saved me, Little Flower. You saved me."

THIRTY

CHARLEIGH

One Week Later

I'm staring through the front window of my sunlit flower shop with a smile on my face. It's my first day back to work since the fire at my apartment, and it feels good to be back. Although I'm still struggling to keep up with my load of clients and the regular day to day operations of running my flower shop, this place feels like home. It's small, but it's mine.

"Did you see this one?"

I twist, looking over my shoulder as Selene bursts through the opening leading to the backroom. She meets me by the display table I'm standing beside and passes me her phone.

I read the headline to the article she has pulled up.

UNCOVERED: YEARS OF LIES AND FRAUD UNEARTHED ABOUT NEW YORK REAL ESTATE MOGUL CYRUS TEMPER AFTER DEATH IN FIRE ONE WEEK AGO

My shoulders drop with a heavy breath, and I hand Selene's phone back to her.

"No, but I feel like I've read a similar headline years ago."

The news of Cyrus Temper's death has captured the attention of every headline in the city. It's been plastered everywhere. Newsstands, TVs, radio, social media. Cyrus's story is everywhere. My apartment set ablaze. Reporters and journalists have been hounding me and Asher for interviews, but we've turned down each one, unable to bring ourselves to explain the connection of why Cyrus was there that night, and why he tried to kill Asher and destroy me.

The only ones who know are the police and those closest to us.

"Have you finalized the insurance claim on your apartment yet?" Selene asks, picking up one of the loose flowers in front of her and stuffing it into the blue, glass vase sitting in the middle of the table.

"I did." I inhale deeply and add another flower. "I'm just glad to get this over with and have a place to stay."

She gives me a soft smile. "Even if you didn't have Asher's home to call your own, you know you will always have a home with Julianna or me. London even said she would have if she lived here."

I give her a warm smile and place my hand on her arm. "Thank you."

"Of course." She smiles back, tucking her blonde hair behind her ear. "I'm going to head out. I have one last chapter to finish drafting up before I need to head over to the community home to see my grandmother."

"Okay," I say, looking back down at the flower in my hand.

Selene leaves, and I drag the stem of the flower between my fingers. Although its life source has been severed, it still lives. Temporarily, at least.

I close my eyes and bring the petals to my nose, breathing in. Despite losing my home, I am thankful to have Asher's place to call mine. I've never felt more complete than I do with him, and even though I lost everything in the fire, I was able to save

Asher's last letter when I stuffed it into the front pocket of his shirt.

The bell above the front door jingles, but it doesn't stir me. I'm lost in the smell of the flower when I feel his body behind me and his voice hit my ear.

"Open your eyes, Little Flower."

My mouth immediately lifts to a grin, spreading from one ear to the other. My heart leaps like it did when I was a teenager.

When I open them, Asher's hand is in front of me, holding a black folder. His gold watch glints in the sunlight pouring into my shop.

I spin around and look up at him.

My breath is stolen when my eyes meet his golden flecked ones. His jaw isn't as nearly clean shaven as it usually is. A light stubble is peppered along his angled jaw, and his brown hair is slicked back, revealing those eyes that make me weak kneed.

"Hi." I melt.

"Hi." He leans forward and kisses me. I can tell he fights to pull away, lingering a half second longer than a quick peck. He wraps his free hand around my lower back, gripping onto me before pulling away.

I feel his absence immediately.

"What is it?" I ask him, grinning.

He holds the folder between us, urging me to take it. I flick my gaze down to it, then back to his before taking the folder. I take a step back and open it.

The first page is a listing for the first shop Asher ever showed me—the one I never got to see from the inside.

When I look back up at him, I melt all over again. It's the happiest I've seen him in the past week.

While I've worked over in my mind what happened with Cyrus, Asher hasn't. It's been more difficult for him, and after admitting to me in the middle of one of his sleepless nights, he's surrendered to seeking out a therapist. He'd confessed the fight with Cyrus brought up a lot of memories of the night he lost his mother, and the guilt he had for her death. And although Cyrus tried to kill him, he feels almost as guilty for his death as well, after leaving him there unconscious.

My attention falls to his neck, noticing the fading bruises of Cyrus's fingers are nearly gone. But I know even long after today, they will remain, much like the night his mother died.

Asher's smile hasn't faltered, not even when he nervously adjusts the dark forest green tie wrapped around his neck. "What do you think?"

I look down at the listing with confusion. "I don't under-stand. I thought this one sold."

"It did." He clears his throat. I can practically feel his body humming with excitement when he looks down and flips the first page. "The contract fell through right before closing. The buyer backed out, and it went back on the market this morning." He points to the second page. "This is the inside."

I quickly glance back down at the listing.

The first picture is of the front of the building, just as I remembered it: two large wooden doors with windowpanes, rustic yet classy and upscale. The next picture is of the inside, featuring a large, open floor plan; at least triple what I have now. The following images are taken from different angles, but when I flip the page and see the backroom, there are several large coolers and enough space for four of my prep tables. It has everything I could ever need.

"What do you think?" Asher asks, his voice hushed.

"I love it. It's exactly as I hoped it would look on the inside."

"Well, we can go look at it whenever you want." He rubs his chin. "You may change your mind when you see it in person."

I swing my gaze up to his and lower the folder. "I don't need to see the inside."

His smile falls. "You don't?"

I laugh, clutching the lapel of his suit. I jerk him against me, rolling on my toes. "Have you ever just seen something or met someone and known it or they were meant to be yours?"

His eyes flash, and the corner of his mouth lifts into a knowing half-smile. "Only once."

"Well, it's happened to me twice," I confess, stepping back and sitting up onto the edge of the table. I scoot back and tug on Asher's tie until he's standing between my legs. My thighs vibrate and hum with him between them, and I'm already soaked. I'm thankful I'm wearing a skirt, sans panties. Makes for easier access.

"Tell me about the first time." His velvety voice lingers between us as he leans forward, bringing his mouth to mine.

I smile, and my teenage heart returns. "Why don't I show you?"

THIRTY-ONE

CHARLEIGH

Two Months Later

I had just signed the last document to close on my new flower shop when Asher received the phone call. Without hesitation, we packed our overnight bags, and Asher arranged his private jet to fly out as soon as we made it to the airport. A few hours later, the wheels of his jet land on the West Coast.

The Californian sun presses against my skin differently than it does in the north. It's warm and inviting, never wavering in its welcome. It doesn't threaten to leave or suddenly vanish.

We haven't stopped long enough to take in the change of scenery before we slide into Asher's waiting car and race to his father's house.

Asher is quiet on the drive over, and when we pull in front of the enormous Beverly Hills mansion, he grabs my hand and leads me inside.

I'm wondering what thoughts must be going through his mind when we step through the front door. One of the housekeepers holds it open for us, and I watch on as a nurse appears in the hallway, ushering us through the massive house. I take in the wrought iron, grand staircase, the marble floors, and the glass chandeliers. I squeeze Asher's hand as we leave the grandiose entrance and head toward the back end of the house. We're moving quickly, but I can't help smiling at the pictures hanging on the wall.

Asher and his father wading in the water on surf boards.

Asher's UCLA graduation photo.

Asher laughing as he lifts a piece of sushi to his mouth.

Asher mid-cannonball into their backyard pool. Although his face is scrunched, I can tell it was taken not too long after he'd left Connecticut.

But when Asher's hand slips from mine the second we meet the threshold to the backroom, my eyes fall to the picture on the end table, beside Christopher Egan's bed. One of him and his son smiling at the camera, with the same tilt to their grin and the same gold-flecked eyes.

"Asher," Chris croaks. He lifts his fist to cover his mouth, coughing into it. An oxygen canula is connected to his nose, and he takes a few seconds to catch his breath before speaking again. "I wasn't sure when you were landing."

"We left as soon as possible," Asher says, leaning down to give his father a hug.

Chris lifts his arms and wraps them around his son.

Asher sits in the chair beside his father's bed.

"We?" Chris asks. His eyebrows arch before his eyes land on me. My cheeks heat with both Egan men staring at me.

"You're Charleigh, I assume?" he asks.

I step into the room, nervous as I move to Asher's side. "I am." I smile.

"How did you know she was Charleigh?" Asher asks, eyebrows knitted.

"Oh, come on." Chris coughs. "In the past ten years, you've only ever mentioned one woman. It may have been the one time, but a father doesn't forget the look in their son's eyes when they're in love. You were heartbroken, but I saw how much she meant to you."

He wags his finger at Asher when he says to me, "Don't let my son fool you. He was a wreck when he came to me, and it wasn't just because of the fire. I didn't think he was ever going to get over you. He was like a lovesick puppy. Took forever just to coax a genuine smile out of him."

"Oh, my God, Dad." Asher groans, heat spreading across his cheeks.

I cover my mouth, unable to hold back my laughter. "Honestly, Mr. Egan. It's good to know I wasn't the only one suffering."

"Oh." He waves me off. "Call me, Chris. You're going to be my daughter-in-law one day, after all."

My heart practically stops.

"Well, that's if my son doesn't drag his feet." He winks at me before turning to Asher.

Asher glances up at me and chuckles. "I'm sorry."

"For what?" I laugh. "I think this is a very interesting and fun conversation."

"She's a smart one." Chris smiles with his mouth closed and breathes through his nose.

"She is," Asher says, but adjusts in his chair. He places his hand over his dad's, and his face turns serious. "Now, tell me what the doctor told you again."

Chris closes his eyes and presses his head back against his pillow. He rolls it to the side and looks straight at his son. The bags under his eyes droop farther. "There isn't much time."

Asher's breath catches and he swallows. "I want a second opinion." He shakes his head. "I don't believe there isn't anything else to be done." He hangs his head, unable to keep himself together.

"Hey, hey, look at me." Chris moves his hand out from

under Asher's and squeezes it. "Look at me." Asher does as he says, lifting his head. "I don't want a second opinion, and there isn't anything else to be done. I'm tired, son."

"But, Dad…"

I place my hand on Asher's back. My heart breaks and tears sting the corners of my eyes. In the few moments since I've met Chris, he's shown more compassion to me than my own father ever did. The love he's giving Asher is a love I've never experienced, and somehow, I feel his loss already, knowing Chris and Asher don't deserve this.

"Don't be sad," Chris soothes Asher. "I'm not. I've lived my life, and I'm so sorry my past caught up to you. I'm sorry about Cyrus."

"Dad, don't. Stop. None of that matters. I know the truth. I never doubted you."

Tears line Chris's exhausted eyes. "I've only ever loved you and wanted what was best for you."

"I know you have."

"I can go peacefully knowing you're loved and taken care of by this one." He nods toward me.

I give a weak smile, sniffing to keep myself from crying.

"I'm proud of you, Asher," Chris says in a hushed tone. "Don't ever question that."

"I promise, I won't."

"Good."

Chris gives his son a smile, and my chest tightens, seeing the love he has for Asher. My heart aches for something I never had with my own, and suddenly, I need air.

"I'll give you both time to catch up," I say to both men.

They both give me a smile, and Asher kisses the back of my hand before letting me go.

I step out of the room and wander the house before the housekeeper escorts me upstairs and into Asher's old bedroom.

A sadness drags me down, glimpses of mine and Asher's past colliding with our present.

Loving Asher has always been easy despite the pain that comes with it, but being in Asher's old bedroom makes me realize losing him for those ten years may have torn us apart, but Asher found beauty in his life. He needed to lose me to find himself. He found happiness. A happiness that kept him breathing.

When I sit on the edge of the bed and look around, though, taking in the pieces of Asher's life I thought I'd never get to see, exhaustion takes hold, pulling me under. I lay back on the pillow and allow sleep to take over.

THIRTY-TWO

CHARLEIGH

One Month Later

Asher and I stayed with his father until the end. I'd just returned to Chris's house after running to a farmer's market I spotted along the beach when I came home to Asher standing at the end of the hall.

Tears streamed down his face, and his body sagged as if he'd been carrying the weight of the world on his back. The gold flecks in his eyes dimmed, and it was then that I knew.

Christopher Egan was gone.

I ran to Asher, and he swept me up in his arms. I placed my hands around his face and told him to let me in, to share in his pain, so he didn't feel like he had to carry it all.

This time, he did.

He wrapped his large arms around me and just held me, with my legs curled around his waist, as if he was going to fall apart if he didn't. He sobbed into my shoulder, then took me into his father's room.

Chris looked like he was in a deep sleep when I lifted his hand and kissed the back of it. I leaned down and whispered in his ear, thanking him for loving me like his own daughter in the few short weeks I'd known him. I thanked him for showing me how it felt to be truly loved by a father.

Then Asher and I spread a few of his ashes along his favorite beach in Santa Barbera, as he'd asked us to do, before bringing him back home to New York with us.

It's been three days since we left California, and the fall chill in the New York air is already biting at my skin, but it feels good to be home. It feels good to be home in Asher's apartment, with pieces of Chris still lingering in the hallways.

Cracking my eyes open, I twist in my bed, turning to Asher's side. The sheets are pulled back, leaving the space where he left earlier. I run my hand over the silky sheets, excited to get back to work today.

Asher hasn't returned to his job since we've come back home, but he's taking his time. I can tell his father's loss has hit him hard—harder than he expected.

For now, he's promised to come down to my new flower shop to help me plan out the details of how I'll be setting it up.

I turn back over and grab my phone from my nightstand.

My girl's chat is blowing up, the constant pinging too annoying for someone who hasn't had their first sip of coffee yet.

> Julianna: Honestly, it's about time you've added her to the chat.

> Selene: I wasn't sure if London wanted to be included.

> Julianna: Wow, Selene. Are you trying to keep your sister hidden from your best friends?

> Selene: 😏 Of course not. It's just that she doesn't live here, and I didn't want to flood her phone with our never-ending messages.

London: Which you're both doing right now. LOL, but I don't mind. Thank you for including me. 🖤

Julianna: I've got your back, London, and so does Charleigh. If that girl ever wakes up.

Selene: She should be up by now.

Julianna: Charleigh.

Julianna: Charleigh!

Julianna: Wake up, love! It's a big day!

Me: I'm up! LOL But it wasn't the messages that woke me.

Selene: Good morning, Charleigh!

Julianna: Yay! To catch you up, London is now in our group chats. We just have to work on getting her to move here.

Selene: Don't bother trying, Jules. I've tried, and she won't leave her husband. He refuses to trade Boston for New York.

Julianna: What?! Why????

Selene: Beats me.

London: Same here. I've talked to him, but he refuses. It's strange considering he went to college there and his family has history there, too.

Julianna: Well, boo. Does that mean you're still coming to Charleigh's grand opening, though?

Me: I'd love it if you were able to make it, London. If not, I understand.

London: Absolutely!

Me: Good!

Selene: Hey, Jules…

Julianna: What?

Selene: You or your brother don't happen to plan on inviting a certain someone with the same name as a city in Italy, do you?

Me: Yeah, we all saw how that turned out last time.

Julianna: Hell, no. In fact, Hell will freeze over before I'd ever invite that man anywhere. Plus, my brother won't be making that mistake again unless he wants to find his body buried beneath six feet of dirt in one of those cemeteries along the Hudson.

Me: Lol, I'll see you guys later at the new shop. I'm excited to get started on the planning. Love you three!

I shut the screen off and drop my cell on the nightstand, eager to find Asher. I know he's still home because I hear movement coming from downstairs, as well as the scent of fresh coffee lingering in the air.

I slip into his favorite gray T-shirt and head down the stairs. The cool air pricks my bare legs, goosebumps spreading across my skin.

When I make it to the bottom step, I see Asher in the kitchen. He's dressed in his black slacks. His sculpted abs are visible thanks to his unbuttoned, white-collared shirt. I haven't seen him in a suit since before we left for California. Funnily enough, it's an odd sight, like seeing two different versions of Asher. Both ones I love equally.

"Good morning, Little Flower." He grins behind his mug, the steam lifting from his coffee before he presses it to his mouth.

I run my fingers through my tangled hair and wrap my arms around his waist, looking up at him. "Good morning."

His eyes roam over my face. "You look beautiful this morning."

I giggle and stand on my toes. "I doubt it, but I appreciate it, anyway."

Pressing my lips to his, I lean into him, moaning. We've gone through enough pain to last a lifetime, but life with Asher is beautiful now. I could get used to this.

I pull back from him, and he places his mug on the kitchen island. His fingers graze my cheek when he tucks my hair behind my ear.

"Remember when I said you'll look good on New York?"

"Of course." I smile, my heart fluttering. "It was the first paper heart you ever left for me." I ache between my thighs, wanting him inside me, but I hold off, knowing I need coffee first.

Asher wraps my hand up in his and pulls me into the living room, his mouth tugging into a smile. "It still applies, don't you think?" he asks, stopping in front of the window facing the entire city. He nods behind him with a coy, teasing grin on his mouth. I dart my eyes over his shoulder, gasping at the sight of the paper heart taped to the window.

My eyes move to his before taking a step forward. The small heart stands out against the clear glass and the backdrop of New York City.

I read the four words written on the front.

From Asher, with Love

I swallow, tears already streaming down my face. I never thought I'd ever receive another paper heart from Asher. All of them were lost in the fire. Seeing it brings back a flood of memories—the good ones. The ones where Asher kissed me for the first time. The ones where he told me he loved me. The ones of him climbing through my window while I tried to stifle my laughter. The ones where he traced my collarbone.

With shaking fingers, I reach out and tear the heart from the window, turning it over in my hand.

Will you marry me?

My breath stops, and I cover my mouth before spinning around. Asher is bent down on one knee, a ring pinched between two of his fingers. The large, square diamond is surrounded by a string of tiny golden gems. The gold band shimmers in the morning light.

His eyes fall to the ring. "My father helped me pick out this ring the day after we flew in to see him. But the truth is..." he pauses, steeling his chest and inhaling a deep breath. "The truth is, I already knew I wanted to marry you. I've known I wanted to marry you since the first time I saw you huddled under that oak tree, with your wide eyes and dirt-stained jeans. I just got a little lost along the way. I love you, Charleigh. I never stopped, and I will spend the rest of my life loving you, making sure I never lose you again. To anyone or anything. You are mine forever."

I fall to my knees in front of him and press one hand to his face. I place the other around his, holding the ring and hold it between us.

He pulls me close, his mouth almost touching mine.

"So, what do you say, Little Flower?" he whispers, his breath dancing across my skin. "Will you marry me?"

Turns out I was right.

Four words *can* change everything.

THANK **you so much for reading *From Asher, With Love*!**

Want to read more of Asher and Charleigh? Hop on over to https://author-brittany-taylor.kit.com/8c3abe1aec **to get your bonus scene!**

BE **sure to look for more from the NYC Billionaires coming soon!**

PLAYLIST

- "Forever" by Lewis Capaldi
- "All Too Well (10 Minute Version) by Taylor Swift
- "All For You" by Cain Ducrot
- "Lose You To Love Me" by Selena Gomez
- "Hold Me While You Wait" by Lewis Capaldi
- "My Tears Ricochet" by Taylor Swift
- "Liar" by Jelly Roll
- "Driver's License" by Olivia Rodrigo
- "Burning Down (Alex's Version)" by Alex Warren
- "Hammer to the Heart" by Teddy Swims
- "Wildest Dreams" by Taylor Swift

ACKNOWLEDGMENTS

As always, I'd love to thank these people for all their help, friendship, work, and encouragement that made this book possible...

To my husband and two boys, you keep me motivated every day with all your support. I love you all! To my incredible assistant and friend, April. Thank you for all the work you do to keep me together and for all your wonderful ideas and confidence in what I do. To my beta readers (April, Lori, Amy, Joan, and Ana) for reading this book through its transformation and for your insight. To my agent, Nikki, for helping collaborate with me on how to take my career to the next level and for your unwavering support and belief in me. To my editor and friend, Vicki James. I don't deserve you. You are an amazing editor, author, and confidante. Thank you for polishing each of my books.

To all the Bookstagrammers, Bloggers, TikTokers, THANK YOU for all the incredible things you do!

And to you, my readers. Without you, none of this would be possible. Thank you for reading. xx

ABOUT BRITTANY

Brittany Taylor grew up all over the world including places such as California and England. Her love of reading started at a young age. Finally deciding to fulfill her lifelong dream, she took the plunge into the writing world and published her first book when she was twenty-eight. Today she resides in Maine with her husband, two sons, two cats and one dog.

www.brittanytaylorbooks.com